Perfect for You

Dec wanted it to be relief that flowed through his veins, but despite the icy water, he felt ignited. And hard. So hard he ached. From the moment he'd captured her in his arms, he felt like *he'd* been the one swept away. One touch of her sweet body and he felt like he'd been tossed into the center of a storm he couldn't escape.

Shivering from the cold and the aftereffects of being slammed beneath the surf, she looked deep into his eyes. "Thank you for saving me," she whispered.

When her tongue swept out to capture a droplet of ocean from her full, kissable bottom lip, his good intentions burst into flames and he just fucking broke.

With one hand firmly on her ass, the other slid up her body and gently captured the back of her head. They both stared into each other's eyes and Dec knew she could read his intent.

"Don't say a word," he growled. "Not. One. Word."

Dropping his mouth to hers, his mind completely shut off and pleasure took over.

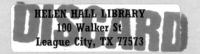

By Candis Terry

CANDIS TERRY

perfect for you

A SUNSHINE CREEK VINEYARD NOVEL

AVON BOOKS

An Imprint of HarperCollinsPublishers

Excerpt from *A Better Man* copyright © 2016 by Candis Terry.

PERFECT FOR YOU. Copyright © 2017 by Candis Terry. All rights reserved. Printed in the United States of America. No part of this book may be used or reproduced in any manner whatsoever without written permission except in the case of brief quotations embodied in critical articles and reviews. For information, address HarperCollins Publishers, 195 Broadway, New York, NY 10007.

First Avon Books mass market printing: March 2017

ISBN 978-0-06-247184-0

Avon, Avon & logo, and Avon Books & logo are registered trademarks of HarperCollins Publishers in the United States of America and other countries.

HarperCollins is a registered trademark of HarperCollins Publishers in the United States of America and other countries.

17 18 19 20 21   QGM   10 9 8 7 6 5 4 3 2 1

This one is for my readers. Thank you for opening my books and allowing my imaginary worlds into your lives.

Acknowledgments

No book is written alone, and I have a team of the most inspiring and brilliant people who make me look a whole lot better than I really am.

The beginning of a new series is scary and I'm honored to have my hand held by my incredibly smart, savvy, and beautiful editor Amanda Bergeron. I don't know how I got so lucky to have our stars cross, but I am ever grateful.

Sometimes I need to hear the voice of reason. Thanks to my amazing agent, Kevan Lyon, who keeps me informed, grounded, and leads my future to a brighter place.

There are people you know who will be friends for life. I'm lucky to have several and yes, I plan to keep them there until I go to the big bookstore in the sky. My publicist Caroline Perny, you are simply the best. I adore you and I thank you from the bottom of my goat-loving heart. Pam Jaffee and Jessie Edwards, you freaking rock! Elle Keck, where would I be without you to keep me straight? Happy blueberry Pop-Tarts! Lisa Filipe, from the moment we started chatting, I knew we'd be BFFs. Thank you for working so hard for me and cheering me on. Shawn Nichols, you are a total marketing badass and I sincerely appreciate you. To the pair of gorgeous ladies who create my gorgeous book covers, Gail Dubov and Nadine Badalaty, thank you so much.

And always, thanks to my family—the Hubster, Picklehead, and Binks—for your love, your patience, and your forgiveness. I love you all more than you will ever know.

perfect for you

Chapter 1

In Declan Kincade's world the real problem with leisure time was finding the time for it.

At the window of his Newport Beach high-rise office, he watched the sunset glisten across the rolling ocean waves. Down on the beach, like a ritual changing of the guards, the sun worshipers packed up their towels, tanning lotion, and umbrellas to head home while the locals grabbed their boards for their moment in the sand and surf. Despite the June gloom of overcast skies, early summer was the perfect time of year for Southern Californians to play along the coastline before the hordes of vacationers swamped the beaches and local bars.

Not that Declan knew much about having fun these days. In fact, he hadn't had a good time in . . . hell, he couldn't remember. He'd spent nearly eight non-stop years working on his career, and building his financial investment and wealth management company in

Southern California. Recently—as if he didn't already have enough to do—he'd added the task of putting together the beginning stages of an additional Chicago-based office.

Not that he was complaining, but lately he had started to feel the wear and tear on his brain. At the age of thirty-three, it seemed like he had entered his golden years without all the significant life experiences. The recent tragic deaths of his parents had taught him that life was too damn short, and he realized he'd better start taking advantage before it was too late. But sometimes putting ideas into action didn't come easy.

Hands in the pockets of his tailored slacks, he stepped closer to the window and settled back on the heels of his black oxfords. Rather than standing there looking down, he wished he could be strolling on the Newport Pier, breathing in the fresh salty air. He imagined the sound of the waves crashing against the pier's massive pylons. He imagined stopping to watch the fishermen bring in their daily catch while the hovering gulls screeched for scraps. He imagined stopping at the local oyster bar for a cold brew and a quiet moment to watch the last of the bikini clad beauties shuffle back to their cars. Instead he would spend one more evening within his plain white office walls in a meeting scheduled to start in . . . He glanced down at the Citizen Signature watch clasped to his wrist . . . four minutes.

Imagining life was no longer enough. He'd reached a point where he needed more. Something . . . different. He needed to participate instead of being just an observer. The problem was, he'd forgotten how.

Those on the beach below his high-rise window probably had their own daily challenges, yet they'd found a way to merge fun and responsibility together to enjoy life to its fullest.

When had he stopped trying?

Things never came as easy for him as they did for his four brothers. Before he'd been diagnosed with dyslexia in the seventh grade, his school years had been difficult. Frustrating. He'd wished for things to be simpler, more fun. While Jordan, his fraternal twin, had breezed through his homework so he could run out to play with the others, Dec had sat at the kitchen table for hours struggling over each word, each number.

Back then he'd felt different, the odd man out, even if physically he was his brothers' match or better. Maybe even back then he'd subconsciously pulled away from those he was closest to. Away from those he wanted to be more like. Those who didn't have to work so hard just to be . . . normal.

Once the doctors had figured out what was wrong with him, they taught him a learning system that helped. He wasn't God-given smart. He'd had to work at it to prove to himself and everyone else that the learning disability wouldn't encumber him his entire life. Those challenges had made him the man he was today—successful on the page but lacking in matters of the heart.

When he was tired he still struggled, but at least he'd learned to plow his way through. All his life he'd worked hard, really hard, to fit in. Somehow he never did. As a substitute, work and career became his main focus.

His source of gratification.

His reward.

Early on he'd figured if he could become successful in the one thing that challenged him the most, he'd prove to himself and everyone else that he could compare with the rest. He just hadn't realized, in doing so, how hard he'd pushed away all the other important things in life.

Behind him the office door opened.

"They're here. Are you ready?"

The question willed him to turn instead of just giving a nod. Over the past four years he'd heard that husky female voice a million times. But lately the smooth whiskey tone took his imagination to forbidden places. Because now, Dec couldn't help being mentally poked by his twin brother's recent observation about his executive assistant.

She's hot as hell.

It wasn't that Declan had never noticed Brooke Hastings's voluptuous hourglass shape, long legs, and deep brown eyes.

Of course he had.

His libido was in fine working condition.

It wasn't that her bubbly personality hadn't made him laugh at times he'd really wanted to pull his hair out. And it wasn't that he didn't have an appreciation for her high IQ or how she always seemed to save his professional ass when he really needed it. But Brooke was his executive assistant, the one person who kept his career on track. And even if his newly engaged brother insisted he chose pleasure over work, Dec knew mixing business with pleasure was a very bad idea.

And yet, somewhere along the way, Brooke had become much more than *just* an employee. She'd become an essential part of the reason he got up every morning and came to work. Over the past few weeks, when he hadn't been looking, she'd escalated to being everything he'd ever wanted but could never have.

"Dec?" Brooke's head tilted slightly. A waterfall of honey blond hair fell over the shoulder of her silky white blouse. "Are you okay?"

Hell no, he wasn't okay.

Because right now, even though he knew it was wrong, he couldn't help wondering how all her soft shiny hair would feel wrapped around his hands while he pulled her in and seduced her right out of that hip hugging skirt. He couldn't help thinking about how warm and soft her body would feel to touch and hold all night. He couldn't help thinking about how rewarding it would be to hear her laughter any damn time he wanted, or have her flash those dimples in his direction.

Like a bad habit, he had to stop those thoughts before they created a real problem. Brooke was too damn valuable in too many ways for him to allow his sudden need for something forbidden damage the amazing working relationship they'd built over the past four years.

"Dec? Are you ready to meet with the Flavios?" When she stepped inside his office he blinked to take his eyes off the luscious curves that made a simple button-down blouse look like something that should be removed.

Slowly.

One button at a time.

With his teeth.

Damn.

"Yeah." He took a breath that did nothing to clear or stabilize his thoughts. "Bring them in."

"Are you sure?" Her head tilted again in an are-you-positive-you-haven't-gone-off-the-deep-end way. Which wasn't the first time she'd regarded him that way recently.

"I'm good. Let's do this."

Before she disappeared to the lobby to escort their clients into his office, she flashed him a grin that showed off a perfect set of dimples. He'd seen those dimples five days a week for four damn years. So why did he suddenly have the urge to press his lips against them and then follow up with a slow slide of his tongue down her long, delicate neck?

He'd never thought of himself as a masochist before, but with all these wayward thoughts, he had to concede it was a strong possibility.

Less than a minute later Brooke escorted James and Josh Flavio into his office. The father and son duo were looking for investment advice on adding a beachside Caribbean-style restaurant to their growing food service empire.

"Gentlemen." Declan extended his hand. "Welcome."

With the perfunctory introductions out of the way, he gestured to the conference area. While the men chose their seats, Declan watched Brooke settle into the leather chair at the end of the granite table and cross her legs.

Her bare, tan, smooth, shapely legs.

The black high-heeled, ankle-strap sandals she wore bordered on dominatrix, and that intrigued the hell out of him. Not that he was into the whole Christian

Grey red room thing, but he sure as hell wouldn't mind seeing Brooke in a little black lace and leather.

When she opened the file folder she'd placed on the table, he noticed the slender length of her fingers and the pale pink polish on her nails. Last week she'd worn Tiffany blue polish. The week before that she'd worn bloodred. Just last night those colorful fingertips had starred in a dream from which he'd awoken hot, sweaty, and horny as hell.

A white-gold filigree band graced the ring finger on her right hand and a silver bracelet with a charm that said *Fearless* encircled her left wrist.

Their past working lunches revealed she preferred chicken salad over egg, her steaks medium rare, and Caesar salads over garden. He knew when she crossed her legs she swung her right foot in tune with the music in her head. And when she was intently focused she tapped the end of a pen against the soft cushion of her lips. He also knew that after the office closed at night and everyone else had gone home—except him—she'd often stay to finish her work barefoot.

What he didn't know was what made her *fearless* as her bracelet proclaimed.

Extreme sports? Overcoming anxieties? Taking risks? Why didn't he know? And why was he wondering about it now? Especially since he had plenty of other things to think about. Like the fact that he had clients sitting at his conference table waiting for him to morph into the financial magician they were paying him to be. Or that his parents had died barely three months ago and he and his brothers were struggling to keep the family vineyard afloat. Or that he was knee-deep in the plans for a new Chicago office.

Yet here he was. Instead of keeping his eye on the ball, he was eyeing his assistant like she was a five-star meal he couldn't wait to devour.

Damn his twin.

This was all Jordan's fault.

For four years Declan had kept his mind on business and his hands to himself. A task that seemed impossible now.

Aside from knowing he'd be lost without Brooke, he didn't know the really important stuff about her. Like what she did in her spare time, where she'd been born, or what kind of upbringing she'd had. He didn't know if she lived alone, had a roommate, or lived with a boyfriend. Hell, he didn't even know if she had a boyfriend.

For four years he'd lived perfectly happy in his self-induced work cave and had kept everything on a strictly professional level. Now all he could think about was how much he'd like to caress Brooke's shapely curves in a very non-businesslike manner.

"Would you like me to record the meeting?"

Caught daydreaming, Dec's head snapped up. "What?"

Her lips tipped in a saucy smile. Okay, maybe it was just a regular smile. But for what he'd just been imagining, saucy fit the scenario.

"I asked if you'd like me to record the meeting."

"Gentlemen?" He glanced at the two men at the table. "It's your call."

"Josh can take notes," the father said.

"I'll be happy to do that for you." Brooke smiled. "That way you can focus on the discussion."

"We'd appreciate that," Mr. Flavio said.

"Then let's get down to business, shall we?" At that moment, Dec made the mistake of looking at Brooke again. While she reached for her laptop, her breasts pushed together just above the buttons of her shirt. When the tip of her tongue slipped out and swept her bottom lip, he couldn't give a shit about anything other than how badly he wanted a taste of her.

He knew how and when he'd started seeing Brooke in a new light, but he didn't understand why he couldn't control his thoughts or desire. Till now he'd been the epitome of control. It wasn't like it had been eons since he'd had sex. And even if that were the case, it wasn't like there weren't other women he could call on to relieve the ache.

Obsession with anything other than making a name for himself had never been an issue. Until the idea of *Brooke* had been lodged in his brain. And frankly, he wasn't too damn happy about this current preoccupation.

Only one thing in this muddled up mess was clear. As soon as he got back to the vineyard he was going to beat the shit out of his brother—one punch for each insane thought he'd planted in Dec's head.

*S*omething was bothering him.

While Brooke took notes during the meeting, Declan took care of business in the clever, professional manner he'd adopted before she'd ever walked into his office for a job interview.

On a normal day he was cool, confident, and a class act. Lately he seemed a bit distracted. Edgy. Even grumpy. He'd *never* grumbled at her before, yet in the past few weeks it had become his favorite form of communication. Not that he wasn't handling the Flavios' questions and concerns properly. And not that he wasn't offering great financial advice. But there was something in the way his deep blue eyes kept flicking up to meet her gaze.

She'd worked with him long enough to know when something was off. When that particular something wrinkled his brow and created tension at the corners of his eyes. But never had the look been directed at her. At least not with such intensity.

Had she done something wrong?

Maybe she shouldn't have taken that day off last week when she'd come down with food poisoning from the deli sandwich she'd snagged at the convenience store on her way home from work. She never took a day off unless it was absolutely a puking-in-the-trashcan necessity. Her hurried selection from the store's cooler and lack of checking the expiration date had caused her to miss an important meeting. When she'd returned to work the following day, Dec had kept his distance.

Maybe he'd just thought she had contagious cooties. Or maybe he'd become dissatisfied with the quality of her work.

No. That couldn't be it.

From analyzing documents, to preparing research

reports, to supervising the clerical staff, even to organizing baby showers and employee recognitions, she knew she was an integral part of the team. A part of the business Dec would either have to take care of himself or hire someone else to do. As his executive assistant she was more than just a message taker or a calendar coordinator. She kept his days managed and fluid. And she'd helped his business become one of the top financial companies in Southern California. Plus, she'd never had a bad or even a problematic performance review.

Still, an employee rarely knew when the ax was about to fall. Especially if they thought they'd been doing a good job.

Was she about to be fired?

God, she hoped not. She'd just booked a diving vacation in Costa Rica. She couldn't afford to lose her job now. Then again, no time was a good time.

A direct question from her boss forced her to temporarily push the concern aside and do what the man paid her to do.

As the hour-long meeting with the Flavios crept along, Brooke struggled to stay on task. Each tick of the clock increased her edginess about what was going on inside Dec's complex mind. The distraction made her anxious and until now she'd *never* allowed herself to become preoccupied during work hours.

Well, that wasn't entirely true.

She allowed herself to be plenty distracted by her boss—her gorgeous boss—who'd never been anything other than a gentleman. Who'd never displayed any intent other than getting a job done well. He'd never looked at her with anything more than his professional game face. He'd never made an inappropriate joke or a suggestive pass.

Even though she'd be totally open to it.

He worked too hard and, yes, he seemed a bit rigid and reserved, but that just made her want to dig deeper. To discover which buttons to push to get him to cut loose a little. He had so much passion for the financial world and his business that he must be equally passionate about everything beyond the office walls. Or was that just her wishful thinking?

A horrified thought crashed through her brain.

What if she'd been too transparent about her infatuation with him? What if she'd made him feel awkward with the longing looks she knew she sometimes couldn't help? Like now, when he was relaxed in his chair looking confident and powerful. What if she'd inadvertently let her silk sheets fantasies about him out of the bag?

No. That couldn't be it. It wasn't like she'd ever drooled or anything. She'd been careful.

Hopefully.

Maybe.

She glanced up from her keyboard, watching him as he began to wrap up the meeting. His presence commanded a meeting in a way that had more to do with his brain and less to do with his nearly black hair and blue-eyed good looks. He was smooth and smart, and the Flavios were inhaling his every word like he was some kind of economic demigod. She saw him as a god too, but hers leaned more toward the sexy superhero kind, even if she'd never seen him in anything other than a suit. The dark blue tie he wore today matched the color of his eyes. He had amazing eyes. Especially when he smiled. Which, come to think of it, wasn't all that often.

Unbidden, her fearless alter ego dove into the fantasy of what it would be like to coax a smile of satisfaction from those sultry lips. Or maybe, if she blindfolded him with that blue silk tie, what kind of smile she could entice by exploring his athletic body at her leisure. With her tongue.

A quiet little hum accidentally slipped from her mouth and he pierced her with a dark glare.

Yep.

No doubt about it. Something was definitely wrong.

When the men finally stood, signaling the end of the meeting, Brooke hit PRINT on her laptop. Perfect timing before her misplaced thoughts got her in even more hot water.

"I'll grab the notes off the printer." When she pushed away from her chair she could feel the heat of displeasure in Dec's eyes as he continued to talk with the Flavios.

Her hands trembled as she pulled the papers from the printer tray and she wondered if she could get back the deposit on her vacation. She should have read the fine print, but now she was just thankful she hadn't paid for the whole thing. Sure, she'd been saving money so it wouldn't hit her pocketbook too hard, but she'd been saving because she had her own professional dreams and aspirations. Not that she didn't love working for Dec, but she didn't want to be someone's assistant forever. No matter how wildly he stirred her blood.

Dec inspired her to believe in herself. He paid her well, gave her amazing financial advice, which she put to good use, and since she shared a house with her best friend her rent wasn't astronomical. She was on a good economic path to her future. But without a job her savings would go kaput fast, and her dream of someday becoming a business owner would fade into the sunset. On top of all that, she'd just be sad not to walk into the office every day and be able to see Dec sitting behind his enormous sleek black desk.

With her mind reeling over the potential problem, she took a calming breath and tapped the sheets of paper into a neat stack.

As soon as she walked back into Dec's office his dark brows pulled together again. Looked like the end of her workday wasn't going to end up half as good as the beginning.

Mostly because when she'd woken up this morning she'd been employed.

*B*rooke slid one set of the meeting notes into a manila envelope and handed it to Mr. Flavio. The other set she kept in her hand to be filed away before she went home—probably unemployed and heartbroken. Maybe she was imagining things. Maybe Dec's intense glares weren't meant for her. Maybe he was just under pressure and she just happened to be in his blue-eyed line of fire.

"Gentlemen," she said. "If everything is wrapped up here, I'd be happy to see you to the door."

The Flavios shook Dec's hand then began to file toward her.

"Brooke?" When she turned to face her boss, his lips were flattened in an implacable line. "Once you see the Flavios out, please come back to my office."

"Of course."

The walk back to Dec's office made her heart thump like a frightened rabbit's. With the spare set of meeting notes clutched in her hand, she knocked on his office door.

"It's open." Dec's terse response delivered a punch of proof that she had plenty of reason to worry.

Though everyone had gone home for the night and no one remained in the outer office, Brooke closed the door behind her. No sense letting the bad juju escape. And no sense waiting for the hammer to fall. Time to take matters—and the state of her employment—into her own trembling hands.

Shoulders rigid beneath his charcoal Hugo Boss, the man who held her immediate future in his hands stood near the window gazing at the beach scene below. He didn't acknowledge that she'd entered the room.

And that ticked her off.

"Are you firing me?"

His head snapped around, eyes shooting blue sparks. "What?"

"Are you firing me?" Clutching the copies of the meeting notes tighter, she propped her hands on her hips and lifted her chin. "Because if you are, I'll fight for my job. I won't go down easy. I've worked hard. And you'll go a long way before you find someone as dedicated to the success of this company as I am."

"What the hell are you talking about?" He stepped away from the window. Came closer, then backed off like he'd been hit with a wave of heat. "I'm not firing you."

She blinked. "You're not?"

"Hell no."

Relieved, her hands dropped to her sides. "Then what's with all the glaring eyes and menacing frowns?"

"What frowns?"

"Like that." She pointed. "The one on your face right now."

"Of course I'm frowning now. Because I think you might have gone a little crazy. Either that or you had a drinking lunch."

She gasped. "I don't drink on the job."

"Maybe you should. It might loosen you up a little."

"I don't think *I'm* the one who needs to loosen up."

His brows slammed together. "Are you saying I'm too tense?"

How in God's name did the man not realize that *tense* was his middle name?

"Well, I did just sit through that entire meeting wondering why you were going to fire me."

"You can't be serious."

"Dead."

His long, and obviously perplexed, pause immediately made her want to smooth things over. That was her style. Had always been her style. She couldn't stand it when people were mad. She'd always taken a peace-maker role, even when she knew her efforts would be wasted.

"Am I that difficult to work for?"

"Occasionally you *do* make me want to drink my lunch." Her attempt at humor went nowhere. "But you're not the worst boss I've ever had. At least you don't make me clean toilets."

"I don't believe that's in your job description."

"Good. Because that's where I'd have to draw the line."

"I don't know why you'd think I'd fire you." He moved toward his desk. His big hands slid over the top of his executive chair and gripped the leather tight. "Unless there's something you're not telling me."

She tsked. "So suspicious, boss man."

"Do I have reason to be?"

"You don't trust me?"

He hesitated and Brooke knew she really didn't want to hear his response. The persistent hesitation in his eyes made her believe that overall, her boss wasn't a very trusting kind of guy. And now that it felt like his suspicion had dropped a dark cloud over the room she decided to lighten things up.

"Maybe you're right," she said. "Maybe this was all just a ploy to get a raise."

"You should go for it." He knew she was kidding and showed it with the barest hint of a smile. "Perfect timing."

All things considered, it wasn't his half smile that caused the delicious shiver to ripple up her spine. That strike of awareness was brought on by the slow, sensual ride his gaze took over her body. Like he was considering a test-drive in a racy sports car.

Or was she imagining things again?

As long as she was walking on a razor's edge, she guessed it wouldn't hurt to test her theory.

"I hope you know by now that I don't *beg* for anything." She watched his face for any hint of a change when she added, "Well, that's not necessarily true."

Though his expression tightened, awareness flashed in his eyes like a hot streak of lightning. When he cleared his throat and held out his hand, Brooke noted the response and wondered just how far she could push the proverbial envelope.

"Are those the meeting notes?" He gave a sharp nod.

"Oh." As though she'd forgotten, she looked down as she extended her hand to give them over. "Almost forgot." She'd probably go to hell for that little white lie. Or maybe her ticket for the downtown train would be stamped for what she was about to do.

Moving her fingers apart, several sheets of paper *accidentally* floated to the carpet. As she bent down to retrieve them, she made the most of the pose and gave him the best opportunity for an eyeful. To her shameless delight, his gaze followed every movement like warm honey melting over every dip and curve she possessed.

Dec had never looked at her that way before, and she liked it a whole lot more than his recent scowls. While he may not have been considering firing her, she still didn't know what prompted his obvious displeasure.

While he may be good at hiding his soft center, Brooke was equally good at paying attention to the slightest details. The little things he did that showed his heart. Like the unexpected bonus he'd given Andrea in human resources when her husband had broken his leg on his construction job and couldn't work for three months to help support their family. Or all the donations and personal effort he put into the many charities he supported.

But how far could she reasonably push him on a personal level before he finally hit the gas or put on the brakes?

Was she willing to risk it all to take that chance?

"Sorry about that." Once she gathered up the papers and handed him the notes, their fingers touched and his eyes sparked again.

While it wasn't confirmation that he'd crossed the boss/employee line—in her mind—it certainly had them teetering on the edge. And it definitely offered encouragement.

After he glanced at the notes then dropped them on his desk, she asked, "So if the unemployment line isn't in my near future, what was it you wanted to see me about?"

When he looked up, he was back in full Declan Kincade professional mode.

"I know it's been a burden for you to hold things up here at the office and cover for me since my parents died. I wanted to thank you for that."

"You don't need to thank me." She wondered if he even knew of the pain that etched into his handsome face at the mention of his loss. Or how much she wished she could take all that agony away and see him smile. "I can't imagine how difficult this has all been for you and your family."

"It hasn't been easy. And apparently it's not getting any better. I spoke with Ryan earlier today and he says I need to get back up there as soon as possible."

Without all the details, Brooke had sensed there was more going on in their family than what normally occurred with such a loss. She'd been happy to go the extra mile when he needed her. And, no question, she'd go that mile again. She suddenly felt ridiculous and petty focusing on whether she'd still have a job tomorrow or whether he'd been looking at her in a suggestive way when all he'd been concerned with had been the state of his loved ones and their family legacy.

"How can I help?" she asked.

"I know we have a lot of meetings scheduled in the next couple of weeks and that some are ones that have already been rescheduled from when I was gone before. I hate to have to reschedule again."

"I'm sure your clients will understand."

"I don't want to take that chance. It's not fair for them to put aside their financial futures just because of my little situation."

"But it's not *little*, Dec. And if someone doesn't understand then maybe they're not the kind of client you really need."

"I wish it was that easy. But we need every client we have if we're going to open that Chicago office within the next year."

"Maybe now isn't a good time to move forward on that project when you already have enough on your plate."

"You don't understand."

But she did.

She knew he needed that distraction right now. He needed something else to focus on aside from the current issues and the overwhelming sadness of his loss.

She'd gladly distract him and let him focus all that energy on *her*. But she understood what he meant. She empathized with him. And because there was the slightest chance that she was probably, most likely, absolutely, positively already in love with him, she wanted to step up and do what he needed her to do.

"Right now I'm just trying to figure out how to pull everything together and be out of town at the same time." The tension in his voice matched the rigidity in his jaw.

"Well . . ." She gave her idea half a thought then said, "I could go with you."

"No. Not necessary."

His instant rejection stung, but it didn't stop her from forging ahead.

"Why not? It would enable us to keep working while you deal with your family situation. It might ease some of the pressure from constantly having to call and check in with me. I could set up Skype meetings with your clients so you don't have to reschedule. Basically I'd be right there handling things for you like usual."

A long pause hung between them while he considered her proposal. "I can't ask you to do that."

For me wasn't spoken, but Brooke heard the words loud and clear.

How did she let this man know she'd do *anything* for him without sounding too desperate or presumptuous?

"You don't have to ask. I'm offering. My job description doesn't say I'm only to perform my duties within these office walls, does it?"

"I doubt I added that particular clause."

"Then if there's access to the Internet, all I'd need is my laptop and my phone and we're in business."

He studied her, obviously weighing the pros, cons, and sheer insanity of the whole thing.

"Come on, Dec. It makes total sense."

To her relief, he caved. "If you're sure it wouldn't interfere with your schedule."

"Your schedule is my schedule." She gave a nonchalant shrug. "What difference does it make where it's handled?"

His shoulders visibly relaxed a smidge. "Then, if you wouldn't mind before you go home, I'd like to book our flight."

"Not a problem." She went to her laptop, which was still open on the conference table, and opened her browser. "How soon would you like to leave?"

"As soon as possible."

She browsed a few airlines' websites and those flights from local airports were booked for the next few days.

"Aside from going standby or chartering a jet there's not much available for the next forty-eight hours."

"Not surprised." Once again he'd moved away from

his desk to the window and stood there, hands in pockets, looking out.

"There is another possibility."

He glanced at her over his shoulder. "Which is?"

"We drive."

"Drive?" He spoke the single word like the idea was preposterous.

"Sure. How do you usually get around when you get there?"

"I rent a car."

"Well . . ." Quickly she searched the drive time and distance to Vancouver in her browser. "It's roughly a fifteen-hour drive. You can either waste time waiting on standby in the airport or shelling out a fortune for a charter. You'll need a car once you get there, so driving is probably faster, more economical, and a reasonable alternative."

He remained absolutely expressionless and silent.

"If you're worried about the time behind the wheel, I can help. I promise I haven't had a traffic ticket since they issued my license."

"It's not that I don't trust your driving."

"Then what's the issue?"

"That's a long time. In a car."

"Afraid you'll get bored?"

"No."

"Are you afraid your butt will fall off?"

"No."

"Aha." She pointed. "You smiled."

"No I didn't."

"You did too."

His brows slammed together again as though finding something humorous was a sin.

"Be realistic, Dec. Driving is a solid option." She'd pushed just enough and hoped he'd bend. "My only goal is to give you everything you really need."

Even if what he really needed had never crossed his mind.

Chapter 2

*M*orning peeked its sunny little head above the horizon way too soon for Dec, who hadn't slept all night. His sheets were tangled, a headache poked him between the eyes, and dread pounded his brain like a cheap whiskey hangover.

On a normal day he was an early riser. Even on weekends he had a pot of coffee going and the financial news up on the TV before the alarm went off.

Today was anything but normal.

Today he'd set himself up for a disaster. How he'd allowed Brooke to convince him that driving to Vancouver was a good idea was anyone's guess. At the same time, he had to admit he hadn't felt this heightened level of anticipation since . . . he couldn't remember when.

After he'd left the office last night he'd needed an outside opinion that his plans weren't out of line. Or at least a ride to the loony bin. Though his brothers were miles away and busy with their own lives, he'd needed someone—anyone—to talk him off the ledge of what-the-hell-did-I-just-do.

After Brooke had driven out of the parking lot in her little red car, he'd made a call to his most level-headed brother.

The conversation with Ryan began with the usual small talk of business and family. He learned that Ryan's little girl, Riley, was having trouble sleeping because of nightmares. Jordan and his fiancée, Lucy, were sampling wedding cakes. Ethan was clearing out the old barn, apparently in search of the lost treasure. Parker continued to split his time between working long hours with his food truck business and juggling duties at the vineyard. And their baby sister, Nicole, was still contemplating taking off to Nashville to start her music career now that she'd graduated high school.

Dec believed now was a horrible time for Nicki to make such a life-changing decision. Especially since her entire world had been thrown into upheaval. Not only had she lost the mother she'd been very close to, she was still reeling from the comments made by their father right before he'd died. Comments that had led Nicki to believe he didn't love her and that maybe she wasn't really even his daughter.

The more the conversation with Ryan went on, the more Dec believed going home was the right thing to do. Even if that meant spending fifteen hours in a car, elbow-to-elbow with his smoking hot, sweet smelling assistant.

Before he'd ended the call, he'd casually asked if Ryan thought bringing Brooke along with him on a thousand-mile road trip would be throwing himself into the fires of hell. His big brother had laughed then hesitated before giving Dec an unexpected response.

Little brother, I've seen your assistant. And believe me, the trip to hell would be worth it.

In the morning light, Declan wasn't so sure.

After losing an internal all-night debate about canceling the trip, he pulled up in front of Brooke's address in a suburb of Orange County. He noted the simplicity of the home, the well-trimmed lawn, and the huge black truck parked in the driveway next to Brooke's Honda.

Stupid shit.

He'd conveniently dismissed the reality that Brooke could very well be involved with someone who wouldn't appreciate her taking off with another man. Her employer at that. No question his initial reaction to the idea blurred the line between business and pleasure. And no matter what his brother thought, Brooke was a valuable employee.

Period. End of story.

He sat in the car and contemplated all the reasons this was a bad idea, but the wheel was already in motion. He needed to get back to his family. Decisions needed to be made. Puzzles needed to be solved. Business needed to move forward. And for *that* he needed his assistant. Having her travel with him wouldn't be any different than any other day at the office. He could maintain control of his thoughts. He could keep his desire for her at bay. No matter how good she looked, how wonderful she might smell, or how delicious she might taste.

Fifteen hours was a drop in the bucket.

He could do this.

Before he went all Hulk Hogan and started grunting, he walked to the front door and rang the bell. When a man opened the door he wasn't surprised.

The guy on the opposite side of the threshold equaled Dec's six-foot-three height, was clean-cut, in good physical shape, and obviously annoyed.

For a second he and the man stood there, sizing each other up before Dec introduced himself. The lack of a reciprocating introduction was definitely intentional and Dec didn't blame the man for the snub. If someone like him had shown up to take *his* woman on a long road trip to another state, he'd have something to say about it.

Like a big hell no.

"Brooke sweetie, your *boss* is here," the other man said as if he could reach into Dec's mind and grab hold of the not-so-professional thoughts hovering there.

Yep. That clinched it.

Dec pulled down his imaginary professional hat and waited for Brooke to come to the door. Without a word to Dec, the guy disappeared somewhere in the house. When Brooke appeared, Dec had to take a step back and hold on tight to his good intentions.

For four years Brooke had shown up at the office with a professionalism that matched her straight skirts and button-down blouses. This morning, however, she looked like something straight out of a country music video. Her honey blond hair looked freshly washed and tousled so that it hung down her back in long sexy waves instead of the sleek straight look she usually wore during business hours. A snug white tank top accentuated her perfect breasts. Around her narrow waist she'd tied the sleeves of a red plaid shirt. Her long tanned legs were topped off with a pair of short cutoff jeans. And her feet were covered with gray-and-blue sneakers.

If *he* was her boyfriend he'd never let her out the door looking like that. Not that he had a problem with the way she dressed or would ever have the right to tell her what to wear, he'd just be too busy taking off her clothes, hauling her into the bedroom, and making love to her until the sun went down. Yet the man in the house remained glaringly absent as his sexy-as-sin girlfriend tossed Dec a smile that flashed her dimples.

"Hey. Look at you." Her dark eyes moved appreciatively over his body. "I've never seen you in anything other than a suit and tie. Jeans and a T-shirt look good on you. I'm glad I suggested we go casual for the drive."

He was glad too. But for completely different reasons.

"Come on in." She waved him into the house. "I just have to grab my stuff and I'm ready to go."

Dec stepped inside of a house furnished nice and neat without looking antiseptic. A few real houseplants were placed on shelves and some nice black-and-white photography decorated the walls. Basic black leather furniture had been strategically positioned for the best viewing of the large flat-screen TV. And with a smattering of decorator pieces, the place didn't look overly feminine or masculine. More like a combination of the two.

Still, the boyfriend remained MIA.

"Let me help you with your bag," Dec said, wondering why the boyfriend wasn't offering to help his woman.

"Awww. You're sweet. But I can get it."

Sweet?

He'd never been called that in his life.

Pensive, determined, private, and successful? Yes. But sweet? Nope.

He watched her hips gently sway as she walked down the hall.

Yeah, she might be taken, and he might be her boss, but damned if he didn't look anyway.

Moments later she came back down the hall with a bright orange tote bag slung over one shoulder, pulling a red suitcase, and cradling a little tri-colored dog. A real dog that looked at him with utter surprise in its bright blue eyes. Not a stuffed animal like something she might cuddle at night. Well, maybe she cuddled something but he definitely wasn't going to allow his imagination to go there. Especially not now when he knew she had a boyfriend. Even if the unnamed idiot couldn't seem to come out of hiding to say goodbye when she called out that she was leaving.

Amid her protests, Dec took her suitcase and tote bag, leaving her to carry the dog, who had something big, fuzzy, gray, and slobbery hanging from its mouth.

"Who do you have there?" he asked with a tilt of his head toward the canine. "And *what* is *that*?"

"*This . . .*" She chuckled then gave the dog a kiss on the head. "Is Moochie. She's a mini Australian shepherd who disregards the 'mini' moniker when there's a cat on the fence. And *that* is her favorite toy. It used to be an elephant before she pulled out the squeaker and all the stuffing."

Eyes wary, the dog looked up at him.

"She looks a little freaked out." Dec put Brooke's suitcase next to his in the trunk of his red convertible Infiniti Q60.

"It's the bright color of her eyes that makes her appear that way." Brooke resettled the little dog on her hip. "I hope you don't mind if I bring her along. I don't have anyone to watch her while I'm gone and I don't have the heart to put her in a kennel."

"What about your boyfriend?"

"My . . ." She glanced back at the house. "Kyle?"

Dec shrugged. "He didn't introduce himself."

"Kyle is my best friend and roommate. He's *not* my boyfriend. In fact, he's engaged to be married." She chuckled. "To Marc."

"Marc?" Dec's head snapped up. "I didn't get that vibe from him. The glare he gave me seemed more of a protective one for *you*."

"He quit throwing out *the vibe* when he met Marc. They're a great couple," she said as he tossed her tote bag into the backseat. "And he's not overly protective of me because he knows I can pretty much hold my own."

Dec thought of her *Fearless* bracelet and wondered if there was a connection. However, when she leaned into the car, all thought stopped and his attention immediately shot to the rear view of her Daisy Dukes.

"Tough girl, huh?"

She scooted inside the car and looked up at him. "There's a lot you don't know about me."

Apparently.

"By the way, the answer is no."

"No?"

"No, I don't have a boyfriend. Just in case you were wondering."

Of course he'd wondered. He wasn't dead for God's sake.

"So . . ." She tucked her enormous purse by her feet. "Are we officially on the clock right now? Do you want me to pull out my laptop and get to work? Wi-Fi might be spotty but I have other things I can accomplish."

"Too distracting for me." Like he wasn't already on overload? "I need to focus on the traffic."

"Sweet. So I don't have to act all professional and boring until we get there?"

Since when had she ever been boring?

And what exactly did she have in mind?

"You're free to sit back and relax."

"I can relax when I'm asleep." She threw him a grin. "Right now I want to have fun."

Well, that didn't bode well for the control he expected to maintain.

"I thought maybe before we jumped on the freeway we could stop for something to drink and some travel snacks," she added.

"Like water and protein bars?"

"I was thinking more like caffeine and pork cracklings."

"I don't even know what the hell those are."

"You don't know what you're missing, boss man."

"Clogged arteries?"

The wind blew through her hair as she tipped her

head back and laughed. "I never knew you've been so sheltered. Guess there's a lot I have to learn about you."

Before his mind traveled to dangerous places, he spotted a Starbucks and pulled into the drive-thru. Along with a plain black coffee for himself, he ordered her usual latte.

"What if I wanted something different?" She wrinkled her nose.

"Do you?"

"No." She settled deeper into the passenger seat. "I just don't want you to think that I'm one of *those* girls."

He pulled up to the drive-thru window and handed the server his credit card. Distracted by something the woman at the window was saying, he asked, "What kind is that?"

"You know . . . predictable and boring."

Heaven help him.

"I like predictability," he said, veering into safer waters.

She glanced at him across her bare shoulder. "Do you also like boring?"

He paused a second too long and she pounced.

"I didn't think so. I may not know what you do in your off hours, but you don't seem like the type to sit at home and watch reruns of *Two and a Half Men*."

"Two and a half what?"

She laughed. "Do you watch TV at all?"

"Of course."

"Let me guess." Playfully she turned in the seat to face him. "*Once Upon a Time*, *Game of Thrones*, and *Dancing with the Stars*?"

"More like CNN, *Bulls & Bears*, and *Face the Nation*."

"Boring."

"TV should only be used as an opportunity for expanding views or education."

"I promise I won't tell all the porn stars you said that. Then again . . ." She crooked a brow. "Is that what kind of education you mean?"

Before he could respond she added, "Kidding! Please tell me that you at least channel surf once in a while and secretly end up watching *Naked and Afraid*."

Naked and *afraid*. In his mind, two words that didn't belong together.

"I'm actually familiar with that one. It's one of Parker's favorites."

"Parker being brother number . . ."

"Four."

"Ah. Well, at least he gets it."

Oh Dec got it all right. Watching shows with naked people struggling to stay alive was supposed to broaden your horizons. But if Dec wanted to see someone naked he wanted to be the one to dirty her up. And since that thought led right to his traveling companion he allowed himself to be dragged into the subject matter. He had to. Otherwise the drive was going to be a hell of a lot longer than he needed.

"Does your choice of TV viewing have anything to do with the *Fearless* bracelet you wear?" he asked, handing her the caramel brûlée latte.

"Ha!" She let out a deliciously devious laugh that stirred everything behind the zipper of his jeans. "You have no idea."

Maybe not.

But he certainly couldn't wait to find out.

In a strictly professional sense, of course.

*B*rooke had to take a deep breath before she sipped her latte. Not because of the heat of the drink. Not because yesterday she thought she'd be fired. But because today she was sitting in the front seat of her incredibly gorgeous boss's sexy convertible thinking very *un*bosslike things about him. Like how the sunshine gleamed in his nearly black hair. Or how the Ray-Ban sunglasses he wore made him look lickably hot. Or how nice the snug baby blue T-shirt lay across his wide shoulders and broad chest, and how the fabric rippled smoothly over what she suspected was at least a six-pack of sexy abs. Or how flawlessly the short sleeves hugged his defined biceps. Or how the well-fit jeans cupped him in places that ignited her imagination and curiosity. Or how she'd like to remove each one of those clothing items to see if beneath he wore boxers, briefs, or nothing at all.

She knew he was a runner from the countless charity marathons in which he participated. And even though he was long and lean, he didn't have that skinny look that some runners developed. He didn't look like a gym rat, either. So curiosity sparked at exactly how Dec developed and maintained all those finger-tempting, mouthwatering muscles.

But she digressed.

She really needed to focus on being the ever helpful assistant so that he could focus on the important things.

Just because he'd given her a once-over a couple of times didn't mean anything more than a man looking at a woman. No big deal on the grand scale of things. All those wayward thoughts in her head needed to stop.

Needed to, but most likely wouldn't.

There was just something about him she couldn't leave alone. Not that she expected anything from him—a raise, romance, or anything else—she just wanted to see him smile. Laugh. And learn to let go of those reins he kept so tight in his hands. She wanted his life to be enjoyable as well as successful.

She'd spent far too many years trapped in a world where a smile was perceived as a sin. To know that Dec may be caught in that same whirlpool broke her heart.

When they stopped at a gas station near the freeway, Brooke tried to sober up and cut out all the goofing off. But the utter dismay on Dec's face made her do a complete three-sixty and end up right back where she'd started.

Determined to make him smile.

Furthering his education in the finer things of life in the snacking world was currently up at bat.

The moment they walked inside the convenience mart, Dec's eyes went wide and Brooke quickly assumed he'd never gone farther than the gas pumps. She imagined his cupboards and refrigerator filled with healthy, boring items like kale, brown rice, and tasteless protein powder.

Time to turn things upside down.

"I can see you're a virgin," she said without cracking a smile.

His head snapped around and he looked at her like she was wrapped up in silly string. "Excuse me?"

"Relax, boss man. I've seen enough of the women you date to know you're not *that* kind of virgin. I meant that you're a convenience mart virgin."

He looked around at the rows and rows of sinful snacks as if someone had dropped him in a galaxy far, far away. "I've never had a reason—or a desire—to venture inside before."

"Yeah. I figured. No worries. I've got your back."

"Really."

"Would I steer you down the wrong path?"

His scowl told her he thought it was a definite possibility. One he didn't want to encounter.

He was right, of course.

"First . . ." She cut her eyes across the store. "I need to mention that while those sub sandwiches in the cooler over there look innocent enough, make sure you always read the expiration date before you indulge."

"Speaking from experience?"

"Don't ask." She waved her hand. "Shall we?"

"I think I hear your dog barking."

"You drive a convertible, you're parked out front, and I can see her from here. She's not barking. And if you'll stop dragging your feet, this will only take a minute."

"Said the executioner to the dead man walking."

"Ha. Good one." She made an arc with her hands. "Did you know you can create an entire food pyramid meal in here?"

"Hard to imagine."

"It's true." She led him down the closest aisle. "You can start here with the bread group. Rice Krispies treats, donuts, granola bars."

"I don't think granola bars drenched in chocolate count."

"*Anything* drenched in chocolate counts." She expected resistance, so to avoid losing momentum, she took off toward the next aisle. "Down this aisle we have the vegetable and meat groups."

"Potato chips and beef jerky?"

"And don't forget the corn nuts." She grinned despite his persistent frown. "Over here we have the dairy section."

Clearly ready to bolt for the door, he shoved his hands into the front pockets of his jeans. "Let me guess, smoothies?"

"Don't be silly. Chocolate milk and ice cream."

"I don't see any eggs."

She grabbed an egg and cheese burrito from the freezer and held it up. "Voila."

"Dangerous. And fruit?"

"I recommend you bypass the nutritious bananas at the checkout stand and go directly for the glazed apple pies."

"You've really got this all figured out. Do you dine here frequently?"

"In moments of sheer desperation. At my house dining alone is an all-too-frequent matter. And cooking for one just isn't much fun."

"You cook?"

She shrugged. "I can hold my own with a frying pan."

"Now there's a chilling thought."

"Are you always this—"

"Cautious?"

"Reluctant."

"I don't believe it's out of line when someone's trying to kill you."

"I would *never* do that." She feigned indignation. "Lead you astray?" She shrugged. "How about we ease you into things with a bag of these?"

Suspiciously he eyed the bag of Combos. "I'm not even sure I want to know what that is."

She sighed dramatically. "So much to learn. So little time."

*M*uch to Dec's dismay they left the convenience mart with a large bag guaranteed to be a gastrointestinal nightmare. Brooke's dog caught scent of the snacks they'd also picked up for her as soon as they got back in his car.

"Want to know how Moochie got her name?" Brooke opened the bag and set a dog snack on Dec's thigh. "Watch."

From the backseat the little dog's impatient whining turned into an attention-getting sneeze, a dance, and a comical growly bark. Dec didn't move as Moochie put her front paws on the center armrest and gave him another goofy little growl. She nudged his arm with her long nose and pleaded with her big blue eyes. When he remained motionless, the dog hefted her entire little body onto the armrest.

Having never had a pet before, he didn't know what to expect. And since her owner had completely jumped off the business rails, anything could happen.

The dog gave him a flirty little bark while she crept closer and closer to the snack on his leg. Then she placed her front paws on his arm and licked his chin. He chuffed a laugh then told the dog to go ahead and get the snack. That's all it took for her to snap it up and then devour it while sitting on his lap, gazing up at him with canine adoration.

"She's got quite the personality." Dec petted the dog then backed out of the parking space. "Until Jordan gave Nicole a kitten, we never had pets."

"Never?"

He shook his head. "Parents didn't want any, and when I moved out I never had time."

"So who keeps you company at night?"

Was she fishing?

He glanced across the car too late to know. She'd conveniently dropped the sunglasses that had been perched on her head down onto her small, straight nose.

"Usually the light of my laptop," he said.

"Declan Kincade, that's just sad."

What had she expected him to say? That he was never alone and had plenty of willing women to warm his sheets?

They'd already veered too far from the boss/employee line. He had to keep that in mind at all times. Because this fun, flirty side of Brooke was going to be very hard to overlook.

He'd been denied many things in his life. Forbidding

himself at least a taste of Brooke was going to be like sitting in front of a decadent slice of chocolate cake with a shark cage between them.

Just before he swung the Infiniti onto the freeway onramp, she said, "Pull over."

"What?"

"Right there." She pointed to yet another gas station.

Against his better judgment—because today he seemed to be minus a few marbles—he complied. "Did you forget something?"

"No. You did."

He braked to a stop near the driveway. "I'm sure I didn't."

Mischief written all over her, she folded her arms across her breasts and grinned. "Would you consider yourself the adventurous type?"

Uh-oh.

"Depends on what kind of adventure you're talking about." Between the sheets? Hell yes. Trying to figure out what really went on inside Brooke's quick mind? There'd never be enough time in the day.

A small shrug lifted her shoulders. "Life in general."

"In that case I prefer to gather information and make calculated and appropriate decisions."

She leaned in just slightly and his senses were filled with sweet, warm woman. "Of course you do."

"Exactly where is this all going?"

"Calculated and appropriate decisions might be great for business or emergency situations. But when it comes to your personal life?" She shrugged again.

She might have a point, but the implication had

temptation written all over it, and he was not about to willingly walk into that inferno.

"My personal life is just fine."

Her head tilted and those loose, sexy curls tumbled over her shoulder. "Is it?"

"Yes. It's fine. Great. Perfect." He tightened his hands on the wheel. "Can we go now?"

"Not so fast." She pulled the sunglasses off her face and tucked one of the handles down her shirt and between her breasts.

Yep.

No question.

She was trying to kill him.

Her eyes locked onto his. "When is your family expecting you in Vancouver?" she asked.

"There's nothing life-threatening on the table, so I didn't give them an exact time. I just said in the next day or two."

"In that case . . . how about we test that theory?"

He looked skyward. *Dear God, please don't make me ask.* "What theory?"

"Whether your life is fine. Great. Perfect."

"Mimicking me isn't going to get you that raise."

"Were we still talking about a raise?"

Yes. But probably not the kind she meant.

"*Were* being the key word."

She chuckled. "Then in light of me continuing to live on a tight budget, how about you turn this car around?"

"Why would I do that?"

"Because you're dying to be adventurous."

"I think you've misjudged me."

"I'm going to keep hope alive that I'm right."

"I really wouldn't do that if I were you."

"Oh come on." She started to touch his arm but at the last second, pulled her hand away. "It will be fun."

"Supposing I agree—which I won't—exactly where is this *fun* supposed to take place?"

"On the road to Vancouver," she said enthusiastically. "Via the scenic route."

"I don't believe I signed up for the scenic route."

"Have you ever driven all the way up the coast?"

"No."

"Then why would you be opposed?"

It would take him all day to count the reasons.

"Dec. Come on. You have a convertible, aka a *fun* car. Not only is it a convertible but it's *red*. Double score in the fun factor."

"Have *you* ever driven all the way up the coast of California or Oregon?" he asked.

"No. Then again I drive a Honda. And while we might have the same taste in the color of cars, I guarantee the driving experience is patently different."

"And driving up the coast is something you're determined to do?"

"Absolutely. It's on my bucket list."

"You're too young to have a bucket list."

She laughed. "I've had a bucket list since I was ten."

He tried to picture her as a little girl and couldn't. She was too grown-up and sexy now in her cutoff shorts and breast hugging tank top. "What kind of kid does that?"

"If you take the coastal route to Vancouver, I might tell you."

He had no idea she was such a tease. As her boss,

he frowned at the level of pleasure that rippled through his blood at that thought. But that didn't stop him from considering the possibilities in the rearview mirror. Against every sane thought he possessed, he flipped a U-turn and headed toward Pacific Coast Highway.

"Woohoo!" Brooke lifted her arms in victory. Her shriek of sheer joy and the delighted expression on her face sent a wild shot of adrenaline through his heart.

In that breath-stealing moment, Dec thought they might be in for a grand adventure.

In a professional sense only.

"Maybe we should stop and get a map."

A sigh drifted from Brooke's pretty pink lips. "Just drive, boss man. Live a little. I'll make sure you get off in all the right places."

Holy shit.

Her words might have been innocent, but they had him picturing something entirely different than pressing the pedal to the metal.

"You said you've never driven the coastal route," he said.

"That's true."

"Why not?"

"It's hard to find someone who wants to take a play day and just go." She fed another snack tidbit to Moochie. "What's your reason?"

"Too busy."

"At least I made it to Malibu one time for a suntan."

He turned his head and found her with her face tilted toward the sun, her sunglasses in place, and a smile playing at the corners of her lips. "You drove all the way to Malibu just for a suntan?"

"Of course not. I drove all the way to Malibu so I could stop at the Santa Monica Pier, ride the carousel, and go to trapeze school. And so I could eat oysters at Gladstones in Malibu on the beach. The suntan I got was just topping on the cake."

"Then how do you know the way to Vancouver?" Sure, the answer was simple. There was a phone app that would give them directions to the damn front door easily enough. Curiosity may have killed the cat, but the way her mind worked fascinated him. He didn't want to feel that way, but God help him, he did.

"I *don't* know the way," she said. "But I think the discovery will be fun."

"You big on taking risks?" Yeah. He knew the answer. But he felt compelled to ask anyway.

She held up her arm and her *Fearless* bracelet flashed at him in the sunlight.

"Does that have anything to do with you coming up with a bucket list at ten years old?"

"It has everything to do with it." She sank down more into the seat and lifted her face to the sun. "Go ahead and ask me. I know you're dying to."

"Apparently I'm not."

"Sure you are. Admit it. You want to know what makes me fearless." She leaned in. "*And* you want to know what else is on my bucket list."

Of course he did. He wasn't dead for God's sake.

"I've never known you to have so many miscalculations at the office."

"But we're not at the office." She grinned. "And that

look on your face tells me you want to know what makes me tick. You want to dissect me and figure me out like you do with all those numbers you play with every day."

"I don't *play*. I analyze."

"Playing might be a lot more fun." She folded her arms. "So go ahead. Ask me."

"Is that a request? Or a demand?"

"Neither. It's your sheer curiosity."

"What if I'm not curious?"

"Then it might be fun if you learned to be."

If there was ever a moment in his life where he felt like he was sliding down a slippery slope, this was it. "If I ask will you let it go after so I can focus on getting to Vancouver?"

"Maybe."

Jesus.

This went beyond a can of worms. This was like an invitation to a party he couldn't afford to attend. "What makes you fearless?"

"The story is too long to tell."

Squeezing the steering wheel he dared to look at her. "So you brought it up why?"

"Because this road trip is for us to learn more about each other."

"No. I believe we agreed this road trip was a faster option to reach Vancouver than going standby with the airlines."

"But that's not much fun. I like my version better."

Someone picked up a sledgehammer and smashed him between the eyes. "Brooke?"

"Yes, Dec?"

"Would it be too much to ask for a moment of silence?"

"I'm afraid so."

"Then could we just listen to the radio? I'll let you choose the station."

"How about we listen to music *and* talk?" She leaned forward and turned the radio to a country station where Florida Georgia Line was sippin' on fire. "I'm surprisingly great at multitasking."

The coastal highway was busy as Dec maneuvered between cars to get ahead of the sightseers. "I need to focus on driving."

"So you're saying *you're* not great at multitasking?"

"I'm not saying that at all. Point being, I'm trying not to say anything."

"So . . . back to my bucket list."

Yep. This was going to be the longest damn drive of his life. He didn't even bother to wonder if he'd be sane at the end.

"Why don't you just give me the CliffsNotes and hit on some of the highlights."

"They're all highlights."

Dear God. "Then give me your top five."

Moochie crawled up from the backseat and into Brooke's lap. The dog looked up at her adoringly before her long pink tongue slipped out and licked the bottom of Brooke's chin.

"Top five? Okay, here we go." She held up her index finger. "I want to hug a sloth—"

"Wait." He took his eyes off the road and turned them toward her. "Did you say a *sloth*? Like the animal?"

"Does that seem weird?" Her head tilted as though she wondered why he'd even question that.

"A little."

"Well, I think they're adorable."

"Duly noted. Continue if you must."

Finger two popped up. "I want to see the aurora borealis. Sleep under the stars on the top of a mountain. Kiss the Blarney Stone." Four fingers wiggled and her thumb joined the party. "And own my own business."

"Now there's something I can get behind."

"But the number one item on my list is that I want to marry the love of my life."

Pushing aside the distasteful image of Brooke wrapped in some faceless guy's arms, he dared to engage. "What? No jumping from airplanes or climbing Mount Everest?"

Her nose wrinkled. "You only said the top five."

"Jumping from a plane *is* on your list?"

She nodded. "So is diving the Great Barrier Reef and wrestling an alligator. Although that scares me pretty bad so that one might eventually come off the list." She stroked the top of Moochie's head and received another chin lick for her efforts. "What about you? Do you have a bucket list?"

"No."

"Why not?"

He shrugged. "Never thought about it."

"Seriously?"

He nodded.

"Well, now is as good a time as any to start one. So what's the first thing you might put on your list?"

He could hardly tell her that on top of his list would be stripping her naked and having mind-shattering sex, so he came up with something totally unsubstantial. "Maybe I'd drink my way across the small pubs in Ireland." Because drinking himself into oblivion right now seemed like a really good idea.

"That's a great start. I might even be tempted to join you." Her dimples winked as she laughed. "And then you could come with me to kiss the Blarney Stone."

When she looked at him with so much hope and enjoyment in her eyes he was tempted to go anywhere with her. But kissing some old rock seemed a waste of good kissing time.

"What else?" she asked.

He thought for a moment and knew that in reality there was really only one thing on his mind that didn't involve her. "I'd like to honor my parents by making our family business a success again."

"You will." Her voice softened with genuine affection. "And I'm sure your parents already knew what a special son you are."

Apparently not, considering the fact that his own father hadn't asked him for help in his area of expertise when he'd needed it.

Dec frowned behind his sunglasses.

Where his parents were concerned, he really wasn't sure of anything anymore.

They made it to Santa Barbara before Brooke begged Dec to pull over. She and Moochie both needed a potty break and they could also use a chance to stretch their legs. She'd never been this far north, but like all the travel magazines promised, the scenery was breathtaking.

And that included her handsome albeit grumpy driver who asked, "You hungry?"

She nodded even though her stomach had been plied with a snack pack of Swedish Fish and she still had a sugar high going.

"Maybe we can find an outdoor patio so your dog can come along."

"Sounds great. She likes to be involved. If she's not, she pouts."

"Seriously?"

"Yep."

"Wonders never cease."

After they parked and made a quick restroom stop, they passed a beautiful dolphin fountain and headed toward the wharf. The day was clear, the mountains rose into the blue sky at their backs, and the warm midday sun gleamed across the vast Pacific Ocean.

Brooke couldn't believe she had this opportunity to share something so beautiful with the man she'd crushed on for nearly four years. She may have fantasized about it, but to actually have it come true made her want to drag her iPhone out to take some selfies as proof. If she didn't feel she'd already pushed enough of Dec's buttons today she wouldn't hesitate.

Midway down the wharf they stopped so a little girl could give Moochie some love. Of course, the pooch, who loved children, returned the favor with several slurps up the darling little towhead's chin. The child giggled and Brooke did too. Dec watched the action from several feet away with a blank expression.

"Don't you like kids?" she asked as they walked away.

"I'm fond of my nine-year-old niece. And although I was sixteen when my little sister was born, she was a lot of fun."

"Have you ever thought about having any of your own?" she asked.

"My own?" He answered as though she'd asked if he had sex with aliens.

"I'll take that as a no."

"Kind of like a bucket list—never entered my mind."

"You don't think you'd make a good dad?"

"I have no idea."

"Huh."

He lowered his sunglasses and peered at her over the black frames. "Clarify 'huh.' "

"Well . . . usually people from large families either want a large family themselves or they completely steer clear of it."

"I'm not steering anywhere. Neither marriage nor children are on my radar."

"Ever?"

He shrugged those broad shoulders.

Well, that was disappointing.

He lifted one dark brow inquisitively. "You?"

Brooke snagged her lip between her teeth. Answering his question would no doubt lead to more inquiries about her family, and she wasn't ready to go there yet.

Maybe she'd never be ready.

For years she'd been judged based on her mother and father's beliefs and behaviors, and the community in which she'd lived. It wasn't a place she'd ever felt safe or loved, and she never planned to return.

Since she'd escaped she'd done her best to maintain radio silence on the issue. The less people knew, the less opportunity they had to criticize. Dec's opinions mattered. And he was the one person she couldn't bear to have judge her. Though she trusted him, she knew not everyone looked further than the dirty details. The situation over which she'd had no control had left a stain on her past. And as everyone knew, stains were impossible to ignore.

"I already said I wanted to find the love of my life and get married." She let out a little more of Moochie's leash.

"And do you have huge aspirations to be a mother?"

"I don't know," she answered honestly. She hadn't had the best role model with her own mother. Then again, she'd pretty much struck gold with her foster mother. So she was torn. "I'm willing to give it some serious consideration when the time is right. I like kids. Until they turn into teenagers. Then they scare me."

"Tell me about it."

An elderly couple strolled by, holding hands, and smiling in that special way two people who'd spent a lifetime together did. Brooke felt a little pang in her heart. She wanted to be just like that someday.

Dec never even noticed them.

"My sister, Nicole, became a little crazier each year

she grew older," Dec said, obviously not paying any attention to the couple who'd just passed them by. "Things haven't gotten much better since she turned eighteen."

"Well, don't get your hopes up. She's not out of the woods yet."

"Is being a difficult teen a subject you're familiar with?"

"Nope." She'd been too afraid she'd be sent back where she came from to be difficult. "Don't get me wrong, I was no angel." Sometimes she'd had to push the envelope just to see if the Hastingses would truly never send her back for any reason as they'd promised. "But usually when I was given rules I stuck to them."

A gull swooped and screeched, startling Brooke a little and causing her to bump into Dec. His hand came up to steady her.

"How about you?" she asked quickly, fanning down the flames his unintentional touch had ignited. "Rule breaker?"

"Totally." Obviously the bump hadn't affected him at all.

"How did I already know that?"

Without a response, he stopped in front of a seafood restaurant with a rooftop patio.

Looked like tall, dark, and bossalicious might have some secrets of his own. Which gave her another avenue to explore.

"How about this place?" he asked.

"Looks great. I'm hungry," she said, knowing the only thing that would truly taste as good as it looked was *him*.

He waited for her to take the stairs ahead of him.

Brooke knew the gesture was because he was a gentleman, but part of her hoped he'd let her go first because he wanted to watch her go up the stairs in her short shorts. In any case, she made every step she took visually count.

"Wow." She gasped as they reached the rooftop patio. "Great view."

"Excellent view," he replied, looking at her legs and not the mountains and ocean.

That single deviation from his usual business persona to a sexual alpha male gave her hope. It also made the ladies in the lingerie department stand up and shake their lace.

When his eyes finally made it back up to her face and he was once again in full control, he asked, "Hungry?"

"You have no idea."

A server instructed them to select any table they wanted and said she'd be back shortly with their menus and water. After Moochie did a cute little dance, the server added that she'd bring a bowl of dog water and maybe even a snack.

They selected an umbrella table by the rail where they could watch the anchored boats bob on the water and a pair of sea lions frolic near a buoy.

"You ever wonder what it would be like to live on the ocean?" Brooke asked Dec.

"Nauseating?"

She laughed. He may not show it often, but the man had a wickedly dry sense of humor she truly enjoyed. "Do you get seasick?"

"No idea." His big shoulders shrugged. "I've never been out in a boat. The closest I've come is a rotted canoe my brothers and I took out on the lake when we spent the summers at my grandfather's place."

"Being that none of you drowned, it sounds like fun." She lifted her sunglasses to the top of her head. "Did you camp out too?"

"We did. 'Bout burned down the forest trying to figure how to make a campfire once or twice." A nostalgic smile brushed his lips. "Most of the time we were big adventurers. Indiana Jones had nothing on us."

"I'd love to see what you looked like as a child."

"No you wouldn't." He shook his head. "I was tall and scrawny, and it took forever for my face to grow and match the size of my two front teeth."

"Well, they're perfect now."

"Braces. Two years of metal tweaking torture."

"I can't picture you as a metal mouth."

"You'll get your chance. My mom has pictures all over the house. There's one in the hallway with me in braces and lime green rubber bands. Guess I thought those were cool back in the day."

This might be the most personal info she'd ever gotten out of him. Yes, she'd known he was one of five brothers and had a sister, but she didn't know what kind of household he'd grown up in. She'd guessed, but didn't actually know if his parents had been overprotective or easygoing. She didn't know exactly how close he and his siblings were. And she didn't know what kind of kid he'd been. Troublemaker? Teacher's pet? Class clown? She could picture him as either of the first two, but not the last one. As an adult he was way too uptight to have ever been the funniest guy in the class.

Maybe the distance and time away from the office and the fast pace of the big city would do him good. He already seemed a little more relaxed. At least, relaxed for a tightly wired, always-on-the-go professional with colossal aspirations and a driving force for only God knew what.

"Did you wear suits and ties back then too?" she asked with a grin.

"Nope. Back then you couldn't get me out of my jeans or a baseball uniform."

"You played baseball?" Why did this even surprise her? It wasn't like he'd suddenly shown up on earth in Giorgio Armani with a master's degree in his hand.

He sipped his ice water and nodded. "Earned a full ride scholarship for it at San Diego State. That's when I decided to move to California for good."

"Ah. So you were an Aztec."

"I was. But I only played one season."

"Injury?"

He shook his head. "My brother Jordan had already been drafted into the NHL. Everyone knew he had mad athletic skills and would make a career with his brawn. I decided I wanted to make one with my brain."

"So you don't have that special twin connection with him?"

"My twin and I are polar opposites in every way. Especially now that he's getting married."

Brooke had met Declan's twin and concurred they

were nothing alike. Jordan Kincade had been a typical playboy jock that graced celebrity magazine covers with a different woman on his arm in every issue.

But if a total player like Jordan had been tamed by love, who was to say Dec couldn't be next in line?

*B*efore his twin had become engaged, Dec had never given marriage much thought. Correction. He'd never given marriage *any* thought. How could he ever consider committing himself to one person when he was already completely devoted to his career? It wouldn't be fair to anyone. Especially someone he would obviously care about. Since his parents died, his views on the holy sanctity of marriage had shifted, warped like an old record left in the sun. His mom and dad had been married for thirty-five years. They'd been great parents and had a wonderful, supportive relationship.

Or so he and his siblings had always thought.

Now the façade had slipped and there were more questions than answers, leaving Dec to wonder why bother with the fuss of getting married in the first place. In his mind, a brief, passionate relationship was better than investing time with someone who may not actually be in it for the long haul.

Not that he planned to be in any kind of relationship—brief or otherwise—anytime soon.

At that moment their server appeared with a water bowl for Moochie and was ready to take their lunch orders. Brooke ordered Maryland-style crab cakes and a Diet Pepsi.

When it was his turn he told the server, "I'll have the seared ahi and black coffee."

Brooke gave him a funny look. Not ha-ha funny, but what-the-hell-is-he-thinking funny.

"What's wrong?" he asked, fearful of what she had cooking in that fanciful off-the-clock brain of hers.

"Do you mind if I order something different?" she asked, scrunching her nose in a comically rueful way.

"Go ahead."

"Cancel both of those orders," she said.

"Hey, wait a—"

She held up a finger. "Instead, could you bring us the Triple Trouble Tacos? Is your salsa hot or mild?"

"We have both," the server said, flashing Dec an occasional look. "The hot is made with habaneros. We do serve a special order salsa with ghost peppers and—"

"No." Dec stopped the nonsense before it went any further. He was not about to create a five alarm fire in his mouth and scorch off his taste buds. Who knew when he might need them for something more delicious? Something other than food.

"No ghost peppers." Brooke grinned, knowing she already had him backed into a culinary corner. "And if you could just serve it on one big platter then give us a couple of smaller plates that would be great."

Since he'd once observed an adolescent Ethan lick the popcorn bowl he'd been sharing with Parker because he'd been pissed off, Dec didn't share food off the same plate with anyone.

"And instead of soda and coffee, could you bring us a . . ." Her finger trailed across the menu before it stopped. "Shipwreck and a Voodoo Crush?"

"Right away."

When the server left their table, a sly smile pulled at the corners of Brooke's luscious lips.

"I don't even want to know what's in those drinks," he said. "But you do realize we have to drive when we leave here."

"And we have all of that . . ." She lifted her hand and extended it to indicate the wide expanse of sand perpendicular to the wharf. "With which to walk it off."

Wanting to smile at her brashness, he leaned back in his chair. "Pretty ballsy changing my order, Ms. Hastings."

The sunlight caught like spun gold in the wavy strands of her hair. He liked that her face was makeup free, but mostly he liked that she didn't need a mask to feel confident. Not that he ever planned to date Brooke, but he'd dated a lot of women who'd refused to leave the house until their makeup had been perfectly applied and every hair was in place.

In his mind, all that preparation took away an opportunity for spontaneity. With his busy schedule, sometimes that's all he could manage—a last minute invite. Brooke had so much sexy going on she didn't need all that stuff. And today she'd pretty much proved that she was game for the whole spur-of-the-moment thing. Impressive.

"How many business lunches and dinners have I sat through with you, Mr. Kincade?"

He shrugged. "Too many to count."

"Bingo." She pointed. "And do you know what you order almost each and every time?"

"No."

"Seared ahi."

"And the problem with that is?"

"Boring."

"I like ahi."

"Good for you. But why not expand your horizons? Eating the same old same old every day is like having missionary sex every time the mood strikes."

And why did she need to bring that up? Because his imagination definitely didn't need a push in that direction.

"Shake things up." She waved her hands upward like she was about to take flight. "Be daring. Live a little."

Damn she was animated. How the hell did someone get like that?

"I'm happy with things the way they are."

"Are you really?" As she leaned into the table, the unyielding fabric of that tight white tank top across her breasts dominated his attention.

He didn't respond.

Couldn't.

He was too . . . distracted.

"You know what they say; all work and no play . . ." she said with a shrug, leaving the remainder of that statement hanging like a noose.

"So you're saying that eating fish tacos is suddenly going to *shake things up* in my life?"

"Breaking your same old song and dance routine will. After you've opened up the door, anything can happen. Aren't you the least bit curious?"

The server interrupted them to deliver a large plate of steaming soft tacos, bowls of salsa and sour cream, and two giant froufrou drinks with slices of pineapple and maraschino cherries speared by pink umbrellas.

Oh hell no.

He was *not* going to drink something that would immediately revoke his man card. But when Brooke plucked the cherry from her glass, dangled it in the air, and captured it with her tongue, he had second thoughts. By the time she settled the bright pink straw between the soft cushion of her lips and sucked the orange frothy drink into her mouth, he figured he'd be game for just about any damn thing. As long as he could watch her do *that* all day long.

A long blink brought his brain cells back together. "No."

"No, what?"

"I'm not curious."

"Oh come on. Play along."

She sure liked to use the word *play* a lot.

She sucked on the straw again then looked up at him with an impish grin. "If you actually came up with some bucket list items you might act on them. Think about all the fun you could have."

"How about we just stick to *your* list?"

She dragged a blackened salmon taco onto her plate, shook a spoonful of salsa on top of the fish then took a bite. Eyes closed, she hummed her approval. Dec didn't know how someone just biting into a tortilla could be so sensual, but Brooke made it look easy.

"This is delicious." She waggled her taco. "Your turn."

"Evading, Ms. Hastings?" He dragged a lobster taco

onto his plate, took a bite, and nearly moaned when the buttery flavor rolled over his tongue. When Brooke took another bite, he began to understand the implications of how sexy food play could really be.

Especially when she licked her fingers.

"The quandary is," Brooke said after another sip of her umbrella drink, "that I do have a list. Which means I've already given the topic plenty of thought. Which means I'm much more fascinated with you and yours."

"I'm pretty uninteresting," he insisted.

"Are you?" Doubtful and challenging, she raised a sleek brow.

"Depends on who you ask."

"I'm asking *you.*" She took another bite of taco and he couldn't have stopped himself from watching her lips close over that tortilla any more than he'd be able to stop breathing and survive.

"Everything in my life is pretty routine," he debated.

"You want to know what *I* think?" Taco in hand, she tilted her head as though he was a puzzle she had to put together.

"I have a feeling I'm about to find out."

Her straight white teeth tore off a chunk of taco and while she chewed she studied his face. Once she swallowed and sipped her drink, she grinned. "I think you're *afraid* to have fun."

He scoffed. "I'm not afraid of anything."

"Except having fun."

"Why do you keep saying that?" The growl in his tone should have stopped her.

It didn't.

"Because when you describe yourself, you use words like *uninteresting*, *routine*, and *busy*."

"Fear has nothing to do with it. That's how I see myself."

"Well, I see you as sharp, intelligent, diligent, stubborn, devoted to family, passionate about helping others, and . . ." She paused while her dark eyes roamed his face then dropped to his mouth.

Jesus. The look she gave him was so hot he wanted to break every damn rule he'd forced upon himself.

"And?"

"And . . ." Her full, luscious lips curved into a smile. "Chicken."

"Chicken?"

"Yes. I'm doing everything I can right now to keep from flapping my wings in your honor."

"Brooke?" As he leaned in just slightly to make his point, he had to do everything he could not to crack a smile. The idea was absurd, but he expected she knew that. "I am *not* chicken."

"Sez the man who won't let himself go enough to toss some items in a bucket list."

"Fine. If you want to play this . . . game, I'll bite. But since you're such a big talker, how about you go first."

Discovering more about Brooke was something he found he could do all day. It wasn't just her answers; it was the way she responded. She had more passion in her little finger than most people did in their entire bodies. And as a man who really shouldn't be attracted to her but was, he'd like to see how deep and far that passion went.

"If I go first, you *have* to give me an answer. No more dancing around." She reached her hand across the table. "Deal?"

"Deal." They shook, and it was everything Dec could do to let go.

"Okay. Let's see." Deep in thought she looked skyward then turned those melted chocolate eyes back on him. "I'd like to visit Hobbiton."

"And *Hobbiton* is?"

"I take it you're not a fan of Bilbo, Gandalf, and Gollum."

"Who?" His brother Ethan had been a fan of the series of books so he vaguely knew who the characters were. But getting a rise out of her by playing dumb was more fun than owning up.

She sighed. "Hobbiton is the movie set where they filmed *Lord of the Rings*. Next to Disneyland it's the coolest place ever."

"I never really got into reading that much." Because it took him damned near forever to learn. "Haven't seen the movies. Haven't been to Disneyland."

"For someone who lives in Southern California, that is an unforgivable sin," she said emphatically. "You don't like fantasy?"

"Depends on what kind we're talking about."

"Now there's a conversation that begs to be discussed over a glass of wine." She chuckled before her expression tightened. "When I was young, I wasn't allowed to read anything other than educational or religious books. When I finally discovered fiction, I devoured all the classics. Reading is still something I prefer to do rather than watching television."

He could almost picture her with her wavy hair pulled up on top of her head, dressed in PJs, sitting in a comfy chair by the fire, and lost in the book in her hand.

"I liked being read to when I was a kid," he admitted. Because it was far more enjoyable than trying to put the letters together and comprehend them too. "During the summer, my grandmother read us stories like *Treasure Island* and *The Adventures of Tom Sawyer*. Then my brothers and I would go out and pretend we were explorers and adventurers. Usually it led to a broken wrist, a bad sunburn, or a rash of poison oak."

Brooke laughed. "I can imagine with the five of you so close in age it was a lot of fun."

"We definitely had our moments."

"Okay, Mr. Evasive." She pointed a tortilla chip in his direction. "Your turn. What's the first thing you're dropping into your bucket list?"

He'd never been much of a dreamer. Spare moments were always spent planning, preparing, and making things happen. He glanced out at the ripples glistening across the ocean and went with the first thing that came to mind.

"Swimming in the ocean in the moonlight."

"Not afraid of sharks. Check."

"Only those in the boardroom."

Her eyes glimmered. "With or without clothes?"

"In the boardroom? You really are adventurous."

"In the ocean."

"Depends."

"Now we're getting somewhere." She lifted her glass, sipped, and looked at him over the rim. "And before you go thinking that with me nothing is off-limits, I do have boundaries."

"Which are?"

"I try to stay away from being thrown in jail. Or getting my heart broken."

She didn't say it but he could hear the unspoken word *again*.

His stomach tightened. "Who broke your heart?"

An almost imperceptible shrug lifted her shoulders. "Someone who claimed to love me, but lied."

"Those aren't words to speak lightly," he said, wanting a name and address so he could pay this asshole a personal visit.

"No. They're not." She tucked the straw between her lips and drained her glass. "And I've never said those words to anyone because of that."

"Yet earlier you said your bucket list included marrying the love of your life."

"Because someday—hopefully—I'll be brave enough to say those three little words to someone special." She flashed him a cautious smile. "It's not that I don't believe in them, it's just that I really have to believe in the person who will—hopefully—say them back."

The guy who'd broken her heart must have been a total idiot. Brooke was special. The kind of woman who'd inspire a man to change his wicked ways.

If that was even possible.

After lunch, Dec had taken only a few steps down the wharf before he realized that Brooke and her little dog weren't beside him. While his internal clock might be saying it was time to get back on the road, Brooke's internal clock was on a completely different schedule.

He caught up to her with her nose pressed to the window of a little pink shop called Fantasy Island.

"We need to get back on the road."

"We will, Captain Obvious. Just walking off that shot of rum first." She looked up at him. The gold in her eyes sparkled in the sunshine. "Don't tell me you're not dying to see the rest of what this place has to offer."

Idly he glanced to his left where the wharf ended and the ocean continued.

"Oh my God." She thrust her fists on her hips. "You didn't even give it a thought, did you?"

"No."

"I'm going to have to completely reprogram you."

"It's time to go," he insisted.

"Nonsense." She scooped Moochie up into her arms. "We're going inside."

Judging by the frilly stuff in the front window, he really didn't think this version of *Fantasy Island* was his style.

"I'm not going in there."

"Then stay outside and bake in the sun. *I'm* going in."

Once she disappeared through the glass door, curiosity got the best of him.

Surprisingly inside the place was more than he imagined. One side of the shop was obviously for the small fries in the girl kingdom with tutus and wands, castles and crowns. On the big girl side where Brooke currently stood were dresses and jewelry, perfume, and lingerie in the form of costumes. Really sexy, next-to-nothing, every-man's-fantasy costumes.

Though he was a man who appreciated women's lingerie, he tore his eyes away from the silk and sexy. Especially when Brooke walked right into the midst of it and his imagination drove into warp speed. While she wandered around with Moochie tucked in her arms, he wandered off to the safest place in the store.

"Do you see something you like?" the woman behind the counter asked him as he peered into the glass display case. Without warning his gaze came up and found Brooke holding up a light pink short and see-through little number.

"Yes," he said without hesitation. "Yes, I do."

The woman's gaze followed and she smiled. "Are you looking for a gift for *her*?"

He hadn't been.

But when he looked back into the display case he spotted a silver bracelet with two charms. Next to it was a display of charms of all types. He pointed. "Can you add *that* charm to *that* bracelet?"

"Absolutely." The woman slid the items from the glass case. "This will suit her well."

Hesitant to actually purchase the considerably personal item, he turned and looked across the store at his assistant.

Nine-to-five Brooke was something to behold. After-hours/road trip Brooke was even better.

Fate sealed, he pulled out his credit card.

* * *

*O*nce they left the princess shop, Brooke settled her newly purchased fairy crown with its streaming and sparkling pink ribbons on her head. Then she set Moochie down on the wharf so she could trot alongside. The dog had other ideas. Immediately she put her front paws on Dec's leg and looked up at him with adoration and a cute little whimper.

As Moochie tap-danced with her hind feet Dec asked, "What's *that* mean?"

"*That* means she wants you to pick her up and hold her. I think she has a crush on you."

"How is that even possible?"

Brooke laughed at the confusion crinkling his forehead. "She's female. And I'm guessing you do pretty well charming the ladies." Grumpy or not, she knew he could charm the pants off of her any day, any time. In fact, if he wanted to right now, it would totally not offend her.

"None with fur."

"There's always a first time. No worries," she said. "She can walk. The exercise will do her good."

Moochie gave him another pitiful little growl and continued her wiggle dance.

"Shit." He picked up the dog and snugged her against his chest. "Sorry. I can't resist that face."

Brooke could swear she heard her dog sigh. And that was even before Moochie looked over at her with a smug *Yeah, I've got this* look.

"Sucker."

On an average day, Dec was gorgeous. Today, with

the blue T-shirt hugging his pecs, the sun gleaming on his nearly black hair, the sunglasses perched on his chiseled face, and a cute pooch in his arms, he stole her breath.

And apparently she wasn't alone.

Completely unaware of the lusty looks he received from the women who passed by, he led the way toward the end of the wharf.

"Look." She pointed to a building. "A wine tasting room. Dare we try?"

"We need to get back on the road."

Totally what she expected him to say. Breaking Dec out of his "all work, no play" zone wasn't going to be easy by anyone's standards. Too bad for him she had plenty of game and lots of determination.

"Oh come on." She headed toward the rustic building that loosely resembled a sailing ship. "Loosen up a little. It's a beautiful day. The road isn't going anywhere. And your family doesn't expect you to get there at breakneck speed. If they get mad, I'll take the blame. It's what I do."

The heat of his eyes scorched her from behind those sunglasses.

"What do you mean, it's what you do?"

"You don't believe your clients love you all the time, do you?" She shrugged. "I'm your buffer. If they have an issue, they yell at me so that by the time they get to talk to you, you're still the Prince Charming of the financial world."

"I don't want you to be my buffer. That's harassment. The company doesn't approve of that in any form."

"Easy, cowboy. It's not a big deal. I can handle it."

"It's unacceptable. How often do you save my ass like that?"

"Pretty much daily." She prodded him toward the tasting room door. "Now, let's get down to some serious sipping."

"I'm driving. No sipping."

"Too bad. I guess that just means more for me."

"Not this time." He turned an about-face and headed back toward the parking lot with her dog still tucked in his arms.

Brooke sighed. She thought she'd had him right up until she'd spilled the beans. Apparently he'd had no idea how often he rocked someone's boat and she had to settle the stormy sea.

Well, he knew now.

Time would tell how many steps that set them—or at least her—back.

Chapter 3

The sunset smoldered on the horizon in fiery shades of tangerine and gold before the velvety darkness of night descended. Then the coastal route became a moonlit display of a black velvet sky with the near full moon casting a spotlight over the Pacific Ocean.

The hour had grown way past dinnertime and Dec had snacked on corn nuts until his teeth hurt. He needed a real meal. A glass of Maker's neat wouldn't hurt either. The hours on the road had started to wear on him. And that didn't even come close to the impairment of his rationality from being in such close proximity to the woman in his passenger seat.

Listening to her had been entertaining and insightful, but inhaling her sweet scent and looking at all the tanned skin that rose above and below her tank top and shorts was pure torture. As they drove into a charming little seaside town, he knew he needed a break before he actually broke and did something he'd regret.

"How about we grab a bite to eat?"

"I vote we find a place to stay for the night." Brooke snuggled her little dog closer to her chest and petted her affectionately. "You look exhausted."

"I won't take that as an insult."

"Good. Because it wasn't meant as one. You've been driving for almost . . ." She peered at the clock on the dashboard. "Eight hours. So I should either take a turn and give you a break, or we should stop for the night. I'm sure your family would prefer you to arrive rested and in one piece."

"I can keep driving," he said, unfamiliar with someone other than a family member worrying about his well-being. "I just need to refuel with food and caffeine."

"We could just stop in a gas station and you could ply yourself with a few dozen Red Bulls and a bag of chips."

"Bad idea."

"So is you continuing to drive when you're tired." She peered through the windshield and pointed toward a little visitor's information hut. "How about you stop here and ask if there are any restaurants open late and we can discuss?"

"It's not open for discussion. But I'll stop and ask about a place to eat."

After several minutes inside the visitor's information center, Dec went back to the car armed with brochures and pamphlets he didn't want or need. The older woman inside the center had been so sweet and insistent he couldn't say no. "There are some restaurants a couple of miles ahead where we can grab a bite to eat," he told Brooke.

"I've already got reservations for dinner." Brooke held up and waggled her phone.

"You're kidding," he said, although he really wasn't surprised. At the office Brooke was all over everything and had most things taken care of before he even knew he needed them.

"Do you doubt my executive assistant talents?" she asked with a smirk, knowing she was totally kickass at what she did.

"Never."

"Good. Because this is the kind of stuff I do. I've been making your travel arrangements for four years. I've learned all the super-secret handshake places to go on the web to find what you need."

What he needed was to get out of the damn car before he weakened and dragged her into his arms for a slow, wet kiss.

The charming, tree-lined street leading to their destination was dotted with beachy cottages, waterfalls of bougainvillea, and sweetly scented tufts of night blooming jasmine.

While Dec listened to driving directions via his phone, Brooke dealt with the energetic crackle in her veins.

She'd pulled a fast one on him, and who knew how it would go over. He'd either be too tired to argue or he'd be pissed. Since she'd been dealing with the latter for days, she didn't feel the slightest bit intimidated.

Even if she should.

When the Google Maps lady told them they'd arrived at their destination, Dec leaned forward and glared through the windshield. "This doesn't look like a restaurant."

"It's not." Brooke clutched Moochie tighter. "It's an inn by the sea."

"With a restaurant." He turned his head and those distrustful eyes nailed her through the darkness. "Right?"

"There's not an actual restaurant inside the inn. But the lady on the phone said they can either have food delivered or there are a couple of restaurants nearby."

His eyes narrowed. "Then why are we stopping here?"

"Because I booked a reservation. Good thing too. Last one for another hundred miles."

"I told you I was okay to drive."

"And you're hardly irritable." She sighed when the tension in his jaw twitched. "Look. You're tired. You need a break. It's obvious you don't trust me enough to drive your car—"

"I never said I didn't trust you."

"You never said I could drive your car either." She gave a small sharp jerk of her head. "So like it or not, we are stopping so you can get some rest. We'll get up early and finish the drive tomorrow so you can arrive fresh as a daisy."

"Do I look like the daisy type?"

Not even.

"Doesn't matter, boss man. We're doing this."

He pulled into a small lot near the inn and stopped

the car. Before he could rip into her for going against his wishes, Brooke unhooked her seat belt and opened the car door. "It's gorgeous."

The Colonial-style inn was secluded, nestled at the end of a cul-de-sac street, and only steps away from the beach.

"I've always dreamed of staying in a place like this," she said.

"Get back in the car. We're not staying."

"Of course we are."

"I'm not arguing with you about this."

"Good." She snapped on Moochie's leash and set her little dog on the ground, knowing her teeny tiny bladder was probably bursting. "Come on, Mooch."

"Brooke," Dec called out in a growl that sent a shiver down her spine. "I'm serious."

"Me too. I'm not going to end up roadkill because you're too damn stubborn to admit defeat." She tossed the words over her shoulder and kept walking. A double dose of guilt clawed at her conscience as she headed toward the inn.

If he was irritated now, he was going to be royally ticked off when he discovered the truth, the whole truth, and nothing but the truth.

*B*ecause she kept walking, Dec had no choice but to follow. He cussed once or twice because she was right. He needed to call it a day. But the hell if he'd give her that satisfaction.

He caught up with her inside the lobby where a small

check-in desk was located near the double doors. The rest of the large open room had nooks of comfortable seating for reading, and a long sofa in front of a stone fireplace. As soon as Dec closed the door behind him the sound of waves crashing onshore muted. Celtic harp music played softly through hidden speakers.

"Mr. Kincade?" At his nod, the older woman behind the desk waved them in. "We're so pleased you're joining us tonight."

He tossed Brooke a dirty look. "Thank you."

"As I explained to Ms. Hastings over the phone it was a stroke of luck that we had a last minute cancellation. Apparently the groom got cold feet. We have the last available room in town. Good thing you called when you did."

One room?

Holy fucking shit.

"That's . . ." He looked at Brooke, who refused to look back. "Great."

The woman behind the desk held out her hand. "If I could just see your card to verify the security code?"

When he reached for his wallet Brooke whispered, "Since I kind of sprang this on you, let me get this."

Dec scowled. "Absolutely not."

He handed his credit card to the woman, who smiled at the both of them.

"Is this your first visit here?" the woman asked.

Dec wasn't usually one to share information with strangers so he merely muttered an "Mmm-hmm."

"Honeymooning?"

While Dec choked on a response, Brooke piped up.

"We're going up to his family's vineyard and decided to take the coastal route. Neither of us has ever experienced it before."

"That's wonderful. Friends of ours have a small winery nearby. I'd love to send you up a bottle."

"That would be so nice. Thank you."

When Dec turned toward Brooke with a let's-not-give-out-too-much-information scowl, his thoughts froze. A smile beamed across her beautiful face. She loved meeting and talking to new people, which was just one of the many reasons he valued her as his assistant. He'd never considered himself a people person. Brooke waved that flag like a neon sign and he knew that her presence in his company was one of the reasons a lot of clients kept coming back.

But right now, that was not the thought that had him in a quandary. He either had to shut down this whole ridiculous idea and keep driving or find a way to spend the night with Brooke and keep his sanity intact. Not to mention fighting his attraction and keeping his hands to himself.

"Would you like help with your bags?" the woman asked as she handed him back his card and the room keys.

"We can manage," Dec said. "I believe you mentioned there was a restaurant nearby?"

"There are several just a short walk into the village. However, if you're tired from the long drive or would like some privacy, I can arrange to have dinner delivered. The suite has a nice fireplace, and you're on the second floor so you also have a beautiful patio overlooking the ocean. Or I could have your dinner served in the garden courtyard. We have a fireplace out there too."

Shit.

Dec looked at Brooke hoping she'd choose a restaurant. Sitting across from her in a bustling environment would be a hell of a lot more bearable than a private setting with a fireplace, wine, and the ocean waves crashing on the shore. "Preference?"

"The suite."

Could she have at least given it some thought?

He must have scowled because she quickly gave him a cautious look. "If that's okay with you."

Okay? Hell no. "Sure."

"Excellent." The woman behind the desk set two menus on top of the counter for them to peruse. "I personally recommend both of these places."

Dec slid the menus in front of Brooke. "Italian or seafood?"

"How about you choose the meal?"

Now she had a frightened rabbit look on her face, as though she feared he'd take a bite out of her for her sheer sneakiness.

He hated that look.

Even if taking a bite of her sounded far tastier than anything on either menu.

His decision was quick. It was late and Italian food was too heavy. And no, he wasn't about to order seared ahi. He'd learned his lesson. "How about a couple of lobster tails, grilled salmon, maybe crème brûlée and . . . a slice of caramel fudge cheesecake."

So much for going light.

The woman behind the desk grinned. "Oh, you're going to love that."

"Wow." Brooke readjusted the sparkling fairy crown over her silky hair. "You must be really hungry."

He was starving.

But it didn't have a damned thing to do with food.

*B*rooke followed Dec up the stairs to their room.

Their room.

She'd been mildly nervous before, but now her heart was sprinting like a racehorse in the last lap.

Was he pissed or just mildly irritated that she'd pulled one over on him? His total silence since they'd retrieved their luggage from the car gave her no indication. She'd grown used to his scowls, so those weren't helping either. Maybe she'd pushed him too far this time. Then again, maybe this was exactly the nudge he needed.

Not that she imagined a man like Declan Kincade needed a push if he found a woman interesting. So maybe he really just wasn't interested in her.

Naw.

She'd caught him looking plenty of times. And if the suggestion in his eyes gave her anything, it was the courage to keep pushing.

As he unlocked the door and rolled their luggage inside the suite, she watched the play of muscles in his strong back and bulging biceps. At that moment all she could really do was imagine how those arms would feel wrapped around her body.

Catching her in the act of checking him out, Dec cleared his throat. Despite the fact that her skin was probably flushed, she feigned innocence as she stepped into the room.

"Oh. Look at that view!"

The open curtains framed a dreamlike portrait of a moonbeam glittering across the ocean. Brooke couldn't resist—and she also needed an escape to pull herself together. Setting Moochie down, she opened the sliding glass doors and stepped out onto the terrace where a bistro set with cushioned chairs waited for company. Brooke stepped to the rail, curled her hands around the cast iron, and took a deep breath. A hint of jasmine floated on the salty air and she wished she could bottle the delectable aroma.

Below, the waves rolled in and crashed against the sand of a deserted beach. As the sea foam washed back out, it erased the footprints of anyone who might have walked there.

It was so romantic.

The clean cotton and lingering sunshine heat of Dec's body radiated as he came up behind her. "I set your bag on the luggage rack in the closet."

The deep timbre of his voice caressed her skin and created a path of tingles down her back before she could stop them. She feared that no matter how much she dreamed, wished, hoped, or imagined that the looks he occasionally sent her way were of the suggestive kind, he really might never blur the hard line between boss and employee.

She should have a talk with the overzealous ladies

in her egg basket and wipe all those thoughts from her mind. Then again, she'd pushed this far and had only come up against a modicum of resistance.

She didn't wear a *Fearless* bracelet for nothing.

Was she really willing to risk it all—including her job—just for one night with this man? Or did she foolishly believe she could turn it into something more? Maybe the bigger question was could she keep pretending that she saw him only as her boss?

For years she'd tried to figure out more than what he might do on a day off or what tools he needed for a meeting. All this time she'd felt like a kindred spirit with him. This road trip had definitely confirmed that both of them—at some point in life—had needed a refresher course on how to have fun. Both of them had family ties that at times could seem a little constrictive. But who was Declan Kincade beneath the suit and tie? What did he really want out of life? What did he need? What made him happy?

And could she be it?

"Thank you," she said, remembering that his statement required a response.

When he came closer to look out over the panoramic view, her body responded with another tingly jolt that verified everything about her was into him. Even so, did she really have what it took to take him to the edge and push him over, regardless of the consequences?

"That's quite a view." His deep voice hummed through her like a swarm of happy honeybees.

"It's breathtaking. The perfect spot for a few days of fun in the sun. Too bad we can't stay."

"Why not?"

She turned and, not realizing exactly how close he stood, her breast brushed his arm. "Do you mean that?"

Without any hint of acknowledgment that their bodies had touched in a very personal way, he took a step to the side and wrapped his hands around the fence. "I meant *you* could stay. There's no reason you have to go with me. You work hard and rarely take any time off. You deserve to relax a little. I can save my own ass," he said in reference to her earlier disclosure.

Totally *not* what she wanted to hear.

"Not that I'd consider it, but how would I get home? We're almost eight hours away."

"I'm sure there's a car rental nearby. Google it."

"I'm not Googling anything." Bubble burst, she went back into the suite and he followed. "I'm going all the way with you no matter what."

Well, that didn't come out exactly right.

"Don't make up your mind until morning. The offer will still stand."

Going their separate ways was the exact opposite of what she had in mind.

"Since there's only one bed . . ." He jerked his thumb toward the suite. "I'll take the sofa."

"There's no way I'd let you sleep on the sofa."

"Well, I'm not going to let *you* sleep there."

"No worries." She flashed a let's-get-this-happy-train-back-on-track smile. "I wasn't planning to."

"Brooke?" His dark brows came together. "In the office you are the most organized, on-the-money person I've ever met. Outside the office . . ."

Say it.

Her hopeful heart perked up.

Say you want me. You need me. You can't live with-out me.

"You confuse the hell out of me."

Poop.

She'd failed. Unless confusion was the gateway to breaking him down.

"At the office you pay me to be organized and on-the-money," she said. "You're not paying me right now. And it's five o'clock somewhere."

"And that means . . . ?"

"I told you, I don't want to become predictable and boring. So don't expect me to spoil all the fun." She flashed a flirty smile. "Besides, as Mae West used to say, 'Between two evils, I always pick the one I never tried before.'"

"Are you calling me evil?"

"Don't be silly." Catching his look of bewilderment, she scooped Moochie up off the bed, going for the old will-he-or-won't-he-check-me-out *bend and snap* she'd learned from the movie *Legally Blonde*. "And don't bother trying to figure me out. It will only drive you crazy."

His dark eyes followed her every move. Then he dropped his shoulders and rolled his neck as if she'd caused him physical pain. "I'm starting to get that."

Brooke took a quick tour of the suite, giving him a moment to relax, reflect, and figure out that in some wickedly sexy universe, they belonged together. One that possibly started with the giant four-poster king-sized bed in this room.

The suite's dusky blue Cape Cod décor and polished

wood floors managed to feel both elegant and homey. The fireplace glowed with dancing flames and cast a romantic mood over the entire room.

She stepped into the bathroom and gasped. Elegant granite countertop, double sinks, huge soaking bath, and huge glass shower.

"Oh my God. This bathroom is five times the size of the one at home." She opened the shower door and looked inside. "There's a ceiling mount rain head and six body sprays in this thing. And colored LED lights." There had to be a whole lot of serious sex going on in that thing. Luckily that thought stayed in her head and never made it out of her mouth.

From the other room she thought she heard him chuckle. Then again, she could just have road trip lag in her ears.

"Does this being unpredictable and not boring thing you keep going on about mean you're a bubble bath or shower kind of girl?"

Good question, hot and hunky. She smiled. "Depends."

"On?"

She closed the shower door and came out of the bathroom, hoping to see some kind of smile on his face. Instead, it was slammed in a frown, as though he was pissed he'd asked the question and couldn't retract it.

"On whether you've driven me crazy at work that day," she said. "Or whether I need some *me* time. Or whether I have five minutes to pull myself out of bed and get on the freeway. How about you?"

"I haven't taken a bath since I was about five years old."

"Seriously?"

He nodded. "One bathroom for five messy boys meant quick showers."

"Well, you don't know what you're missing. Especially if you add at least a dozen candles, some mood music, and a tasty glass of wine." She hitched a thumb over her shoulder. "And that LED light show in there."

"I thought people only did that in the movies."

"Life is what you make it, Dec. You can either enjoy it like a long, hot bath, or you can stand back and let it zip by like a cold shower. I do my best thinking wet and naked."

Boom! Drop that in your all work and no play bag of tricks, boss man.

Rarely was the man at a loss for words. But before he could intelligently form a response to her audacious remark, a knock sounded on the door.

"Would you mind getting that?" she asked sweetly, stopping just short of batting her eyelashes. She noticed the briefest hesitation before he did as asked.

An older gentleman stood there holding an ice bucket with a bottle of wine chilling inside in one hand and balancing a large tray with several covered dishes in the other.

"Oh!" Brooke inhaled. "That smells delicious."

"I guarantee it will taste even better than it smells," the man said. "And the wine will leave you smiling too. Where would you like me to set all this?"

"On the terrace, please," Brooke answered while Dec pulled out his wallet for a tip. When the man disappeared with a nod and thanks, Brooke settled Moochie in her little doggie bed. "She's not going to be happy about missing out on this dinner."

"One taste won't hurt, will it?"

Brooke laughed. "One taste of something this rich would be a disaster. Sensitive stomach. I, on the other hand, am dying to dig in."

Dec motioned toward the patio doors and she didn't hesitate. "You do have excellent taste in food, Mr. Kincade." Uncovering the plates allowed the aromas to waft up on a curl of steam. "When you aren't stuck on seared ahi."

To her, his quiet chuckle sounded golden. Dec laughed as rarely as he smiled. For her, getting him to respond to anything with levity was a great gift.

After she sat down at the table, he joined her. "None of us knew much more than hot dogs and casseroles. Both my parents worked. With five constantly hungry boys, they had to be frugal with the meal planning and the time it took to prepare them. It wasn't until Parker came back from doing time in a culinary arts and life skills training program in Idaho that things started to change."

"Sounds interesting." She dipped a bite of lobster tail in butter and popped it in her mouth, moaning as the rich flavors rolled across her tongue. "Tell me more."

At his hesitation, Brooke looked up and found him staring at her mouth. It was then she felt the slow slide of butter oozing from the corner of her mouth. Her tongue darted out and licked the melted butter away.

His laser focused gaze followed before he blinked and brought his attention back to their discussion.

"We went from mama's surprise noodle casseroles to chicken curry salad and perfectly grilled flank steak."

"That's quite an upgrade."

Obviously having pulled himself back together, he nodded. "The best part was that Parker had changed. Before he went into the program he'd been a trouble-maker down to his shoelaces and had the bad attitude to go with it. The program gave him not only the skills to cook, but it taught him how to be a good employee and how to run his own business. He's made good use of all those skills. In the process he dumped the mean, angry guy and is now the fun, outgoing guy."

"You're very proud of him."

"I'm proud of all my brothers. My sister too. We're a pretty independent bunch."

"And successful."

"In our own rights. I guess it depends on how you define successful."

You had to love a man who loved his family. Even if Brooke didn't love him already, she'd be won over in a flash just by the smile on his face as he talked about them.

"What about you?" he asked.

"Me?"

"You said you didn't really have any family. But you had to come from somewhere."

I came from hell.

Damn. Brooke hadn't realized she'd been setting her own trap. "I had a sister and brother."

His gaze snapped up. *"Had?"*

"We're not . . . close."

"Why?"

She shrugged.

"You don't know?" he asked. "Or you're not going to tell me."

She'd been happy just a moment ago, flirting her pants off with the gorgeous man at her table. How exactly did this conversation get turned in her direction? She glanced over her shoulder. "The moon is really pretty tonight."

"Brooke." The tone in his voice was rife with concern. "You know you can trust me. Right?"

She nodded.

"Then why the big secret?"

Shit. Shit. Shit.

How much to reveal? How much to hide?

She didn't tell people about her past. The only times she'd shared she'd been peppered with humiliation. After that, she worried about people judging her harshly. Or worse, pitying her.

Did she believe Dec was the type to judge? Maybe not. But she couldn't take his pity, and she didn't want him to think less of her for what she'd been through or what she'd done. Still, she couldn't flat out ignore him on the subject. She had to give him something.

Even if it was only a hint of the truth.

"Have you ever met someone you really liked or admired," she asked, "then found out something about them that changed everything?"

Mid-bite, his hand and fork dropped to the table. "Are you trying to tell me your family are mass murderers?"

"Of course not."

"Embezzlers?"

"No."

"Arsonists?"

"No."

"Do they break the law in any way?"

She didn't respond.

"Brooke?"

"Depends on whose law you're talking about."

*D*ec sat back and studied the brilliant, sexy woman across the table.

Whose law?

Wasn't there only one?

"This cheesecake looks delicious." She stuck her fork in the tip of the dessert then held it up. "Want a bite?"

Was her avoidance of the subject because she was embarrassed about her family's reputation? What could possibly be the big deal? He'd never judge her based on someone else's behavior. She should know that. Yet it was as clear as the moonlit sky above them that this was a subject she didn't want to and wouldn't talk about.

At least not right now.

"No thanks."

He refilled her glass of wine then took a sip from his own to clear his head. Or muddy it the fuck up, whichever came first. Aside from how pretty her wavy hair shone beneath the moonlight, or how soft her skin might be, or that she smelled like exotic fruit and dark chocolate, he felt a need to protect. Maybe even on more than a physical level—although that was a rocket to the moon—he was consumed with the mystery of her.

She was the first woman who made him want to crawl out of the iron box he'd caged himself in. She was a woman he wanted to take care of. To make happy. He wanted to take away the occasional darkness that crept into her pretty brown eyes. But as luck would have it, she worked for him. And that meant heart locked, hands off.

"We all have our demons, Brooke. Believe me. If you ever want to talk about anything . . ." A vision of lying with her on that big bed, holding her in his arms, and chasing the demons away darted through his brain and he knew he had to get back on the rails. "My door is always open."

"Ah. Work." She sipped her wine. "That's something you're *very* good at."

"Might be the only thing." No. He had other things he was good at too. But they were definitely off the table.

A frown brought her delicate brows together and it physically pained him not to be able to smooth it away.

"Well, we can't have that, can we?" She pushed away from the table and went back into the suite. "Come on."

"Where are we going?" he asked before he followed her into a higher mountain of trouble.

"Somewhere completely non-work-related." Mischief tipped the corners of her lips. "We have at least one more day before we go back to the whole nine-to-five thing. I just want to do something I'm not able to do at home. Are you game?"

He'd be insane to say yes. "Why not."

Okay, so not exactly a yes, but problematic all the same.

"Sweet." She gave a whistle. Her little dog sprang up out of her portable bed and pranced toward her master.

Before Brooke opened the suite door, she stopped. "Let's make the most of this, okay?" she said, looking up at him with a heat in her eyes that made him want to claim defeat, give in to instinct, and take her to bed.

He'd spent years schooling himself into not giving in to impulse. Now, as he followed her out the door, that perseverance crashed and burned. Because following Brooke in those short shorts was a temptation mightier than reason could handle.

Chapter 4

When the sidewalk ended and the vast expanse of fine grain sand took over, Brooke stopped and pulled off her sneakers. With a dramatic sigh she wiggled her pink painted toes.

"Your turn." She pointed at his feet.

He'd never been a barefoot kind of guy. Still, he kicked off his shoes.

"Now dig in," she said.

He gave her a look.

"Don't be a party pooper." She wrinkled her nose and thrust her hands on her shapely hips. "Wiggle them in the sand."

Who knew a bossy woman could be so sexy? And so dangerous.

Still warm from the sun, the sand felt amazing on the soles of his feet and he nearly sighed out loud. This was exactly what he'd been dreaming about yesterday. A walk along the beach, some good food, and a drink.

However, in that fantasy, he hadn't conjured up such interesting and attractive company.

"Happy now?" he asked.

"Getting there." She pointed again. "Roll up your pant legs."

"Why?"

"Such a Debbie Downer." She tsked. "Maybe I want to see if you're one of those guys who waxes everything south of your chin."

"I can assure you I'm not."

"Good to know. I always prefer a man whose skin isn't softer than mine."

"Prefer them for what?" Shit. Didn't he know that curiosity killed the freaking cat? He needed to keep those kinds of thoughts sealed inside his damned head.

"Oh, you know . . ." Her sly grin had his imagination taking flight. "Things like . . . zipping up my dresses. Helping put my shoes on. Making the bed."

With her, he could picture doing just the opposite— unzipping, taking off, and stripping down.

"So you're saying you're looking for a love slave?"

"Exactly!" She giggled. "Roll your pants up and come on."

Hmmm. Maybe he should fire himself and then apply for *that* job.

"The pants stay."

"Too bad." Brooke took off in a dance down the beach with her little dog in merry chase.

He thought it too bad that she'd taken off the fairy crown. With it she'd look like a pagan princess in celebration of being in her natural environment.

Stuffing his hands in his pockets, he headed down

the beach in her direction. Soon they were walking side by side on the edge of the surf where the chilly ocean washed over their feet.

Arms out, she spun a few circles then took off again like a mischievous sprite, jumping and kicking at the surf as it splashed up her bare legs. Her little dog decided she didn't like the splash of the water and headed toward higher ground where she lay down with her long snout poised atop her front paws.

From the water's edge, Dec watched Brooke play as the waves splashed higher up her legs. He'd always appreciated women on a sensual level and he'd never been shy about making his point when he'd been attracted to one. But he'd never committed. Hell, he never even spent the night if they invited him into their bed. For him, sharing a bed for a full night meant more than just, *Hey, I want to enjoy your company and your body for a few hours.* For him, sharing a bed for a full night meant something permanent. And it was something he'd never considered.

Not even for a heated moment.

Yet, he was about to do just that with the one woman in his life he shouldn't be sharing a bed with. The one woman he shouldn't be thinking about in an *I want to tear your clothes off, push you against the wall, and make love to you, then cuddle* kind of way. The one woman who managed to keep his shit together at the same time that she tore him apart.

Every muscle, every fiber of his being screamed with need as he watched her play. Need not just for release. Need for *her*.

His jaw clenched.

Can't have her, buddy. Sorry. Not now. Not ever.

Her frolicking took her a little deeper into the water where the waves now broke around her knees. A cool breeze fluttered the tails of the plaid shirt she'd pulled on over that breast-hugging tank top. The moonlight shone in her golden hair. And Dec knew he'd never seen anything more beautiful and breathtaking in his life.

"Aren't you coming in?" she called.

"I'm fine right here." The cold water had numbed his toes. He couldn't imagine how she could stand it splashing up her legs.

"Do *not* make me start clucking like a chicken."

"Seriously? You're daring me?"

She laughed and the musicality washed over him like a gentle spring rain. Then she started squawking like a damned chicken. "Come on, boss man. Afraid you'll melt?"

He didn't want to do this. He didn't want to move any closer to her. He was having a hell of a time holding on to his control as it was. Her out there looking like some kind of water nymph was not helping at all.

"At least come in up to your ankles," she said over the crash of a wave. "I promise not to let Jaws Jr. take a bite."

"You're very funny, Brooke."

"I know." She giggled then started backing up. "Little bit closer."

Fuck.

It was the playful finger wiggles she did that made him cave. Without another reasonable thought left in his head he strode into a wave, which immediately soaked the legs of his jeans and made them feel like they weighed a hundred pounds.

"Little bit closer," she coaxed in a sexy voice full of temptation.

Before he knew it he was beside her and in up to his knees. The water was so cold it stung. She was in up to her thighs and he had no idea how she could tolerate it.

"Happy now?"

Bottom lip caught between her teeth, she looked up at him. The moonlight glistened in her eyes. And all he wanted at that moment was to replace her teeth on those plump, delectable lips with his mouth. To soothe away whatever caused her uncertainty then make her forget about anything but pleasure.

"I don't talk about my family," she said unexpectedly. "In fact, I don't think of them as my family at all anymore."

How could someone walk away from family? Even if they drove you crazy, they were always there for you. Something tragic must have happened in her life. He wanted to know more. Needed to know more. But he wouldn't ask. She had to trust him enough to tell.

"It's not that I'm trying to be rude and ignore your questions," she said. "I'm just very uncomfortable about answering them."

"Maybe someday you'll feel comfortable."

"Maybe." Somber train of thought gone, she grinned. "How bold are you feeling right now?"

"Bold?"

The sudden change gave him whiplash.

"Bold." She nodded, backed up a step, and lifted a shapely leg to kick water at him.

At the same time, a rogue wave—much larger than the ones that had been lapping at their legs—came up and caught her off balance. She went under, disappearing as if she hadn't just been standing there.

"Brooke!" Dec's breath left his lungs in a terrified whoosh. He dove into the water and quickly swam to where she'd been before she disappeared. His heart pounded and the salt water burned his eyes as he peered through the murky darkness.

What if she couldn't swim?

What if she'd hit her head when she'd gone under?

A beam of moonlight speared through the watery depths and the flash of a flailing arm caught his eye. He reached out, caught her arm, and dragged her up to the surface.

She came up sputtering and dove straight into his arms. Before he could blink the salt water from his eyes, she climbed him like a monkey. Her arms locked around his neck and her long legs linked around his butt. Goose bumps dotted her chilled body. Her pebbled nipples pressed into his chest. The crotch of her Daisy Dukes pressed tight against the zipper of his jeans. And his hands had a firm grip on her sweetly rounded ass.

With her arms around his neck they were face to face as the ebb and flow of the surf floated around them, pressing them closer then threatening to pull them apart. Her heart pounded against his chest, and he was pretty damn sure his own was talking the same language.

Dec wanted it to be relief that flowed through his

veins, but despite the icy water, he felt ignited. And hard. So hard he ached. From the moment he'd captured her in his arms, he felt like *he'd* been the one swept away. One touch of her sweet body and he felt like he'd been tossed into the center of a storm he couldn't escape.

Shivering from the cold and the aftereffects of being slammed beneath the surf, she looked deep into his eyes. "Thank you for saving me," she whispered.

When her tongue swept out to capture a droplet of ocean from her full, kissable bottom lip, his good intentions burst into flames and he just fucking broke.

With one hand firmly on her ass, the other slid up her body and gently captured the back of her head. They both stared into each other's eyes and Dec knew she could read his intent.

"Don't say a word," he growled. "Not one. Fucking. Word."

Dropping his mouth to hers, his mind completely shut off and pleasure took over. The taste of salt water lingered on her lips as he coaxed them open with a sweep of his tongue. She tightened her hold on him, instinctively moving closer while he delved deep, stroking inside her mouth with a rhythm the lower half of his body craved. She tasted sweet like caramel and cheesecake. Like wine and sex. Like the promise of something he couldn't deny.

A long, lusty moan rumbled against his chest—hers, not his—and the fire in his blood flashed hotter. Right here, right now he wanted to push off her shorts and plunge deep into her over and over until mindless satisfaction consumed both of them.

Now he knew what had been scratching at his insides.

Now he knew how soft she felt and how delicious she tasted.

And now he knew that this moment—this kiss—was all he could, would, ever have. No matter how much it would kill him to let go. Because if there had ever been any doubt in his mind, it was clear now.

She owned him.

*D*esire shot a hot streak through her center and set fire to the tips of her breasts pushed into the hard muscle of his chest.

She was kissing Declan Kincade.

Wow.

Brooke had always wondered, but now she knew what heaven must be like. She'd been his assistant for four years. For each of those Monday through Fridays she'd grown to know the man. She loved his dedication to both family and clients. She loved that his outside focus was charity and the many functions he attended and donated to in the name of children and the ill. She loved his sincerity, his smile, his heart. The more she knew the harder she fell.

Unlike the men in her past, she knew he'd never push unrealistic expectations on someone he loved. He'd protect them, take care of their wishes and desires.

She'd never had anyone like that in her life.

Never.

Being in his arms made her feel as though she'd found her own special happy place. The trick was getting him to feel the same. For four years she'd had reservations about the risks of letting him know how she felt. Tonight, she knew the risks were worth it.

She could find another job.

Finding another Declan Kincade would be impossible.

Hopefully he'd see things her way.

But in that fleeting breath of victory, he pulled his head back and ended the kiss.

For a moment his gaze swept her face then fell to her mouth.

Kiss me again.

Please.

Water clung to the tips of his thick dark lashes, and when those deep blue eyes came back up the heat burning in them scorched her. His erection pressed against her shorts as his arms and hands held her close.

She knew reality would slam down hard and he'd back away fast.

Unfortunately he proved her right.

"Don't think, Dec." She looked deep into his eyes. "I'm begging you. For once in your life, don't think. Just feel."

"Too late."

Distress marred his handsome face and she wanted to kiss away all those lines of confusion and concern.

"So . . . what. Even if I disagree, you're thinking this takes the whole boss/employee thing too far, right?"

"Way too far." With his hands still cupping her bottom and her arms and legs still locked around him, he trudged back toward the beach.

Once they reached dry sand, he released his hold and clearly expected her to do the same.

She clung on.

"Let go, Brooke."

"What if I don't want to?"

He gave her a look and reached up to peel her arms away.

Reluctantly she released her hold from around his neck and slid down his body. The second their bodies separated, he took off down the beach. Moochie, little traitor that she had become, trotted behind.

"Hey, what if I get knocked down by another wave?" Brooke called, trying to restore a modicum of humor into a serious situation.

"Don't go back in the water," he called back without turning to look.

Ever hopeful, she reached into her useless bag of illogical wiles and tried again. "Aren't you even going to thank me for helping you knock an item off your bucket list?"

Hopefulness died a quick death with his four-letter word response and his purposeful stride back to the inn.

Back in the suite, Dec chastised himself while he waited for Brooke to finish her shower. She'd been in there awhile. Singing. At the top of her lungs. Horribly belting out a Carrie Underwood song like a tone-deaf screech owl. He looked at Moochie, who had comfortably stretched out on the bed. "I suppose you're used to that."

Moochie lifted a paw then belly crawled until she ended up in his lap.

Pets had never been a part of his life, but as he stroked

the silky softness of Moochie's fur, he expected he now knew what he'd been missing. Maybe just the continuous motion calmed the nerves tightening his stomach, but he'd take what he could get. Because he knew once Brooke came out of the shower he needed to apologize and they needed to have a talk. He needed to know that what had taken place in that ocean would not have an effect on their working relationship.

At that moment the water in the shower turned off and the singing blessedly ceased.

A few minutes later, the bathroom door opened and steam whooshed out in a cloud of heat. Brooke followed with a plush white towel wrapped around her head and another wrapped around her body. A droplet of water slid down the center of her chest where the tail of the towel was tucked haphazardly between her breasts. As much as Dec wanted to reach out and tug it off, he kept his hands safely on Moochie's fur.

"I see you two are making friends," Brooke said.

"She's a nice dog." Moochie looked up at him adoringly with those crazy blue eyes.

"I think she's in love with you. And that surprises me. She doesn't usually like men."

"What about your roommate?"

"Oh, she loves Kyle." She removed the towel from around her head and used it to squeeze the water out of her wet hair. "The man was born into a family that owned a boarding kennel so he loves animals and she knows it."

"I guess I'm lucky then since I know nothing about pets."

"Looks like you're learning pretty fast to me."

"Brooke? We need to talk."

"Dammit." Her face turned sullen. "It's my singing, isn't it."

"What?"

"My singing in the shower. I know it's horrible but I can't help it. It must have been torture for you to sit out here and listen. I completely disregarded your space. I'm sorry."

He could give a shit about her wretched singing.

"While I don't think Carrie Underwood has anything to worry about, it's not your singing we need to discuss."

A frown pulled the smooth space between her eyes together. "So we're completely back in business mode?"

"One hundred percent." Much to his dismay.

"I suppose now you're going to apologize for kissing me."

"It never should have happened. I'm your—"

"Boss. Yeah. I know." Her shoulders stiffened. "How can I forget when you keep reminding me?"

And now she was pissed. At him. Because he'd been a total horndog dumbshit who couldn't seem to control himself around her.

"Brooke—"

"No worries, *boss*. I'll make sure to stay in work mode from now on."

Before he could respond she went back into the bathroom and shut the door. Hard. A second later the blow-dryer turned on and, if Dec was right, there was a whole lot of cursing going on beneath the constant whir of the appliance.

Moochie looked up at him with something akin to *You really blew that, asshat.*

He couldn't agree more.

*T*hey traded places, and while Brooke considered their sleeping arrangement dilemma, Dec took his turn in the shower.

Dammit.

She punched a bed pillow.

He'd liked that kiss.

It didn't take a brain surgeon to figure out how turned on he'd been. His body had done a whole lot of talking. And if she hadn't been his stupid lowly employee, he wouldn't have stopped at one kiss. But now here they were, living *la vida loca* because Dec felt guilty.

Maybe she should too.

She didn't.

She'd known from the start that it would take a monumental shove to move him off the ledge. So maybe she hadn't planned the wave that had taken her down, but she didn't regret that Mother Nature had intervened. She just wished Dec's common sense hadn't shown up at the wrong time.

Or ever.

He was angry with himself now for letting go, and Brooke knew he'd be angry for a while. She'd seen him stew on things until she'd wanted to yell *stop*. But that was his way of working things out. He needed to overthink, overplan, overrule. With a little luck and maybe a few more nudges in her direction he'd finally get a clue that falling in love wasn't something the head had any control over. He had a big heart, and that was the organ she hoped would eventually reign over anything else that popped up in its way.

If he didn't fall in love with her today there was always tomorrow.

Some things were worth waiting for.

He was worth waiting for.

Even if the girls in the lingerie department would be happy with a little attention in the meantime.

*S*everal minutes later he came out of the bathroom, dark hair damp, and wearing a pair of athletic shorts and a T-shirt. She could almost read his mind—fully clothed would make it easier to resist temptation.

But both of them had been fully clothed in the ocean and it hadn't mattered.

Covertly he scanned her, and the boy shorts and tank top she wore, up and down. A deep breath later he pointed toward the bed where she'd hung extra sheets she'd gotten from housekeeping from corner post to corner post and asked, "What's . . . that?"

"I saw something like this in an old Clark Gable movie. Figured if it worked for him and Claudette Colbert it could work for us. You know, to keep things all business."

"Clever idea but not necessary." He planted his big hands on his lean hips, accentuating the whole perfect physique thing he had going on. "I planned to sleep on the sofa."

"Well, now you don't have to. This contraption worked great in the movie."

"I've never seen it."

"You haven't?"

He shook his head.

"It's a wonderful Frank Capra film about a runaway heiress who falls in with a newspaper reporter looking for a story. He promises to take her back to the man she'd just married, but they end up having to share a room. So they put a blanket up between them and he calls it the Wall of Jericho. Naturally, they fall in love and the wall comes tumbling down."

"Figures."

"You don't believe in happily ever after?"

His broad shoulders came up in a shrug. "I don't believe it happens for everyone."

Neither did she, but she hoped she'd been on Santa's nice list long enough to qualify.

"Maybe not." She pulled back the covers on her side of the bed. "I believe we all create our own happiness. But some just prefer to stand by and let it get away."

"Hmmm."

She hoped that meant he was thinking about it, but when she looked he was studying the bed and scratching the five o'clock shadow on his chin.

"So how are we supposed to do this? The bed isn't exactly split in half."

"It's in half. It's just diagonal, like half of a sandwich. One of us can sleep upside down. That way you get more covered room for your body but less for your legs."

The thoughtful look he gave her flipped her stomach like a stack of pancakes. Either he thought she was out of her mind or . . . he thought she was out of her mind.

"I should probably warn you," she said.

One dark brow lifted. "About?"

"Moochie sleeps with me. On top of the covers. And usually by my feet. But if I make her sleep somewhere else she'll whine all night."

His look of consternation preceded a nod. "I've never slept with a dog before."

"I know." She sighed dramatically. "I've seen the women you date."

"Ha. Funny."

"And one more thing," she said. "Kyle tells me I snore. I don't believe him, but then I'm always asleep so how would I know."

"I can give you a report in the morning."

"Not really sure I need that information." She scrunched her nose. "I have enough hang-ups already."

"Anything else I need to be aware of?" He folded his arms across his chest and the T-shirt fabric barely contained his bulging biceps. "Like you're secretly a serial killer when you sleepwalk?"

"No."

"Then I guess we'd better get some sleep," he said. "Long drive ahead of us tomorrow."

"Right."

Like she would get any sleep lying on a bed next to him?

"Can we leave the fireplace on?" she asked. "I love watching the flames dance. They're mesmerizing."

Might as well have something to do during the night besides fantasize her life away.

"No problem." He went around to his side of the bed and she heard him slide between the sheets.

She could imagine him lying there with his dark hair against the white pillow and the covers only pulled up to his waist so she could see the way the cotton smoothed over his broad shoulders and wide chest. Yeah, she'd take that fantasy with her to dreamland.

She turned on her side, tucked her hand beneath her cheek, and watched the flames lick the inside of the firebox.

"Sleep tight," he murmured.

Doubtful.

Brooke sighed.

Very, very doubtful.

Chapter 5

*W*hen morning snuck through the cracks in the shutters, Dec opened his eyes and for a moment forgot where he was. His right arm was asleep and tingling. He'd been warmer than hell all night because of the T-shirt and shorts he'd worn to bed. Normally he slept naked. But with Brooke . . .

Brooke.

He turned his head and realized that during the night the Wall of Jericho had tumbled down.

He was lying dead center of the bed with her head on his shoulder, snuggled up alongside of him, one arm stretched over his chest and one long leg thrown over his hip. A healthy morning erection tented his shorts.

Ah hell.

He gazed up to the ceiling in a hopeless attempt to regain control. But when she let out a sexy little sigh his body ignored all those previous warnings. Desire ignited with a vengeance.

Her hair smelled like a tropical dessert. Her skin was soft and smooth. And everything male inside him wanted to roll her over and make every cell in her body hum with pleasure. He wanted to taste her skin and plunge deep inside her until they were both exhausted and satisfied. He didn't know how the hell the wall had come down, how they'd both navigated to the same spot, or how they'd became so interestingly entangled, but until she opened her eyes and realized their blunder—or noticed his raging hard-on—he'd take a selfish moment to enjoy.

After a long hungry look, he gently pushed her long fairy curls away from her face. Her lashes were thick and dark. Her skin smooth and clear. Her dimples were hidden but he knew exactly where to find each one.

God, she was beautiful. And funny. And sweet.

If she wasn't his employee . . .

Curled up alongside Brooke's delicious derrière, Moochie sneezed and jarred her master awake. First Brooke stretched, then her eyes popped open and she sprung upright. Neither Dec nor his erection failed to notice the hard peaks of her nipples poking the front of the tank top.

"Oh my God." She ran long fingers through her tumble of messy curls. "Looks like the wall didn't work."

"Definitely not."

"I'm so sorry. I probably pulled it down. I sleep with a body pillow—a giant teddy bear Kyle bought for me a few Christmases ago in case I ever needed a bear hug. He said it was so I didn't go out and find some loser boyfriend again."

"Again?"

She nodded, then sighed. "I almost always learn my lesson the first time."

Almost always?

His curiosity skyrocketed.

Rolling to his side, he propped his head up with a hand. "What was this loser's name and what did he do to make him a loser?"

And why did he need to know and what did it matter?

"Zachary. A professional surfer. And he wanted to marry me."

"He's a loser because he wanted to marry you?" And why the hell did Dec feel the need to hunt down surfer boy just to punch him in his sunscreened nose?

"No. He was a loser because he spent every dime he made on surfboards, wax, and microbrew. And he wanted to marry me so we could *hang loose* and *chill* together forever in the bachelor apartment attached to his parents' house."

"Sounds like the guy had lofty goals."

"He was fun for about three dates."

"So he wasn't a longtime boyfriend?"

"No, thank God." She swept her wild curls back with one hand and scooted to the edge of the bed. "Longtime boyfriends are hard to find in Southern California. Unless you're into gym rats, wannabe actors, models, or . . ."

"Or what?"

"Or guys who put their careers first."

Ouch.

She bent her knees then wrapped her arms around

her legs, inadvertently hiding the best view he'd had since . . . last night when she'd been wet and cold. "So no longtime girlfriends for you?"

"Not since high school."

"Seriously?" When he nodded she asked, "What was her name? And how *long* was long?"

"Cindy and six months. Sadly I was tossed aside for a guitarist with hair down to his waist, who wore black eyeliner and black nail polish and played in a heavy metal band."

"Awwww." Her dimples flashed. "And you had no musicality?"

"Nope. No black nail polish either."

"That is such a sad story."

The tilt of her head and dramatic pout made him laugh. "It was over fifteen years ago. Until you mentioned it I hadn't thought of her since we went our separate ways."

"So you weren't utterly brokenhearted and staring longingly at her picture day and night?"

"Doubtful. You know how it is in high school. Everyone is fickle."

"I guess I went to a different kind of school. Either that or I was too oblivious to notice. Still, everyone needs someone to love or we grow old and bitter."

"Is that so?"

"Yep." She nodded. "That's why I found Moochie. She may not be able to take me to the movies or out to dinner, but she's a great snuggler. And she'll keep me from becoming a crazy cat lady."

He wanted to tell her she did pretty okay in the snuggle department too. But that would be admitting too much and at the moment he was going to have to let her go first in the bathroom so he could pull himself together. Or at least convince his lower half that it wasn't going to see any action anytime soon.

"So no great loves for you in high school?" he asked.

"Of course there was." She sighed. "His name was Mr. Cruz and he was my American history teacher. He had dreamy dark eyes and his tie always matched his shirt perfectly. Of course, the idolization was only on my part."

"Good thing or I'd have to go rearrange his way of thinking."

"Ah. So you *are* a Prince Charming."

"Maybe I just like to fight."

"Maybe you're too modest to admit you'd rescue a damsel in distress without giving it a second thought."

Conversation over.

He knew her mind had gone to last night when he'd pulled her from the ocean. But his went right to that kiss and how much he'd wanted to strip her down and make love to her right there on that beach.

And that could never, would never, happen.

"Time to get dressed and get back on the road."

*B*y the time they pulled into the driveway to Sunshine Creek Vineyard it was late, dark, and not a creature was stirring. With the exception of food and bathroom stops, they'd driven straight through.

No more fun.

No more flirting.

Definitely no more kissing.

The closer they got to Sunshine Valley, the more closed off Dec became. Right now as they entered the gates that led to his family's winery, Brooke thought he looked beyond exhausted and ready to get out of the car on a permanent basis. Mostly he looked like he wanted to get away from her.

It wasn't easy to see much as the car drove down the long winding road into the vineyard and stopped in front of a little brick house.

"This is my grandparents' place," Dec said, putting the car in PARK and turning off the ignition. "It's the original homestead on the property. This is where my brothers and I used to stay during the summers. It's not much to look at but it's private enough that we'll be able to get some work done."

"So . . . we're *both* staying here?" She tried to keep the hope out of her tone. Having Dec all to herself was a dream come true.

Even if he might not see it that way.

He gave her a sharp nod. "There are a couple of bedrooms and a back patio out by the creek. It has WiFi and a landline. So we should be all set." He got out and carried their luggage to the house.

With Moochie in her arms she followed as he unlocked the door, turned on a light, then stepped aside to let her enter.

"As long as there's somewhere to get coffee in the morning, I'll be happy," she said.

"The kitchen is fully stocked." He tossed his keys on a table. "I texted Ryan ahead of time to make sure we were covered."

Of course he did. Heaven forbid Mr. All Work and No Play missed a relevant point.

The place was cozy. A brick fireplace served as the focal point of the living room and the leather sofa and chair looked soft and inviting. While she might not have driven a single mile on the trip, exhaustion pulled at the back of her neck even as anticipation fluttered in her stomach. For however long Dec decided to stay, she'd basically be locked up with him inside this adorable little place. Given the close quarters, who knew what could happen?

Ridiculously optimistic that she could reignite the fire in the man who'd kissed her with such passion after he'd saved her bacon, she strolled through the house until she came upon the bedrooms. "Which one is mine?"

"Take your pick. The front bedroom is bigger but the back bedroom's right on the creek."

"I'll take the one in the back. I love the sound of moving water."

"From what I remember this place is pretty peaceful." He stood with his hands on his hips, looking around at his grandparents' former home. "I can't think of anything that would interfere with your work."

Work.

Brooke wanted to kick him.

She didn't want to think about work right now. She didn't want *him* to think about work right now. Right now she wanted him to forget he was her damn boss and carry her off into one of those bedrooms and make love to her until she couldn't walk straight.

"Like I said, I'm great at multitasking. Noise doesn't bother me." And she hoped to God he didn't plan to keep her locked away from everyone like she had leprosy or something.

"Maybe, but I'll try to make sure no one around here disturbs you." He carried her luggage into the little blue bedroom with a cozy wedding ring quilt on the bed. "You hungry?"

"I could go for a glass of wine or a beer to unwind if it's available."

"I'm sure Ryan stocked the place with the best of the lot."

With Moochie on their heels, she followed him into the kitchen where he opened the refrigerator, pulled out a bottle of Essence, and held it up.

"This is a tasty Moscato. Unless you prefer something less sweet."

"Sounds great." Anything that might numb, slow down, or send her overactive imagination into oblivion sounded perfect. She tilted her head toward the back door. "Any chance of sharing that out on the back patio?"

"Did you bring a coat?"

"Of course." Although she'd much prefer his big strong arms around her.

"Good. A breeze usually kicks up off the creek and the moisture can be chilly. If you plan to stay out there for any period of time, you'll need one."

"You won't be joining me?"

Hesitation darkened his eyes and he looked like a man about to run. "Tomorrow will probably be a long day so I should probably hit the sack."

The man might be tired, but that just sounded like a complete excuse to get away from her.

Hint taken.

"No worries. I usually don't drink alone but I've never been afraid of the dark, so I'll be fine sitting out there with just Moochie. Don't feel the need to entertain me."

"You're sure?"

Brooke nodded and tried not to feel disappointed as she went into her room, unzipped her bag, and pulled out a hoodie. By the time she returned to the kitchen the back door was open, a full glass of wine sat on the counter, and a cheerful fire burned in the iron fire pit on the patio.

The orange glow of the flames silhouetted him. When she stepped outside he looked up. Something flashed in his eyes that pumped up her hope again.

"That hoodie won't keep you very warm."

"I'll be fine," she said, although she'd much rather be cuddled up against the warmth of his body.

"If you need another glass of wine, I put the bottle back in the refrigerator to keep it chilled." He stretched his tall, muscular body. If he faked a yawn she thought she'd just cry. "If you need anything else just let me know."

Running her hands over all those taut muscles would be a start.

"I'll be fine."

Before he closed the door, he hesitated as if he couldn't decide whether to go or change his mind and stay. When he disappeared and the door closed it was clear she didn't have a vote.

* * *

Startled, Dec woke to a commotion coming from the back of the house. He glanced at the bedside clock and realized he hadn't even been asleep for an hour. He'd lain there for what seemed like forever trying to erase the entire road trip from his mind.

Not that it had been bad. Brooke was an easy person to be around. And that freewheeling spirit she possessed was irresistible. A huge part of him wanted to just keep driving north and stop at every little town on the way just to see her face light up at what she called unexpected goodness.

But the closer they'd come to driving through the gates of the vineyard, the more the knot in his chest had increased. The more miles they'd traveled, the more distant he'd grown toward Brooke when it hadn't been her at all that had created his tension.

Being back home brought an onslaught of situations that needed to be dealt with. Everyone—including him—was still broken from the sudden death of their parents. Everyone was still on edge from the discovery that their father had stolen money from his own company. And everyone still wanted to know the hell why.

Though he'd been temporarily able to subdue the issues and enjoy Brooke's company, there were too many internal battles to ignore. In his past, he'd used women to relieve stress or loneliness, but he refused to use Brooke for his own selfish reasons.

As much as he would have loved to sit around the fire, drinking wine with her, and feasting on her beautiful mind and body, he'd needed a break. When they'd started their journey north, he'd never imagined how many cracks in his armor she'd uncover. And he'd never imagined how wide she'd break each of them open.

Brooke may not have a devilish mind, but the devil in him had fought to take every advantage she'd thrown his way. It was that battle that had brought on his total exhaustion.

Now, although he felt groggy and grumpy, it was his duty to get up and make sure nothing was amiss. It was his duty to keep her safe.

Even if that meant keeping her safe from *him*.

He shuffled through the house and toward the commotion. By the time he reached the kitchen the rumble of male laughter snapped his head up. Yanking open the back door, he found his brother Ethan cozied up to Brooke next to the fire *he'd* built to keep her warm. They were both laughing and apparently having a jolly good time.

"What the hell's going on?" His sudden appearance startled both of them.

"Oh! I'm so sorry." Brooke's smile died as her eyes widened. "Did we wake you?"

"*He* did." He jerked his head in Ethan's direction. "What are you doing here?"

His brother gave an innocent shrug. "Keeping Brooke company."

"I wasn't aware she needed any." Good God. Did he just snarl?

Ethan threw him a grin bursting with mischief as he settled his hand on Brooke's arm. "I couldn't stand the thought of such a beautiful woman being left all alone on such a beautiful night."

Ethan's taunt sealed the fucking deal. Dec was now officially pissed.

"I told her if she needed anything to come get *me*." Dec folded his arms across his bare chest, more to keep from throttling his brother than to keep warm.

"But, bro . . ." Ethan grinned. Again. "When I saw the glow of a fire, the firefighter in me just had to stop by and check it out. When I did, it was apparent Brooke needed some company. *You* were the one who chose to go nighty-night and leave her out here all alone."

"Ummm." Brooke stood and Moochie jumped off her lap. "I didn't mean to cause any trouble."

"No trouble at all." Ethan stood too. "Right, bro?"

Dec glared at his good-looking baby brother who, where women were concerned, gained extra points for being a firefighter. Something about the whole saving lives/putting out fires/rescuing kittens thing apparently turned them on. Ethan was right; he *had* left her out here all alone. So he should have no reason to want to rearrange his brother's pretty face. No reason at all. Brooke was his assistant. He was her boss. End of story. If his brother found her an attractive way to spend his time, why should Dec care?

Problem?

He fucking cared.

"Right, *bro*." Dec overemphasized the word. "But don't you have somewhere else you need to be?"

"Naw." Ethan shrugged his broad shoulders. "I can sleep in in the morning."

Confused, Brooke's gaze ping-ponged between them.

"But if you sleep in, how's that going to help the vineyard?" Dec asked. "Didn't you stick around so you could help us get back in the black?"

Ethan was about to respond when Brooke scooped Moochie up into her arms. "I'm suddenly very tired. Ethan, thank you for the wonderful conversation. Good night, Dec. I'll have tomorrow's schedule printed out by the time you wake up."

Ethan said good night.

Dec waited until Brooke disappeared to unload. "What the hell?"

Ethan's grin turned absolutely provoking. "Is there a problem, big brother?"

"Yeah. *You* hitting on my assistant."

"She said she didn't have a boyfriend."

"Are you fucking kidding me?" Dec jammed his hands on his hips. "Please tell me I don't have to pound you into the ground to get it through your thick skull."

"You lost me." Ethan lifted his hands in false innocence. "Exactly what is it I'm supposed to get through my thick skull?"

"I didn't bring Brooke up here for you to make a move on her. I brought her because we have work to do and I need her help. How can she do that if you're going to be trying to take up all her time?"

"And that's really *all* you brought her up here for?"

All Dec could do was glare, because there was no way in hell he would admit things he didn't want to admit. Especially out loud.

"Hell." Ethan laughed. Hard. "Why didn't you say something earlier?"

"You knew we'd be working."

"Not about that, dumbshit. About you being hot for her. Why didn't you tell me you've got a thing for her?"

Dec curled his fingers into his hands. Backed into a corner, he lied his ass off. "Because I don't."

"Then she's fair game, right?"

"No. Go find someone else to play with, Ethan. She doesn't need the distraction."

"Ha." Ethan slapped a hand over Dec's shoulder. "You mean *you* don't need the competition."

"I think you've been inhaling too much smoke and it's affected your brain."

"And I think *you* just need to own up to the fact that you're hot for your hot assistant. If you don't say something then don't blame the rest of the male population when we try to win her over." Ethan gave him a wave. "Good night, big brother. Pleasant dreams."

As Ethan stepped off the patio and disappeared into the night, Dec realized that there was no way in hell he'd sleep tonight. Not with Brooke sleeping in the next room. Not with his feelings toward her obviously being read like an open book. And not when he'd realized he'd set himself up for an epic disaster.

At the crack of dawn Brooke was up and jogging down a peaceful country road with Moochie by her side. Unfortunately she had too much on her mind to enjoy the view. The repartee between Dec and his brother last night had confused her. Dec had barged in—or out as it were, since they'd been on the patio—and acted like she was in some kind of danger. She couldn't imagine he'd believe Ethan was any kind of a threat to her safety. He was a gorgeous, genuinely nice guy who'd merely kept her entertained with witty conversation.

So what had crawled up Dec's butt and sent him into protective overdrive?

She could handle herself just fine. After all she'd once been a thirteen-year-old girl who'd planned an escape from her religiously overzealous parents and their perverse plans for her life. She'd been a young girl who'd braved the dark of night and a long scary road toward an uncertain future rather than be locked into a life of despair. She'd been a girl who'd walked away from everyone and everything she'd ever known, aware that she'd have to abandon it all. Because once she scaled the big stone wall that promised her only chance at freedom, she'd be exiled.

She glanced down at the bracelet on her wrist.

Fearless.

She liked to think it was true, but everyone had their limits.

Cutting across the road she and Moochie headed down a dirt path she'd discovered that ran through the vineyard. The rolling hills added a challenge to her exercise. They also offered a view that was hard to beat. A tree-lined creek that ran the length of the property and through an open meadow presented a scene that not only took her breath away, but gave her a sense of calm she'd never achieved in Southern California. Instead of honking horns and rushing cars there were chirping birds and the crunch of gravel beneath her running shoes. Before she knew it they'd jogged all the way into town.

The little town of Sunshine Valley seemed like something out of a movie. Main Street was lined with an array of eclectic shops, dogwood trees in bloom, and the enticing fragrance of warm cinnamon rolls. As she and Moochie slowed to a walk, Brooke followed the mouthwatering scent toward a pink building with a sign that read "Sugarbuns Bakery" in curlicue letters.

"Mooch? We can run the calories off later, but right now we are definitely stopping in there." Her dog excitedly tapped her front paws against the cobblestone walk. "I promise to bring you a treat," she added as she hooked the dog leash onto a shabby chic bench outside the big front window.

The sweet aroma of cinnamon rolls, freshly baked breads, and other delicious goodies met her at a front door that jingled merrily when she walked in. The inside of the shop lived up to the pink exterior with a décor featuring the colors of cupcake sprinkles. Near the window a couple, obviously in love judging by the googly eyes they were giving each other, shared a plate of icing covered cinnamon rolls. Over at a corner table made of white cast iron, sat a woman with bright orange hair and a 1960s-style blue paisley dress. Her white vinyl go-go boots were crossed at the ankles while she sipped a tall specialty coffee and snacked on a large muffin.

"Welcome!" The woman behind the glass display's rounded body clearly said she enjoyed the sweets she made and sold. The broad smile and healthy glow to her cheeks said she enjoyed her occupation immensely. In Brooke's mind there was no better testimony to an establishment's product.

"I'm Pearl," the woman said. "And you're new in town."

Apparently in a small town everyone knew who belonged and who didn't. Brooke knew she didn't belong, but she'd like to.

"Hi. I'm Brooke." She stretched her hand across the display case. "I was out jogging and couldn't resist coming inside."

"Well." The woman laughed and winked. "We'll hook ya any way we can. Good for business you know. So what's your weakness?"

"Hmmm." Brooke leaned down and scanned the sugar-laden contents of the display case. Each treat looked more delicious than the last, including the cute little mice made of a Hershey's Kiss, a chocolate covered cherry with stem, and slivers of almonds. "The scent of cinnamon rolls drew me in so how about one of those and a tall caramel latte? And do you have anything back there that might be appropriate for my little friend outside?"

Pearl peeked around Brooke to where Moochie had her paws up against the glass door, looking inside and wagging her tailless butt.

"Oh, isn't she a cutie. I've got just the thing." Pearl winked again. "Keep 'em right here behind the counter and they're even fresh." She placed a glass jar of dog treats on the counter. "Make 'em myself so I guarantee they're healthy. The wagging tails tell me they're tasty too."

She popped open the steel lid and placed a couple on a bakery tissue. "So where you from, sugar?"

"Southern California. I came up here with my boss on business."

"Well, lucky you. With everything in bloom this is the prettiest time of the year. Who do your work for? Local company?"

"She works for my nephew." The orange-haired woman now stood beside Brooke at the display case and reached out for a hug. "I'm Declan's Aunt Pippy."

Brooke sighed in relief that the wildly dressed woman with the bright blue eye shadow and plastic fruit dangling from her ears wasn't just a random weirdo, and returned the hug. "I'm so happy to meet you."

Aunt Pippy gave her a once- and then a twice-over. "And I'm so happy you're here. When did you arrive?"

"We drove in late last night. Dec talked to Ryan and arranged for us to stay in their grandfather's cabin."

"Hmmm. So you're both staying in the same private location." Pippy gave a nod that wiggled her bright orange bouffant. "Nice."

Unsure of the implication there, Brooke just said, "It's a very nice place. Perfect for us to temporarily set up an office."

"It's romantic too." She gave Brooke a little nudge with her elbow. "Bubbling creek, tree-shaded deck, fire pit, and the best wine on the planet."

"Heck, if she doesn't want to stay there with Mr. Handsome and Wealthy, count me in." Pearl laughed as she placed Brooke's plated cinnamon roll on the counter then went about making the latte.

Brooke wasn't about to dip her toes in gossipy waters. Especially when she'd also thought of the cabin as romantic. Unfortunately Dec only saw business and responsibilities.

"I'd planned to take my cinnamon roll and latte out to eat on the bench," Brooke said. "I don't want to leave Moochie alone for too long."

"Moochie?" Aunt Pippy's head tilted and Brooke realized the woman's wild hair put on a show all of its own.

"My dog." She motioned toward the door where her sweet pup still stood with her paws on the glass and what looked like a smile.

"Oh, she's precious."

"I think so," Brooke said. "But I'm biased."

"I'm all done with my breakfast," Pippy said. "Mind if I join you?"

"I'd love that." When Pearl placed the steaming latte on the counter, Brooke reached into her running jacket for the money to pay.

"You keep that money in your pocket, sugar. Welcome to Sunshine."

"Are you sure?"

Pearl grinned. "Sure as I am that things are going to get interesting around here."

"Well, thank you. I promise I'll be back."

"Just spread the good word and invite me to the wedding. We do cakes too."

Both Pearl and Aunt Pippy chuckled as Brooke waved goodbye then grabbed her treats and headed toward the door.

"Don't mind us," Pippy said as they sat down on the bench outside. "We're just both surprised Declan brought a girl home. Gives us hopes there'll be another Kincade wedding after Jordy and Lucy's."

"I wouldn't get those hopes too high." Brooke set her latte down by her feet and reached in the bag for Moochie's treat. "Dec only brought me along because we have client appointments set up for this week and he needed to be back here to help out with family business." When Moochie sat and lifted her paw for a handshake, Brooke gave her a bite of the dog treat as a reward.

"Didn't you say you drove up?" Aunt Pippy asked.

"Yes. I talked him into it because I've never made it very far up the coast and I'd heard it was beautiful."

"And my nephew agreed?"

Brooke nodded.

Pippy's smile stretched her brightly painted lips. "Declan really is all about business, isn't he? Takes a bit of a nudge or a poke to get him moving in a different direction."

"True. But he takes very good care of his clients and their investments."

"He's very good at taking care of his family too."

"That's nice to know."

"Which is why if you think he agreed to drive up the coast just to satisfy your sightseeing curiosity, you might want to reconsider."

"Oh. Don't get the wrong idea. He's made it *very* clear that he is the boss and I am the employee."

"But you feel something different?"

"I . . . uh."

Pippy laughed. "That's as good an answer as any."

"I try not to wear my heart on my sleeve. Or anywhere else for that matter. I've worked with him for four years."

"So you're pretty good at hiding your feelings?"

Brooke shrugged. "Believe me. He's not interested." She fed another piece of dog treat to Moochie then she used a plastic fork to take a bite of the warm cinnamon roll. The sweetness melted in her mouth and she nearly did a happy dance. "Oh. This is so good."

"Next time try the butterscotch sticky buns. To. Die. For." Aunt Pippy leaned her head back and sighed. "And didn't anyone ever tell you not to believe everything you're told by a man?"

"Not really." Because growing up, the men in their sect said everything they meant with an iron fist while the women were expected to remain acquiescent.

"Well . . ." Aunt Pippy patted Brooke's leg. "Then let me be the first. Especially when it comes to my nephews. They're beautiful, bighearted alpha males who don't always focus on the right thing. And when it comes to matters of the heart, their stubborn streaks have them digging in their heels."

Brooke sipped her latte. "I'm not sure why you're telling me all this."

"Because *someone* has to open their eyes." Pippy patted her leg again. "Lucy had to knock Jordy off his skates before he got a clue. When you talk about Declan, I can see that in your heart there really is more than just a boss/employee relationship."

"You can get that from just the way I talk about him?"

"Oh, and maybe the way your eyes light up too. Eyes are the window to the soul, right?"

If that was true, then Declan had a very beautiful soul.

"Come on." Pippy stood. "I'll give you and Moochie a ride home so you can get started shaking up my nephew's carefully planned out life."

"I'm not sure shaking him up any more than I already have is such a good idea."

"Oh honey." Pippy cupped Brooke's chin in her palm. "Knowing Declan has someone who will love him and be by his side for the things that are sure to rock his foundation in the future is an excellent idea. Now, come on. I'll make sure he puts business aside today to give you a tour of the vineyard."

Brooke had never met a person before who made such giant leaps with their assumptions. Yet unable to come up with a good excuse to remain right there on the bench, Brooke gathered up her food and her dog and climbed inside Pippy's vintage sunshine yellow VW Bug.

"Hang on tight," Aunt Pippy exclaimed. "I guarantee it's going to be a bumpy ride."

Brooke couldn't help wondering if the reference meant Pippy's driving skills or something a lot more personal.

Chapter 6

When he woke up, Declan found Brooke's note that she'd taken Moochie and gone out for a run. Hours later, his worry alarm had started to ring. He didn't know how long or how many miles she usually ran, but she didn't know the area. Not that there were bad neighborhoods to stay away from, but maybe she'd gotten lost. Maybe he should go out looking for her. Maybe she'd fallen and couldn't get up.

He jammed his fingers through his hair and squeezed. Dammit.

Maybe she'd met another one of his damned brothers and had fallen under their spell too. He hated to admit an acquaintance with the green-eyed monster, but where Brooke was concerned, there might be a strong likelihood.

Unable to stay put any longer, he grabbed his car keys off the kitchen counter. The moment he opened the front door, his Aunt Pippy's VW Bug putt-putted up and stopped. Inside were Brooke and Moochie, who had her paws up on the passenger window giving him her happy doggy face. A sigh pushed the air from his lungs and relief wound around his heart. Looked like he wouldn't have to murder his brothers after all.

At least not today.

Stepping out onto the porch he tried to act normal and not expose the twisted bag of nerves he'd been just a few seconds ago. When Brooke got out of the car Moochie jumped down to the ground and ran right to him. The excited dog wiggled her tailless butt then rolled to her back for a belly rub. He complied with the request as Aunt Pippy honked her horn, waved, then putt-putted off toward the main house.

"Good morning." Brooke's long bare legs ate up the ground between them. "I met your aunt."

"I see that." He gave Moochie another quick rub then righted himself so he could look into Brooke's face. "Did she scare you?"

"Scare me?" A head tilt swung the long blond ponytail at the back of her head. "No. Why?"

"Her driver's license was revoked several years ago for making up her own road rules instead of following the legal ones."

"Oh no." Brooke laughed and the sound tickled his chest. "Did she have an accident or something?"

"Let's just say she broke the law several times in front of the sheriff and he stopped thinking she was just quirky."

"Well, she drove fine. But next time I'll remember that and offer to drive for her."

"How was your run?"

"Great. Except I blew all the effort by stopping in at Sugarbuns."

"Cinnamon roll?"

"Yeah." She sighed. "I couldn't resist. How'd you guess?"

He reached out, swiped off the bit of icing on her bottom lip, and held up his thumb. "Evidence."

"Ah." Her tongue swept across her lips to remove further proof and Dec could barely keep his eyes off her mouth. Especially now that he knew what it was like to kiss her.

Keep it business, buddy.

"You interested in a tour of the place?"

"I'd love that." A grin flashed her dimples. "Can Moochie come, or should I put her in the house?"

"Are you kidding? There are hundreds of acres for that dog to run. Let her have some fun. She was stuck in a car for two days."

"Hear that, Mooch?" The dog did a little back leg dance then trotted toward the vineyard, grabbing up a stick on her way.

"Didn't have to ask her twice."

"She's a working-class dog." Brooke stuck her hands in the pockets of her jacket. "She likes to be busy. I always feel bad when I get home from work too tired to take her for a walk. I didn't think about that when I found her. Those big blue eyes just grabbed me and I had to bring her home."

The fact that he worked Brooke so hard that she didn't have the energy to walk her dog at the end of the day scraped a raw nerve. "Do you have a backyard where you live?"

"We do," she said, "but it's mostly concrete and a pool. Another worry, because she loves to swim and I'm always afraid she'll jump in when we're not there and won't be able to get out."

"Can you fence in the pool?" He tried to erase the horrible image from his mind.

"Not really. We're just renting." She kicked at a pebble and it flew several feet away. "I'll have to find a new place when Kyle and Marc get married. Next time I'll make sure there's enough room for Moochie to run and play."

Dec wondered if she lived with a roommate because she couldn't afford to live on her own or if she just liked the company. He knew the salary he paid her was adequate, even at the top of the pay range, but maybe it was time he gave her a raise.

The road they followed wound down to the vineyard and wove around the rows to a variety of grapes. The vines had sprouted leaves. Next would come the fruit, and then the work would really begin.

"I had no idea the vineyard was this big."

"The entire property is over three hundred acres." Dec waved his hand to the vibrant green meadows and the forest rising up to the nearby mountains. "Some of the ideas we've been tossing around are about how to make better use of more of the property to increase profitability. The wines are great but if you can't get them in front of an audience it doesn't matter."

"What kinds of ideas?"

"Possibly an expansion of the bed-and-breakfast, adding a restaurant, a new tasting room, and a better event area."

"Wow. That's a lot."

He shrugged. "The company is currently in the red so something needs to be done. We've all agreed to invest our own money and sweat equity to bring it up where it needs to be."

She stopped and looked up at him. "All of you?"

"It's our family legacy. That's what families do. Pull together in times of need, right?"

"I . . ." Head down, she started walking again. "I really wouldn't know."

"Brooke?" He caught her arm and brought her around to face him. Her forehead crinkled and he was tempted to place a kiss right in the center of it. To take away what troubled her. To make everything right. "You know you can trust me. I wish you'd tell me what happened."

"Thanks." A forced smile crossed her soft lips. "I'll remember that."

"But you're not going to share?"

"Maybe."

"But not right now."

"Right now I want to know what you're putting next on your bucket list." She started walking backward, which ended up being more of a little dance than an actual stride. One thing he was quickly learning, the woman was highly skilled in the art of distraction.

"You first," he said, curious where that creative mind of hers would travel next.

"Swimming with dolphins."

"Not sharks?"

"No." She laughed. "I deal with enough of those in L.A."

"How extravagant can this bucket list be?"

"It can be as over-the-top as you want." Her hands came up. "It's *your* list. There are no rules or boundaries. It can be as far out there as your imagination will take you."

He didn't suppose making love to her should go on that list let alone be openly shared, but right now he'd definitely put that up at the number one spot. "How about opening the new office in Chicago?"

"What?" She stopped abruptly and jammed her hands onto her curvy hips. "*No.* No business stuff. You have enough of that going on. Think of something fun. Something scary or rewarding. Something that after doing, if you were to die tomorrow you wouldn't have regrets because you'd fulfilled that dream."

"That could be anything." His mind really didn't work that way. The inside of his head was always filled with numbers, deals, and client needs.

"Exactly."

"Fine." He tried to focus, but all he could come up with was peeling those gray running shorts off her body.

The seconds ticked by.

"Dec?" She curled her fingers into his T-shirt and gave him a little shake. "It worries me when it takes you this long to figure out something."

It worried *him* that he'd become so single-minded. "Okay, okay. I've got one. How about . . . pursuing my passion?"

"Perfect! What's your passion?"

You.

"I don't know."

"Then how can you pursue it? Haven't I taught you anything these past couple of days? Why don't you know what it is? How can that possibly be?"

"You know the answer to that better than anyone."

"Because you work too much."

"I don't know if it's too much, but I do work a lot."

"Ai-yi-yi." She slapped her forehead and let out a long, loud sigh. "What am I going to do with you?"

He had plenty of ideas.

"All right, smarty-pants." He folded his arms across his chest. "What's *your* passion?"

"Karaoke."

"Brooke?" He managed to refrain from laughing out loud. "I've heard you sing."

"I know. I suck. But I love it. So sue me."

He did laugh then. With her, he wanted to laugh a lot more than he'd ever realized.

"You know, I feel an obligation to introduce you to new things," she said. "I think you've been living in a suit and tie too long and it's strangled your ability to think outside the box."

"That's not true." Because he could come up with plenty of ideas about how to make love to her. Including using the ties he wore each day.

"Really." She cocked her head and gave him a disapproving frown.

Shit.

He had no comeback, because as much as he hated to admit it, she was probably right.

"That's what I thought. I'm disappointed in you,

Dec." With Moochie on her heels, she took off at a fast pace down the row between the Chardonnay and the Riesling. "Let me know when you figure it out."

"Where are you going?" he called out.

"To find some fun."

*B*rooke knew if she turned around Dec's dark blue eyes would be set in a glare because she could feel the penetrating heat of it on her backside.

On an average day she'd never be a game player. But the more she learned about the man she had a heart deep crush on, the more she realized his aunt was right. Someone needed to jar him loose from the strict confines he'd put himself in. Hard work was good. Admirable. But all hard work and no play at all could be detrimental to a soul. If she didn't care she'd go on with her life and let him figure it out. But she did care. A lot. And no way in hell was she going to stand by and watch the man she'd fallen in love with miss out on life.

Commence operation shake, rattle, and roll.

*"W*hat's with the frown?"

Declan looked up as he entered the winery office and found his brother Ryan and his twin, Jordan, refilling their coffee cups. He pulled a cup off the shelf for himself. "You got enough in there to share?"

"Maybe." Using his quick-handed hockey skills, Jordan snatched the cup away. "If you ask nice and tell us what crawled up your butt first."

"Like you care, Mr. I'm-so-happy-because-I'm-getting-laid-on-a-regular-basis." Yes, he was happy his twin had found the perfect woman. And he truly liked Lucy. But his brother's happy sappy shit could get annoying.

"So the problem is you're not getting laid?" Ryan barked a harsh laugh. "Join the club."

"Yeah." Jordan grinned. "And Ryan's not grumpy as shit."

Dec knew his oldest brother hadn't dated since his wife left him. He'd been too busy raising their young daughter and taking care of his duties at the vineyard. He had every right to be grumpy. Yet he sat behind the desk like he didn't have a care in the world.

"At least you can crawl out of the office and look at beautiful women while I'm stuck here with miles of vines," Ryan said, "a crazy secretive aunt, and a moody little sister."

"Dude." Jordan handed Dec the cup back. "I told you your assistant is hot and you should be—"

"Stop. I don't want you talking about Brooke like she's some kind of easy piece of ass. She's my assistant and I expect you to respect her for that."

His brothers looked at each other then started to laugh.

"What?" God, they pissed him off. Yeah, he loved them and all that shit, but it seemed like they took every opportunity to jab him whenever they could.

"You are in deep, little brother." Jordan punched his arm.

"You're only older by a few minutes. Don't get cocky."

"Well, I'm a couple years older," Ryan said, "and I say you're in deep too."

"I don't know what the hell you're talking about." Although he pretty much did. He just wasn't going to own up to it. Dec filled his coffee cup then carried it over to a chair in front of the desk and sat down. "So, in the scheme of things, where are we?"

Ryan kicked his feet up on the desk. Jordan sat in the chair next to Dec and said, "We're in the office waiting for you to tell us why you're being such a fucking Debbie Downer."

Shit. That's what Brooke had called him the other night on the beach. He knew what the hell his problem was, but he sure as hell wasn't going to sound like a pussy and *share his feelings*.

"I'm tired."

"Late night?" Jordan lifted his cup and sipped.

"Stop smirking, jackass." Tempted to plant his fist in his twin's face, Dec looked away. "In case you forgot I drove all the way up the fucking coast yesterday." And he'd used up his sleeping time on Brooke-induced fantasies for two nights in a row.

"And why did you drive exactly?" Ryan asked. "You normally take a plane because you're in such a hurry. Was there some specific reason you wanted to take your time? Did it have anything to do with a hot blond assistant?"

Great.

Backed into a corner again.

Maybe Dec should just kick the shit out of both of them so they'd stop with the fifty questions. "Can we just get down to business?"

"Can *you*?" Jordan grinned even wider. "I mean you do seem a bit distracted."

Distracted? Hell yes. "What are you guys, like five years old?"

His brothers laughed at his expense then finally decided to cut him some slack.

"How's Nicole doing?" he asked. Since their parents' deaths, their baby sister had gone through a lot of turmoil. Especially where their father was concerned because he'd admitted that something in his past had affected him in a negative way where she was concerned. He'd told her he didn't blame her, but also that he didn't know if he could ever move past it to be the kind of father she needed and deserved. Then he and their mother had been killed in a touring helicopter crash while vacationing in Hawaii. Hell of a thing for a young girl to deal with.

Luckily with the help of Jordan's fiancée, who'd also been one of Nicole's schoolteachers, Nicki had been able to receive her diploma and was now considering her future options. Although her mood swings could still drive the brothers to drink.

"She's still thinking about taking her talents to Nashville," Jordan said. "But Lucy's trying to convince her to at least give college a try first."

"Has she said any more about thinking she's not really our sister?"

"She hasn't said much," Jordan said. "But every once in a while I catch her looking at us like her wheels are spinning in the wrong direction."

"I'll take her out to dinner while I'm here," Dec said. "See if she has anything to say."

Jordan grinned. "You might want to take along your hot assistant too."

"Good God, give it a rest." Dec leaned forward and grabbed a folder off the desk.

"That's the latest financials minus the pilfered money Dad took," Ryan informed him.

Dec opened the file and had just begun to scan the contents when the office door opened.

"Look who we found," Aunt Pippy announced, followed into the room by Nicole, Brooke, and Moochie.

Dec and his brothers all stood as the women entered the room.

"Hey." Jordan wasted no time in wrapping Brooke up in a big hug, much to Moochie's dismay. "Great to see you again."

Ryan, ever the professional, reached out and shook her hand. Moochie didn't like that any better and gave another little growl. For whatever weird reason, Dec felt proud that at least the little dog seemed to approve of *him*.

"Isn't she adorable?" Nicki picked up the dog and gave her a nose kiss.

"I'm not sure Fezzik is going to like dog smell on you," Jordan said with a laugh about the kitten he'd bought her before he'd headed off to his last NHL playoffs last spring.

"He's used to *parfum de dog* from Ziggy," Nicole returned. Then she told Brooke, "Lucy's golden retriever shares his loose fur almost as often as he passes gas. And I lean strongly on the word *often*."

Brooke chuckled.

"We were just about to throw out some ideas for the vineyard," Ryan said. "Care to join us?"

"I thought we were going to wait for Parker and Ethan." Not that Dec wanted his youngest brother anywhere near Brooke after he'd put the moves on her last night.

"The wait is over." Both of the aforementioned devils came into the room bearing gifts of sugar-laden treats from Sugarbuns.

Since the bakery was so popular, Dec thought maybe they should consider giving it some space in the picnic market they'd talked about opening.

"Hey, Brooke." Parker gave her a hug. "We heard you were in town."

Brooke smiled. When Ethan kissed the back of her hand, she freaking giggled. Dec clenched his hand around his coffee cup to keep from doing him bodily harm.

"Have a seat." Ethan pulled out chairs for all three women and Moochie planted her tailless butt on Nicki's lap.

"I didn't want to intrude." Brooke crossed her legs and it didn't go unnoticed by Dec that every single brother watched. "But Pippy and Nicole said you all were rarely seen in the same place at the same time so I thought I'd just stop in to say hello. And to ask Dec when he wanted to get started on the Flavios' investment deal."

Dec grimaced. If he'd handled that detail before he left his grandfather's cabin, she wouldn't have had to make her way up the hill where his obviously enchanted brothers could ogle her all they wanted. "After this meeting will be fine."

"You could never be an intrusion," Ethan insisted, claiming the chair next to Brooke.

If he didn't know his brothers would give him ten tons of shit, Dec would groan loudly. As it was he miraculously maintained his professional demeanor. "So are we ready to put some ideas into action or what?"

"We still need a theme." Nicole stroked her hand between Moochie's little winged ears. "Otherwise we're going to end up going in too many directions."

"Good point," Dec said.

"Our sister's not only pretty," Parker said, giving her a hug Dec knew was meant to quell her misgivings about her place in the family. "She's smart too."

Conversation ping-ponged around the room and it became clear to Dec that their sister was right. Everyone did have vastly different ideas about the future of the vineyard.

Dec's lifestyle choices steered him toward something modern contemporary with sleek lines. Parker favored a Tuscan look. Ryan thought Old West might be a better option. Ethan liked an Adirondack theme. Nicole wanted modern funk, whatever the hell that was. Jordan thought a sports theme would work. And Aunt Pippy suggested a retro sixties look à la Austin Powers.

Dec was more confused than ever. How the hell could they all be related when they had such infinitely different concepts?

"Maybe Brooke has some input," Dec said. "She's a lot more objective-minded."

"Oh. No. I couldn't." Brooke put a hand to her chest

and, yep, every brother's eyes strayed there. "I really wouldn't know."

"Your marketing degree and workplace experience say otherwise," Dec said before any of the testosterone injected dipshits in the room could interject. Plus, as he knew personally, she had a hell of a good imagination. "Now that you've seen the place, I'd love to hear your ideas."

Her eyes widened like he'd handed her a gift.

"Do you all mind?" she asked everyone.

A flurry of concurrences rang throughout the room and she smiled.

"Well . . . the first thing you have to ask is who's your market? Is it people of retirement age with set budgets? Young, unmarried singles? Or maybe young marrieds with double income? Are they locals? Or maybe those who are looking for a weekend getaway? If they're marrieds, which partner will be the one to suggest coming to Sunshine Creek for wine tasting or perhaps a stay at the bed-and-breakfast? Once you decipher that information you'll know whose needs you'll be catering to and what type of theme you should give the place. And then knowing how and where you'll target your market will be easy."

"Brooke's right," Dec said, his admiration for her growing in leaps and bounds. He realized now that everyone in his family had been so rattled by the sudden tragic death of their parents and the discovery that the vineyard was in the red that they'd missed the bigger picture. "We need to do a market analysis. I have an associate who could probably put one together and get the information back to us sooner than anyone else."

"Do you want me to make the call?" Brooke asked, already standing and ready to take care of business.

"That would be great. Try to get him on the phone. I'll be back at the cabin in a couple of minutes."

"Right away."

Dec watched her scoop up her little dog, say her goodbyes, and exit the room. When he turned his attention back to his family, all eyes were zeroed in on him.

"What?"

Nicki grinned. "Nothing."

The brothers chuckled and Jordan clamped his hand over Dec's shoulder. "This sure is going to be fun."

"What the hell are you talking about?"

"Watching you crumble at Brooke's pretty little feet."

Chapter 7

With the restaurant choices in Sunshine ranging from surf and turf courtesy of the Pacific Fish House, to the greasiest cheeseburgers in town from Mr. Pickle Buns, to healthy eating at the Pita Paradise, Brooke chose Cranky Hank's Smokehouse. The place was a favorite of Dec's brothers because it was a *guy* kind of restaurant that served huge servings of barbecued ribs and brisket. Most women would balk at the portions.

Not Brooke.

As the server placed an enormous combo plate of ribs, brisket, and chicken with sides of potato salad and coleslaw in front of her, she grinned and rubbed her hands together.

"I don't know how you're going to eat all that or where you're going to put it," Dec said, in admiration that the woman didn't order just a salad.

"I don't plan to eat it all right now." She squirted some extra sweet and spicy sauce over the top of everything then dug her fork into the juicy, tender chicken. "I'm just sampling. The rest is to take back for leftovers."

"Leftovers?"

"Don't you ever do that? Order more so you'll have some for breakfast, lunch, or dinner the next day?"

His fork, filled with steaming brisket, halted halfway to his mouth. "No. With five hungry boys growing up, leftovers were never a concern."

"I can only imagine. Your parents must have gone broke trying to feed all of you." She picked up a rib with her fingers and sank her teeth into the tender meat. As her tongue darted out and licked away the barbecue sauce at the corner of her mouth, she closed her eyes and moaned. "Oh my God, this is heaven."

His fork remained in midair while he watched her turn a simple bite of food into a sensuous experience and he wondered how she kept doing that. Maybe she really did live on leftovers and convenience store food.

"So if not leftovers, what do you keep in your refrigerator?" she asked, licking the sauce from her fingers. "No. Wait. Let me guess."

It didn't take a rocket scientist to realize that Brooke had the ability to turn everything into a game. And it took even less brain power for him to admit he really liked that about her.

"Yogurt. Eggs. Fat free milk. Carrots. Celery. And lettuce. And in your cupboards you have a variety of powdered protein shakes and brown rice."

"You missed the microwave popcorn."

One smooth, arched eyebrow lifted. "So basically

you eat at restaurants all the time but you don't take home leftovers."

"I never really thought about it before. But yes, you're probably correct. Is that a crime?" He didn't know why he found this conversation so entertaining. Maybe it was because the tone Brooke used wasn't reprimanding, but humored. He didn't know where any of this would lead. But as she took another bite of barbecue glazed ribs and then sucked the sauce from her index finger, Dec was all in. Even if he shouldn't be.

"Not a crime. But it's a shame."

It was even more of a shame that he couldn't suck the barbecue sauce from the rest of her fingers.

"Okay, smarty-pants. Two can play at this game." Once he'd passed the age of ten, it seemed he'd tragically misplaced his sense of humor. In the hardworking years since, no one who knew him would ever call him *playful*. But Brooke's easygoing flair stirred a fire in him that made him want to join in on the fun. "What's in *your* refrigerator?"

She didn't even hesitate. "Yogurt—the non-diet kind with lots of gooey fruit at the bottom. A slice of white chocolate caramel macadamia nut cheesecake from dinner the night before we left. Although Kyle will probably snarf that down. A gallon of two percent milk. Leftover Mongolian that I'll have to throw away when I get home. And a box of pinot noir."

"Wait. You actually buy wine in a box?"

"Doesn't everybody?"

He laughed at the impish smile she gave him.

"I wouldn't mention to my brothers that you drink boxed wine."

"Would they think less of me?"

"No. But they'd probably send you home with a couple cases of the good stuff just so you'd know the difference."

"Then I'm totally telling them."

"So, if leftovers are so good . . ." He leaned in. "Why are there still some in your refrigerator?"

She leaned in too. "Because I got in a car to drive up the coast with you."

"So you're saying if you were at home you wouldn't let those *exotic* meals go to waste."

"Not a single one. Besides, it beats convenience store food and food poisoning." She slid a forkful of brisket dripping with sauce into her mouth, closed her eyes, and moaned again.

Dec almost went across the table to kiss her because, come on, a man already hot for a woman could only take so much.

"Do you even know how to cook?" she asked him.

"I leave that to Parker."

"But Parker lives in Portland. So how can his cooking skills benefit you?"

"Can *you* cook?" he asked, dodging her question because really, he had no freaking idea. In fact, with each bite and moan she performed, he lost a little more of his mind.

"I cook like a rock star," she boasted.

"Really."

She nodded.

"Yet you dine on convenience store snacks and you have leftover takeout in your refrigerator?"

She shrugged one shoulder. "I didn't say I cooked like a rock star every day of the week."

"I'm intrigued, Ms. Hastings."

"You should be, Mr. Kincade."

Yeah, he may not do playful, but whatever this was going on between them he was enjoying the hell out of. "Then how about you take a challenge to cook dinner tomorrow night?"

"Easy."

"It has to be something I've never had before."

"Soooo . . . no seared ahi?"

"You did hear the *never had before* part, right?"

Her head cocked and her eyes narrowed just slightly as if she knew she was being tricked. "How do I know what you've had or what you haven't?"

"Guess that will be up to you to find out."

Mischief lit up like golden sparklers in her eyes. "And what do I get if I prove to you that I can cook like a rock star? Will you cook dessert?"

"I believe I mentioned that I don't cook." But he would be willing to do a taste test using her body as a plate.

"Okay. You're on. Challenge accepted." Her playful grin lit a fuse inside him.

Right then. Right there. Dec knew his brothers were right.

He was in deep.

* * *

"*O*h my God. *Stop!*"

On the way home from Cranky Hank's Brooke shouted and Dec managed to slam on the brakes without deploying the air bags.

"What?"

"Look!" Brooke pointed out the window.

THE MOTHER LODE BAR
KARAOKE TONIGHT
CASH PRIZES!

Dec had put the top up on the convertible, so it wasn't a chill that sent a zap of *oh hell no* up his spine. It was the flashing red-and-yellow neon sign of the dive bar he and each of his brothers—minus Jordan, who'd been absent because of his contract with the NHL— had gotten to know up close and personal when each of them had turned twenty-one.

Back in the day they'd been more hell-raisers than angels, a truth their parents had never witnessed. Most of the time they'd been the polite young men their parents had raised. A help to the community. Servants of goodwill to sweet little old ladies who tried to cross the street. But put them inside the Mother Lode and their behavior went a little west of wild. And more times than not they'd been thrown out on their asses and had come home with black eyes and hangovers. Not that they'd done anything illegal. They'd just been looking for a good time. And they'd found it.

Repeatedly.

Dec bit back a smile at the memories.

"You don't want to go in there," he said, taking his foot off the brake and pushing down on the gas pedal. "It's a dive bar."

"I *love* dive bars!"

"Well, you can't love that one. It's . . . questionable."

"But that's the best kind." She ducked her head to look at him. "Come on, Dec. Live a little. You can add karaoke to your bucket list and fulfill it right now."

"I am *not* putting karaoke on my bucket list."

"But your list only has like . . . two items on it. You need more. A lot more. And I say karaoke is a prime candidate. There's even a twenty-five dollar prize for the winner."

Laughter burst from his chest. "You want me to get up on a stage and make a complete fool of myself for a chance at a lousy twenty-five bucks?"

"Come on." Her smile turned seductive as she leaned across the armrest, danced her fingers up the long sleeve of his shirt, and batted her thick, sooty eyelashes. "Do it for me. I'll even sing a duet with you if you're too afraid."

"I repeat for the umpteenth time, I am *not* afraid of anything." Except these crazy things she made him think and feel. Like what would happen if he pulled her over the armrest into his lap.

"Except singing karaoke." She made chicken sounds.

"Are you kidding me?"

She grinned. "Cluck."

"Fuck. That's it." He flipped a U-turn, careened into the busy lot, and parked next to a dented lime green monster truck with tires big enough to build a swimming hole in. While memories of the good old days splashed through his brain, he noted that neither of them were appropriately dressed for the Mother Lode. Brooke—fortunately for the situation, but unfortunately for his greedy eyes—had little skin exposed in a flouncy blouse, jeans, and sandals. He however . . . "If I'd known we were going to come here I wouldn't have worn a button-down shirt and slacks."

"What would you have worn?"

"Threadbare jeans, biker boots, and a Harley Davidson jacket."

"Are you afraid you'll get your ass kicked?" Her eyes went wide. "And might I add that knowing you even own biker boots and a Harley jacket is a huge turn-on?"

"Are you forgetting I grew up with four brothers? Kicking ass was a way of life." And he definitely needed to remember to haul his Harley jacket out of the closet.

They both got out of the car and he hit LOCK on the key fob. He hit it again as an extra precaution. Still, chances were that when he came out of the bar, his red convertible would either be dented or it would be gone.

"Because if you're afraid, I'll protect you," she promised. "This isn't my first dive bar rodeo."

"Brooke?" Near the door he stopped and cupped his hands on her elbows. He ignored the obnoxious music blasting through the thick wood walls and concentrated on inhaling her sweet scent and savoring her soft sigh as she looked up at him. "If anyone is going to do the protecting, it's going to be *me* protecting *you*. You're my assistant and too valuable to lose to a broken arm from a bar brawl."

She scrunched her nose. "Can I ask you a favor?"

"Daring me to sing karaoke isn't enough?"

She shook her head. "Right now, can you *pretty please* forget that I'm your employee? Right now, can we have just a little bit of fun without the whole boss/ assistant thing interfering? Can't we just walk in there like . . . friends?"

Friends?

And there lay the whole enchilada of a problem.

The more time he spent with her, the harder a time he had remembering the whole boss/employee thing. Every little tick of the clock he spent in her presence was rife with the temptation of hauling her against him and kissing her sweet lips.

"I'll try." No, he wouldn't. And he damn well knew that. He had to think of her as his employee. Had to. No option. Options meant trouble. Trouble meant disaster. And disaster meant the end of the world as he knew it.

"Yay!" She raised her arms in a little cheer and dance that made him want to forget they were standing at the door of the nastiest dive bar in Vancouver and give in to his bottled up emotions.

"Come on." She opened the door, grabbed his hand, and pulled. "I need a couple of Fireball shooters before I get up onstage."

In an atomic blast, his good intentions detonated and fell back to earth in ashes. Because once that Fireball whiskey hit his blood he knew he'd never be able to drink away his snowballing desire for this woman he'd promised to treat as a *friend*.

* * *

To Brooke, dive bars all looked the same on the inside. Beat to shit tables and chairs wrapped around a rickety wooden stage. Neon signs with burned-out letters advertising various makes of beer. A timber bar that usually had some kind of unknown sticky substance coating the surface. And bowls of peanuts no one in their right mind would ever actually consume unless they were stone cold drunk.

There were no seats available, not even a bar stool. As Dec led her through the rough and rowdy crowd toward the bar, his big palm engulfed hers with warmth and security. Even without his touch she knew he really would protect her safety.

Protecting her heart was another matter.

"Two Fireballs." Dec held up the appropriate numbers of fingers for the bartender, who might not have been able to hear over the woman currently onstage singing "Redneck Woman." At least the contestant had dressed the part. Although Brooke wasn't sure a plus-sized seventy-year-old woman in a tight jean skirt, red tube top, and pink boots was really going to gain an advantage with the outfit.

"It's loud in here," Dec shouted.

Brooke laughed. "Karaoke sounds better loud. The volume of the music distorts the actual singing."

The bartender slid their shot glasses to them. Dec leaned in and lifted his in a toast. "Here's to total and irreconcilable humiliation."

Brooke wrestled with the enthusiastic salesladies in the lingerie department trying to give this sexy man her lace panties for free while she tapped her glass to his and downed the fiery liquid. Most people coughed after a shot or at the very least, made a bitter beer face. Not Dec. He simply pressed his lips together and ordered two more shots. She wondered if he was drinking for the courage to sing, or whether it had something to do with the lusty looks he'd given her over dinner. She prayed for the latter and that those looks hadn't been just her overactive imagination.

"I'll personally give you the twenty-five bucks if you sing solo," she challenged.

"I don't need the money." He leaned in, bringing his delicious, warm male scent with him. His blue eyes roamed her face and dropped to her mouth as she licked away the cinnamon taste from her lips. "But if you sweeten the pot you've got a deal."

Was he flirting with her?

The smile on his gorgeous masculine face hinted at *yes*. And since Brooke had never been one to ignore an opportunity she did what she did best—thought fast on her feet.

"How about I add one of my specialty desserts to the meal tomorrow?" Yes. She was thinking along the lines of chocolate syrup and whipped cream—all over his naked body.

"Deal." He stuck out his hand.

"You didn't give it much thought." But she was singing hallelujah.

"Didn't have to." As she put her hand in his and shook, he flashed a smile that was two parts mischief and one part promise.

Annnnnd *yes*. He was flirting.

Finally.

Thank you to the Fireball whiskey gods.

As a deterrent to the direction her naughty little mind had wandered, she grabbed the karaoke song list off the bar and handed it to him. "So what's it going to be, cowboy?"

"Cowboy?" He grinned. "Does that mean I have to sing country?"

She shrugged. "Whatever floats your boat. Although I have to admit you don't really seem like a country music kind of guy."

"Oh really." A low chuckle rumbled deep from his chest. "What kind of guy do I seem like to you?"

Hot,

"Maybe some R and B or . . . talk radio. Yeah. I definitely see you as a talk radio kind of guy."

"Hmmm." His dark brows pulled together as he scanned the song choices. "Then as a so-called *talk radio kind of guy*, I obviously have no idea how karaoke works."

"It's easy. You fill out this piece of paper with your name and your song choice and give it to the DJ. Then you wait for him to call your name."

When he looked up at her, her knees nearly buckled from the sexual heat in his eyes. "You're really going to make me do this?"

"Make you? No. But it would be even more humiliating if I started doing the chicken dance right now because you don't have the right stuff." She slammed down her second shooter. "Just sayin'."

"Believe me." He moved in closer, spoke in a low,

sexy voice right next to her ear, and sent a parade of chills dancing down her spine. "I have the right stuff."

She didn't think he was exactly talking about karaoke, and that was perfectly fine with her. Especially when he moved away only a fraction of an inch. "Remains to be seen."

His gaze dropped, lingered on her mouth, then came back up to her eyes. "All right." He jotted down his name and song request. When she tried to sneak a peek he folded the paper, carried it up to the stage, and dropped it in the song jar.

When he returned he slammed back his second shooter. "Just remember, you asked for it."

She certainly had. And hopefully he was picking up what she was putting down.

"Why do I get the feeling you aren't playing fair?" she asked.

A slow, sexy smile tilted the corners of his lips. "Because I always play to win."

That dance of awareness hit her spine again. This time it headed south and the lingerie ladies were starting a conga line.

"Your turn." He handed her a slip of paper and pen, then at the last second grabbed it back. "On second thought." He wrote her name down then covered the song choice he'd selected for her with his hand.

"How do you know what I want?"

One dark brow slid up his forehead.

"To sing," she added. Yeah. Because that's what she meant. Not.

"You're the one who dragged me in here. You want

to back out now?" He shrugged, then had the balls to make chicken sounds at her before he took the request up to the DJ.

When he came back she had a third round of shots lined up. She'd never gone past two before and she might be/would be sorry in the morning, but she was having too much fun to back down now.

"I don't need this for courage," she said, holding up the small glass. "But what the hell."

He held up his shooter too and gave her a playful grin. "Neither do I."

They clinked glasses, downed their shots, and Dec's name was called over the sound system.

"Don't laugh." He pointed at her then turned to walk away.

"I'll try." Pointless. She was already laughing.

"Wait a second." He turned back around. "I might not need the booze for courage, but I will take *this*."

Before Brooke recognized his Fireball induced intent, he took her face between his big hands and kissed the daylights out of her. The crowd whooped, hollered, and catcalled, but with Dec's hot, sexy mouth on hers, she barely noticed. When he made his way to the stage she locked her knees and leaned back against the bar to keep from sliding to the floor.

As Dec walked away looking all hot and just slightly frayed around the edges, the voluptuous and scantily clad blonde at the bar next to Brooke leaned in and asked, "You think he'd be into a threesome?"

Brooke laughed out loud.

Not because she actually knew Dec's sexual

inclinations—although she certainly hoped to find out—but because she knew if she ever got him all to herself, there was no way in hell she'd share.

When Dec took the microphone he looked completely at ease. Brooke attributed that to either his many financial speaking engagements or the three highly potent cinnamon whiskey shooters he'd downed in less than five minutes. When his gaze cut through the spotlight and the darkness to find her, her panties melted a little bit more.

"I'm not a karaoke kind of guy. But I never back down from a challenge from a beautiful lady." He winked to the crowd. "Especially when there's a reward involved."

The karaoke enthusiasts raised their bottles of beer and hooted some more. And then the music began. Without needing the words on the monitor, Dec broke into a rousing rendition of Brett Eldredge's "Lose My Mind," pointing to *her* in all the right places in the song.

At that point it became undeniably clear why women threw their phone numbers and panties onstage for a sexy man with a microphone. But for Brooke it was more. For her it was Dec's implication that the lyrics of the song might be about *them* that made her weak in the knees.

Because really, who could deny that kiss?

As if she needed another reason, right then and there she fell crazy, madly, and forever in love with the one man she could never have. Because as soon as those Fireball shooters evaporated from his veins, he'd once again be the boss and she'd be out of luck.

Chapter 8

The following morning Brooke woke early, still smiling about the night before, and grateful for no signs of a hangover. Though he hadn't kissed her again, *flirty* Dec had remained on scene for the rest of the evening. Especially when it came to her turn at the karaoke mic.

With apologies to the very talented Miranda Lambert, she'd butchered the song Dec had selected for her. But that was nothing new. She butchered every song she sang. The deep-in-their-cups audience hadn't seemed to mind. And although Dec lost the twenty-five dollar prize to a woman who gave a Marilyn Monroe worthy performance of "Diamonds Are a Girl's Best Friend," they'd both had a really fun time.

At the end of the night Dec had called Jordan to give them a ride home. While Brooke sat up front, Dec had stretched his longs legs out in the backseat and suffered through his twin brother's good-natured ribbing. Listening to the two of them had entertained Brooke and she thought they might be more alike than Dec was willing to admit.

When they arrived at the little brick cabin, Dec had escorted her into the house. Instead of giving her an indication that the night had possibilities, he'd kissed her forehead and thanked her for a perfectly wonderful disaster of an evening. Had he not been grinning at the time, she might have slugged him. When he'd politely reminded her that she'd lost the challenge and he expected grand things for dinner, she'd had to remember that earlier that evening he'd melted her panties with a scorching kiss.

The cinnamon whiskey in her blood had made it easy for her to fall asleep with every intention of getting up early and retrieving Dec's car from the bar's parking lot. Last they'd seen it, it had been scrape and dent free. With a little luck it would still be that way upon recovery.

When she crawled out of bed, Dec was nowhere to be found. Looked like he'd beat her to getting his car back. While he was gone she fed Moochie and took her for a short walk so she could do her business. Then Brooke showered, made herself presentable, and started to put together some breakfast for when Dec came back.

While a vegetable frittata simmered on the stove, Brooke made a call to the office to check on things. Next she called their marketing contact to check on his progress with the stats for the vineyard. She made notes and updates in her schedule then poured a cup of coffee while she made another client call. Back to the work grind. Brooke realized that Dec would quickly fall into his routine, and any headway she'd made into getting him to realize that there was more to life than the hours between nine and five would be washed away like footprints in the sand.

Tonight she had another chance to make a difference. Somehow during the busy day ahead, she had to come up with a menu, a plan, and a proposition where he couldn't say no.

*F*or the better part of the day, Dec spent his time in the office, holed up with Ryan, Jordan, and Ethan discussing matters of business for the vineyard. Once they received the report from the marketing expert, they could proceed with their plans. But as they all sat huddled around Ryan's desk and the coffeepot, they agreed that the vineyard needed a complete overhaul, including bottle labels and distribution.

A huge part of Dec's success was based on his ability to create a well-thought-out business plan. Today he found it impossible to stay focused when all he could think of was how much fun he'd had last night with Brooke and the possibility of spending the evening with her again. She was an extraordinary woman with a multitude of facets he'd yet to discover. Finding ways to do that while keeping the boss/employee issue in mind was becoming harder and harder.

Last night, before he'd gone on that karaoke stage to make a fool of himself, he'd kissed her. For courage, he'd said, which was utter bullshit. He'd just wanted her lips on his. They'd felt so amazing he'd been tempted to carry her out of that bar to continue what they'd started. The burden of guilt had been his only saving grace, and for the rest of the night he'd managed to ignore the temptation.

"Daydreaming?"

Dec's head snapped up. "What?"

Ryan kicked Dec's feet off the desk and chuckled. "We just carried on a complete conversation about the pros and cons of standardizing the wine bottles from high shoulder to sloping while you sat there all glassy-eyed and staring into space."

"Bullshit."

"I call bullshit on your bullshit." Ethan pointed a finger at Dec. "You were ready to kick my ass the other night when you found me outside the cabin talking to Brooke."

"Why don't you just give in?" Jordan asked. "You looked like you had fun last night. Ask her out. Live a little."

"If *you* don't . . ." Ethan folded his arms and leaned back in his chair. "*I* will."

Ordinarily his brothers' teasing repartee was status quo and he'd jump into the fray without missing a beat. But the subject matter was not up for discussion.

"Why don't you guys give it a rest." He stood and the chair slid back on the wood floor with a screech.

"And you . . ." He pointed at Ethan. "Keep your fucking distance from her."

Needing some fresh air after sucking in all the crap his brothers were throwing down, Dec headed toward the door. "I'm out. See you tomorrow."

Leaving a room of adolescent chortles behind him, he stepped outside and closed the door. But even the deep breath he inhaled couldn't clear Jordan's question from his mind.

Why didn't he give in?

How could he tell them that he'd already done enough damage and that fear kept him from going any further? Sure, it was easy to lean heavily on the boss/employee snag, but Brooke wasn't the kind of woman a guy just had a quick fling with then moved on from. Brooke was a keeper. Trouble was, Dec couldn't afford to give in. Losing her was unacceptable. He needed her, and aside from her superior job performance, he just wanted to be around her. She made his days better. Easier. Tolerable. Enjoyable.

Because of dyslexia, all his life he'd struggled to keep things in focus. He'd found that concentrating on one element at a time worked best in his case. Unlike other members of his family who could multitask like pros, he'd never been good at juggling. Keeping his personal life in check while he constructed his career had been imperative.

He'd give anything to be like his brothers. To have that carefree simplicity that seemed to bring so much joy. But he was like a freaking Rubik's Cube. Too complicated. Too twisted. And too much of a puzzle to solve.

His attraction to Brooke had shaken up the order of things.

With family issues, the pieces of his personal life were falling around him. He knew his limits. He had a track record with women and it wasn't pretty. Brooke deserved better. And though she was sweet, sexy as hell, and seemingly receptive to something more, it would kill him if he had to look into her dark brown eyes and find disappointment staring back.

If he lost her and had to watch her move on with someone else, he didn't know how he'd handle it. But despite wanting her more than he'd ever wanted anything aside from his career, he knew he could never have her.

Not even for just a night.

Especially for just a night.

He walked toward his car in the parking lot just as a tall, cool blonde stepped out of a silver sedan parked a couple spaces away.

"Can I help you?" he called out.

Dark sunglasses hid her eyes, but something in the way she moved said she was either lost or confused.

"Hello." She slid a hand to the waist of her jeans. "I was looking for the vineyard office."

"It's over there." He hitched his thumb toward the small "Office" sign hanging above the door on the large building. "But we're closed right now."

"Oh." She looked around then back at him. "Do you work here?"

"Not really. But I'm very familiar with the owners. Is there someone in particular you're looking for?"

The woman was dressed in jeans, a lightweight blazer, and high heels. The well-put-together outfit appeared more business casual than a day-in-the-park relaxed. Her long blond hair fell over her shoulders in soft curls. She was attractive and fit, but seemed completely unfamiliar.

"I'm looking for Carlton Kincade."

Dec's heart thundered in his ears.

"Carlton Kincade?"

"Yes."

Who the hell was this woman, and why was she asking for his dead father?

"Because?" On edge, Dec gritted his teeth. Best to get to the bottom of things ASAFP.

"I . . . It's a business matter."

"What kind of business?"

"I'm sorry." Her head tilted. "Who did you say you are?"

"I didn't."

"I see." She glanced in the direction of the office. "Well then, thank you for your time." She reached into the car and pulled out a large purse that she slung over her shoulder. Then she closed the door and clicked the key fob.

For a moment Dec watched her walk toward the office, then he followed. Apprehension dug nails into the back of his neck as he caught up to her and they hit the door at the same time. Dec reached forward and opened it.

"Oh." She seemed startled even though she had to have known he was right behind her. "Thank you."

He entered the building after her. "The office is this way."

Her heels clicked on the wood floor until Dec opened the interior office door for her. He watched his brothers' eyes widen with curiosity at his return and their unexpected guest.

"Thought you were leaving," Jordan said.

"I found Ms. . . ." He hesitated over the woman's name because she hadn't introduced herself. Then again, neither had he.

"Lili MacKay."

"Ms. Lili MacKay outside in the parking lot. I informed her we were closed but she said she was here about a business matter. So I directed her to the office."

Ryan stood and offered his hand, which the woman shook. "Nice to meet you, Ms. MacKay. What can we do for you?"

Her gaze tracked each person in the room, then she secured her hand around the strap of her purse. "I'm looking for Carlton Kincade."

In that instant, every jaw in the room dropped and Dec knew they were all thinking the same thing.

Why was an attractive young woman looking for their deceased father?

"Have a seat, Ms. MacKay." Ryan motioned to the chair Dec had earlier vacated.

The stiffening in her shoulders made it easy to sense her nervousness, which only amplified Dec's curiosity as he stood at the back of the room, arms folded.

Waiting.

"I'm a little short on time," Lili MacKay said without taking the offered seat. "Is Mr. Kincade available?"

Ryan remained standing as well, and his tone took on an acidic edge. "I'm afraid you'll have to address your business to me, Ms. MacKay."

"And who are you?" A flash of irritation tightened her jaw.

"Ryan Kincade. These are my brothers, Jordan, Declan, and Ethan. And I'm afraid it's going to be impossible for you to see Carlton Kincade."

"Oh? And why is that?"

"Because he died over four months ago."

Lili MacKay released a small gasp, wavered, and dropped into the empty chair. Her hand went to her chest where she absently rubbed its center and stared at the floor. "I'm . . . so sorry. I . . . didn't know."

It quickly became apparent to Dec, as he was sure it had his brothers, that Lili MacKay was deeply affected by the news that their father was dead. Her rapid breathing and inability to speak said that her appearance at the vineyard was obviously more of a personal than a business nature.

So who the hell was this woman?

And what did she want?

After a moment she appeared to recover. She stood, hooked the handbag over her shoulder, and white-knuckled the strap. "Please accept my condolences. I sincerely apologize for the interruption. Thank you for your time."

As she headed toward the door, Dec briefly wondered whether he should stop her or let her go, but the mystery had become too great to ignore.

"I'm sure we can help you with whatever business you came here for." He blocked her exit. "Why don't you have a seat?"

She shook her head and refused to meet his gaze. Of course, he couldn't see much of her expression from behind her dark sunglasses.

"I'm sorry. My business was with Carlton Kincade and only Carlton Kincade. I really must go now."

As she reached for the door handle Dec recognized the distress signs of someone trapped and he let her walk. Once the sound of her high heels clicking on the wood floor dissipated he turned to his brothers, who looked equally stunned.

"What the hell just happened?"

Chapter 9

Dec got into his car in the empty parking lot to go back to the cabin, wrap up his work schedule, and have dinner with Brooke. Since he'd woken up this morning he'd been looking forward to spending more time with her. Not just because they'd had a great time last night, but because as each day passed, he realized that her lively spirit and her unpredictability made him want to explore possibilities he'd never considered. The fortress he'd locked himself in had been created with unbreakable rules and crushing responsibility. Then Brooke came along. And Dec thought that maybe she held the key to open the door and set him free.

Not that he didn't think she could handle it, but it was an unfair amount of responsibility to put on her lovely shoulders. The time had come for him to dig deep inside himself to ascertain what he was really made of. To see if *he* could handle it.

To know if he was worthy.

Before pulling out onto the driveway, he glanced again at the empty parking lot. So much stood in his way. So many unanswered questions. As much as he'd like to blow it all off, he couldn't ignore the obligation to those he loved. He couldn't be that selfish. And he refused to use Brooke as a temporary diversion from everything in his life that had been filed under "Fucked Up." If he spent time with her—and he would—he wanted to give her his undivided attention. He wanted to enjoy her and unravel all those layers that made her so damn fascinating.

The only way he'd be able to do that would be to start chiseling away at everything that stood between them. And right now, at the top of that list was Lili MacKay.

Who was the woman?

What had she wanted with their father?

Why would she only speak to him?

Could she have something to do with their father's behavior toward Nicole?

Was this woman possibly someone with whom their father had had an affair?

She was very young. Probably no more than her early to mid-twenties. Certainly too young for their father, who'd always appeared to be a happily married man.

Appeared being the key word.

If she'd been having an affair with him, why wouldn't she have known he'd been killed along with their mother? The tragic news had been the source of talk around town for weeks.

Unless she wasn't from Sunshine.

But assuming she was *the other woman*, where else

could their father have met her? The only places he ever went were wine competitions. Ryan had always joined him on those trips, making it near impossible for anything to have transpired. There were the times he'd gone back to Philadelphia to visit their uncle but . . .

Why the hell were they all jumping to conclusions? Why did they immediately assume something dark and sordid? He'd been a good father. At least to him and his brothers.

Unfortunately their sister had a different opinion. And that was the real impetus for finding answers.

As Dec drove the convertible out of the parking lot his chest tightened. He dealt with information. Facts. He didn't like to be kept in the dark or uninformed.

Ever.

Lack of data and details made him feel unstable. Powerless. And where his feelings for Brooke were concerned, he was already rowing that boat against a strong current.

While his intent had been to head back to the cabin and just enjoy the rest of the evening, his curiosity and his duty led him in the complete opposite direction.

*B*rooke stood inside the little brick cabin checking things off her list and wrapping up her day. She'd managed to set up a temporary office in the extra bedroom, where she'd followed through with her work schedule and updated her progress to Dec by text every couple of hours. Later she'd borrowed Aunt Pippy's VW Bug and made a grocery store run.

Not that the place had been a superstore by any

means, but it had taken her two trips around the market before she figured out what to make for dinner and dessert. Making good on her cooking boast was important. Even though she could hold her own with a frying pan and a cheese grater, she didn't cook anything like a rock star as she'd claimed. Still, call her old-fashioned, but she wanted to impress Dec.

Now that dark had fallen and the crickets had begun to chirp, there was no sign of the man whom she'd wasted her hopes for a romantic dinner on.

The last text she'd received from him several hours ago had said he'd be back to the cabin within the hour. Though she realized he was a full-grown adult who could take care of himself and really didn't need to answer to her for anything, she'd begun to worry.

Dec never failed to be on time or even early. When he said he'd be somewhere you could count on him like the opening bell of the stock market. So for him not to show up when he'd said he would was rare.

And mysterious.

And troubling.

She'd never been a clock-watcher, and now wasn't the time to start. She wasn't his mother, wife, or girlfriend. So she put everything on hold in the kitchen, prayed for the best, and went into the office to occupy her time working on a new client proposal. If she hadn't heard from him by midnight, she'd call up to the main house and contact his family.

Moochie trailed after her into the makeshift office and settled in on her little puffy leopard print bed. Moments later, snoring confirmed she'd fallen fast asleep.

Sometime later a car pulled up in front of the cabin.

Brooke refused to look at the clock. She debated whether to stay right where she was or get up and greet him. Before she could make a calculated decision that wouldn't have her looking out of line, pissed off, or needy, the front door opened.

Like she'd been poked, Moochie leaped out of bed and trotted off to be the welcoming committee. Brooke could hear Dec praise her little dog, and then his heavy footsteps brought him into the office.

He dropped down into the chair opposite her desk, steepled his fingers and said, "I'm sorry."

Brooke instantly knew she'd been right to worry. Tension crinkled the outer corners of his eyes and his lips were pressed into a flat line.

"For what?" she asked.

"Being late. I know you were planning dinner and—"

"Dec, you don't owe me any explanations."

"*And* . . . if the offer is still open, I'm starving. I don't even care if it's frozen pizza. So how about I go take a hot shower and then help you put it together."

"Anything you want to talk about first?" It was clear that something had happened and weighed heavy on his mind.

"Nope. I just want a shower, and then a glass of wine would be nice."

"I can help you with that. I mean . . . you can take your own shower. I don't need to . . ." Jesus. She'd never been at a loss for words before. But with the exception of when his parents had died, she'd never seen him this troubled. She wanted to help. Even if she had to take one for the team and help him in that steamy shower.

"Thanks." Sluggishly he got up out of the chair. "You're a great assis—"

"Stop." She held up a hand like a crossing guard. "Last night when I challenged you to sing karaoke— which you did amazingly well by the way—we made a deal to leave the whole boss/employee thing at the door for the night. Can we manage that again? Because you seriously look like you could use a friend right now."

He paused at the doorway and looked her over. "I'm not really sure I can ever see you that way."

Pain slammed through her heart like a bullet.

While she reeled and tried to recover from his biting remark, he disappeared down the hall. A moment later when she heard the shower turn on, she buried her face in her hands.

She'd thought they'd moved past the *Yes, I'm paying your salary and I will never forget I'm your boss* barrier. She'd thought that the road trip to Vancouver had been fun for both of them—to a point—and that as *friends*, they'd grown a little closer.

Apparently *thinking* was overrated.

There wasn't enough hot water in the world to ease the tension knotted at the back of Declan's neck. Still, he planted his palms on the shower wall, leaned in, and let the stream pound his muscles.

After he'd left the winery office and his brothers to continue playing the fifty question game about their father's mysterious visitor, Dec had driven into town and gone to every place of lodging until he'd spotted Lili

MacKay's car. It had been his stroke of luck that it happened to be parked in the lot of the Salty Seagull Inn, a family owned operation belonging to close friends of his parents. He'd taken a chance and gone inside to see if she was registered as a guest. And though the inn wasn't technically allowed to give him the information, by turning on the charm, he did learn that she'd indeed paid for a room for three nights. This meant he and his brothers had at least two more days to figure out who the hell she was and where she came from.

Not exactly how he'd planned to spend his time in Sunshine.

Or for the evening.

But when someone came around insisting on speaking to a dead relative then leaving without offering the reason why, it left a person—or persons— no option but to investigate. He'd stopped himself short before knocking on her door and demanding answers. Instead he'd opted to relay his findings to his brothers. Some of them tended to be hotheads, but together they miraculously managed to keep each other in line. And since the mysterious blonde's sudden appearance could be totally innocent, there was no need for irrationality.

Yet.

After several minutes under the hot water, Dec's muscles loosened up and happier images wandered into his mind. Though he knew she was very dedicated, he'd been surprised to find Brooke still working when he'd come through the door. He'd been even more taken aback to find so much concern on her face. He knew he should have called her and told her he'd been delayed. It had been unfair of him to leave her hanging. Especially when she'd offered to do something as nice for him as make dinner.

But in his day-to-day life, he answered to nothing except his own whims and schedule. At times, he knew he appeared very selfish.

Now, for instance.

Before he did anything else, he needed to apologize. Clear the air. And hope she wasn't too pissed off.

By the time he'd dried off and changed into jeans and a T-shirt, a heavenly aroma wafted through the cabin. When he went into the kitchen she was busily concocting something in a big red bowl.

It wasn't the sight of the food that had him taking a second look. It was the woman with the wooden spoon.

In a sleeveless floral dress that hit her mid-calf and a scooped neckline that exposed enough cleavage to arouse his curiosity along with a certain other body part, Brooke simply stunned him.

Why hadn't he noticed when he'd walked through the door?

Dumbass.

With the exception of a few loose strands, her hair had been pulled up in a mess of curls on top of her head, leaving her long, delicate neck uncovered. More than tasting what was cooking in that pan, Dec wanted to savor her soft skin. He wanted to walk up behind her, wrap his arms around her, and pull her tight against him while he feasted on anything bare and everything not.

Need, in too many forms to count, wrapped him up and sent him in her direction.

"I didn't want you to go to too much trouble."

She started at his sudden appearance, then recovered with a small smile that barely brushed her lips. "No big deal. I already had everything ready to put together."

He came closer and a citrus fragrance leaped into the medley of what was going on in the frying pan. "It's a big deal to me."

She shrugged a shoulder. "It's just something I'm throwing together."

"Maybe. But other than my mother I've never had a woman cook for me."

She looked up at him and her eyes went wide with disbelief. "Never?"

Tempted to reach out and stroke his fingers down her long, creamy throat, he shook his head.

"I would have thought all those women you date would be trying to cook their way into your heart."

"They're more interested in eating at swanky restaurants where they can see and be seen."

"So why do you date women like that?" She stopped stirring the mix and tilted her head. "Don't you want something more?"

He never had before. But maybe that wasn't true anymore.

"That type of woman worked for me. I've been too busy building the business to want to take time away from that."

"Believe me." She scoffed. "I know better than anyone about how hard you work."

Dec realized he'd used the term *worked*—as in past tense—when speaking of the women he dated.

Something had changed. He'd never thought about vacations, or leisure time, or even sleeping in on a Sunday morning. He was constantly on the go and it had become his way of life.

What had he missed?

And could he ever get back what he'd lost during that hectic pace?

As Brooke moved around the kitchen he wondered what it would be like to really take the time to get to know her better.

Thought by thought.

Inch by inch.

Intrigued, he leaned over her shoulder to peek at what she was concocting. "What's for dinner?"

She lifted the lid off the skillet. "Pan-seared halibut—not ahi—with mango and avocado salsa, and a side of asparagus tossed with citrus, paired with . . ." She set the lid back down, reached inside the refrigerator, and brought out a wine bottle. "A bottle of Sunshine Creek Vineyard Sweet Serenade. Your Aunt Pippy recommended this one because of the . . ." She read the back label. "Apple and lemon notes that lead to a crisp finish."

"Perfect." He took the bottle, desperate to numb some of the wayward thoughts in his brain. "Mind if I open it now?"

"Go ahead. Dinner is almost ready. I set the table on the back patio. I figured the sounds of the creek might make it more relaxing for you."

"Are you always this thoughtful?"

She propped a fist on her hip. "I've worked for you for four years and you don't know?"

"I do know." He touched her cheek with his finger-tips. "I also know that apparently I am very bad at making a joke."

Her dimples appeared. "But you're good at so many other things it's hard to hold that against you."

"Careful, or you'll have me eating out of your hand in no time."

Did he really just say that?

Detouring around the obvious, he snuck a piece of asparagus and popped it into his mouth before grabbing the corkscrew to open the wine. "Tasty."

"Me? Or the asparagus."

Dec loved her sense of humor, but remarks like that put some seriously dangerous thoughts in his head. "Do you really want me to answer that? Especially after hearing you slice and dice Miranda Lambert in karaoke?"

She chuckled. "Maybe not."

He pulled the wine cork and filled two glasses, handing one to her and lifting his own in a toast. "Here's to my own personal chef."

"Oh no. The next meal is all on you."

Did he get a say in where she placed it on his body? And wasn't he going to try to behave?

"Need some help in here?" he asked. He'd never shared cooking duties before. At least not with a woman who tempted him more than the food. And though he was dead on his feet, he wouldn't mind sticking around just for the view.

"Nope. Almost done. Why don't you go ahead and have a seat out on the patio. I'll bring dinner out in just a minute."

"You sure?"

"As I'll ever be."

When Dec opened the back door he found a truly romantic setting. The patio table had been set with a red checked tablecloth, a votive candle flickered in a glass Mason jar, the fire pit had a small steady fire crackling, and the creek added a relaxing melody. He'd never had anyone do anything like this for him before, and he was deeply touched by the sweetness of her efforts. He'd never been a hearts and flowers kind of guy, but right now, he wished he had a bouquet of spring flowers to give her. Roses were too . . . common. Wildflowers fit her country girl/fairy vibe much better. Unfortunately the only thing close by was a patch of dandelions.

A few minutes later she appeared in her floaty, sexy dress with two plates of the tender halibut, salsa and asparagus, setting one in front of him before taking her seat.

He inhaled the tempting aroma. "Looks and smells great."

"I hope it lives up to my boasting."

"Brooke?" He reached across the table and settled his hand on top of hers. It was a friendly gesture, he convinced himself. Nothing more than sheer appreciation. "The fact that you actually made the effort guarantees that I'll love it."

"Hmmm." Candlelight flickered in her eyes as she smiled and winked. "We'll see what you think after you taste it."

He took a bite and let the lemony flavor roll over his tongue. "It's delicious. You get to keep the bragging rights."

"Yeah?" Her dimples flashed. The praise had pleased her.

"Definitely."

He refilled her glass with the wine he'd carried out. "How'd you learn to cook like this?"

"My foster family. They owned a little European-style café. Everyone in the house helped out as soon as they were old enough."

Her revelation lodged the halibut in his throat and he had to swallow down some wine to clear it. "You were raised in a foster home?"

She nodded without looking up and poked her fork around in the asparagus.

"Was it bad?" Maybe this was why she'd been so reluctant to talk about her past.

"Oh. No." Her head came up then. "They were very nice. I got lucky I guess. They took in foster kids because they really wanted to help, not just the paycheck they got. I think they liked having a lot of kids around. It was quite a spirited house. Lots of chores. Lots of board games. Lots of love."

"So . . ." His fork paused over his plate. "Since you opened the door, is this a good time to talk?"

"Hmmm." She took a bite of halibut and looked up at the sky as though she was thinking it over. When her gaze came back to his she said, "You first."

"About?"

"What upset you before you came home."

Came home.

That had a nice ring to it. He could imagine seeing Brooke every night. Being with her. In fact, he could picture it very easily.

He drained his wine then refilled the glass.

"A woman came to the vineyard office today looking for our father. She was young and beautiful and she wouldn't talk to any of us." Brooke listened intently. She deserved total honesty. And he planned to give her as much as he could without overstepping or dishonoring anyone. "She said she'd come to see him and only him. When we told her he had died she left as quickly and as mysteriously as she'd arrived."

Another bite of halibut and another sip of wine cleared his mind and allowed him to continue. "I knew you were making this dinner and I meant to come straight here when I left the winery office, but at the last second I decided to drive into town to see if I could find out more about her."

"I don't blame you. I'd have been curious as hell."

"We are. The only thing I discovered was that she'd booked a three-night stay at one of the local inns."

Brooke laid down her fork. "Did you get her name?"

"Lili MacKay."

"And that doesn't ring a bell for any of you?"

"No. But it sure as hell got some crazy twisted ideas racing through our heads."

"Like?"

"Like . . . what if she was our father's mistress."

"Dec. Do you think your dad would really do something like that?" A slight move tilted her head and the candlelight shone in her hair. "From what you've said in the past, your parents had a wonderful marriage."

"We all thought they did. But now . . ." He shrugged.

"I don't know. This woman seemed genuinely surprised to learn that he and our mother were both dead."

"Then she couldn't have known your father very well."

"Hard to say." Something gnawed at his gut that suggested the woman knew his father *very* well. But he had no proof. Just intuition. "Remember when I came back from the funerals, I told you we'd discovered someone had been stealing money from the company?"

"Yes."

"It was our father."

"But . . ." She shook her head slowly. "It's *his* company. How could he be stealing?"

"Just because you own a company doesn't mean you can take whatever you want from it. Both he and Ryan took a salary; the rest goes back into the company for expenses, expansions, taxes, licenses, and a million other things."

"Was a lot of money taken?"

"Several hundred thousand over numerous years."

Brooke snagged her bottom lip between her teeth as she waited for him to reveal more. When he didn't she reached her hand across the table and covered his. She squeezed his fingers.

"Don't let your mind go there, Dec. I can see in your eyes what you're thinking. But do you really want to believe something like that about your father?"

"Unfortunately the seed has been planted. There's something else."

"What?"

He took a breath.

Brooke understood. She got it. And she cared. For those reasons he really wanted to leave it all out on the table. To share. Something he'd never been very good at before.

"For a long time Nicki felt our father treated her differently than the rest of us. She said he'd been distant. That he never attended any of her school events, and that he never spent any time with her at all if possible. Before he and Mom left for Hawaii Nicki confronted him. He openly admitted that something in his past prevented him from being the father she wanted and needed him to be, but he didn't clarify what that something was."

"That must have devastated her."

"It did. It still does. Now she may never be able to find out why he felt that way."

"And you're thinking this Lili MacKay could have something to do with that?"

"It's possible." He leaned back in the chair and pushed away his plate. "Hell, anything is possible."

"Is there any way I can help?"

Once he'd heard a song about angels being among them. Right now, that's how he saw Brooke. A sweet, sexy angel.

"Just talking about it helps. My brothers can be hotheads at times. In situations like this they tend to think force is a reasonable response."

"Most alpha males do."

"I guess so." He never considered whether they were alpha males or just plain crazy. They were all the way they were and that was just life.

"Are you done?" She pointed to his plate.

"Yeah. Thanks." He handed her the nearly empty plate. "It was really great."

"There's dessert, don't forget."

"Save dessert for later. How about you grab another bottle of wine, come back, and tell me *your* story now."

Her shoulders stiffened slightly. "I guess that's only fair."

"I don't mean to push."

"No. You're right. It's my turn." She chuffed a laugh and held up the empty bottle. "Maybe we should call the wine Spill Your Guts instead of Sweet Serenade."

With the disclosure about Lili MacKay off his shoulders, Dec felt more relaxed. Could be the wine. Could be the company.

As Brooke turned to go back into the house, the breeze caught her dress and molded it to her body.

With great consternation he realized *the company* did nothing to relax him. *The company* had him tied up in knots and was planting involuntary naughty thoughts in his head.

When Brooke came back out onto the patio, Dec had rearranged their chairs so they sat next to each other and both looked out over the creek.

"Clever." She grinned as she sat down. "Is this so if I don't spill my guts you can do me bodily harm?"

He uncorked the wine and refilled their glasses. "Keeping in mind that we are forgoing the boss/employee thing tonight, I have to be honest and say that there are a lot of things I could do to your body." He handed her the glass. "Harm isn't one of them."

On a gasp, her lips parted just slightly and he was so tempted to lean in and press his mouth to them. To lick off the sweet wine and the essence that made her so damned special. Instead he smiled and tapped his glass against hers. "To world peace."

"I'm not sure what to say to that."

"You're against world peace?"

"I'm all for world peace. It's that other little shock-me-to-my-socks thing you just said."

"I don't believe you're wearing socks." Since he'd moved beyond childhood, he'd never remotely pretended to be playful. But as he glanced under the table, he realized Brooke brought out the playful side in him. And he liked it. "But I do see some blue toenail polish."

"It's called Tidal Wave." She leaned in just a fraction and their shoulders bumped together. "I brought the bottle with me in case you're interested."

"Nice diversion tactic, Ms. Hastings." Thinking of the tidal wave of a kiss they'd shared in the Pacific Ocean a few nights ago, he tapped his wineglass to hers. "Your turn to be storyteller."

"Are you sure you want to hear this? Because it is all kinds of boring."

"Yes." Throwing everything sane to the wind, he reached up and wound an escaped tendril of her hair around his finger. The texture was cool and silky and made him want to bury his face in it. "I want to hear everything."

"Promise you won't judge me?"

Curiosity piqued, he said, "Never."

"Oh boy. Here goes." She squeezed her eyes and her

chest rose on an intake of air like she was preparing for a long hard run. "My birth parents are part of a fanatical religious community that developed their own beliefs. Their own lifestyle. Their own laws. Those laws include the men having all the say and the women being the silent minority. The elders in the community made the rules, amended them to their own satisfaction, and commanded that everyone lived by the laws no matter what. They arranged all the marriages, forbade divorces, and no one had the balls to defy them."

Dec sipped the wine but didn't taste a thing past the bitterness her story put in his mouth.

"*No one* defied them," she said adamantly, avoiding his gaze. "Except me."

"How did you defy them?"

"I never fit." She shook her head vigorously. "I didn't want to be told what I could or couldn't do. Who I could or couldn't be. Or whom I had to spend the rest of my wretched life with. My sister felt the same, but she was too afraid to say anything or stand up for herself. When she turned fourteen the elders forced her to marry a man four times her age. My parents did nothing. They stood by and let it happen. By the time her nineteenth birthday was approaching, she'd already had three babies. When she got pregnant with the fourth six months after her third was born, she died due to complications."

Dec reached out and took her hands in his. Her fingers were cool to the touch and he could feel her pulse pound on the inside of her wrist.

"At least that's the bullshit story her husband and

the elders told everyone," she said, gripping his fingers tight.

"You didn't believe them?"

"I saw her the day she died." A stuttered breath puffed through her lips. "She looked exhausted and sad, but otherwise healthy."

"Do you think her husband had something to do with her death?"

"I do." Tears shimmered in her eyes as she nodded. "Especially since no one except the elders was allowed to see her body. The last time I saw her she hugged me and whispered, 'Don't ever let this happen to you.' She made me promise."

Dec felt sick to his stomach, both for the young girl who'd lost her life and for the one who'd felt the need to save her own. "What happened after that? Was the husband ever investigated?"

"No. The elders stood behind him a hundred percent and the authorities were never brought in for anything."

"Your parents did nothing?" How could that be?

"Nothing. Two weeks after my sister was buried, her husband married a fifteen-year-old. She took over mothering my sister's children and was pregnant almost as soon as she was forced to say 'I do.' My parents abandoned their grandchildren and allowed the new wife's family to claim them as their own."

Dec's stomach turned. His heart faltered. The idea of a man marrying a fourteen-year-old and forcing her to have sex and produce children seemed so dark ages he couldn't fathom it. "And how did you defy them, Brooke?"

"My fourteenth birthday was coming up." Her hands nervously fidgeted with the dress fabric across her lap. "My father came home from an elder meeting saying that I was to be wed to a man who'd joined the community about a year before. He was in his late forties, but even his age wasn't as bad as knowing this man was cruel to the bone. I'd seen firsthand the way he treated animals. Why would I ever believe he'd treat me any better?"

She stopped long enough to sip her wine and blink away the tears. It was clear to Dec that she'd steeled herself against what had happened. She'd completely renounced that part of her life and moved on. It was only the slight tremble in her full bottom lip that gave away the enormity of the emotional scars the situation had left on her.

For her sister she'd cried.

For herself she refused.

"That bucket list I told you I started making when I was ten years old?"

He nodded, wanting to hold her. Wanting to make it all just a bad dream.

"I started creating it because it was my way of imagining a better life. I'd nearly been forced to live the life that had imprisoned and then killed my sister. The number one thing on my list has always been to marry the love of my life, because I *refuse* to let go of the dream that someone out there in this world will love me and treat me with respect. I refused to allow myself to be forced to marry a cruel, much older man who wouldn't care anything for me and would demand I procreate until I was dead."

A slight hesitation and another sip of wine touched her lips. Dec waited patiently for her to complete the story, even while he wasn't sure he really wanted to hear the rest.

"So I planned," she continued. "And I ran. One night I waited until I knew there would be no one out. I crawled out the bedroom window, and then I climbed over the big stone wall that encircled the compound. Then I ran the entire ten miles to the next town in the Arizona heat. Without water. Without anything except the clothes on my back and the fear in my heart. I ran to the police who were familiar with the *community* yet they'd never done anything to stop what went on there. When I appeared at their door, they had no choice but to call child protection services. The next day I was placed with the Hastings family."

"So Hastings isn't the name you were born with?"

She shook her head. "I left everything behind. My name. The little brother I loved. My sister's children. Everything. My parents disowned me and my foster family helped me legally change my name. They're good people. They took care of me and showed me that real love and a good marriage were the complete opposite of what I'd ever seen or had been brainwashed to believe."

"Are you still in contact with them?"

"Of course. They're my family."

He lifted her hand and rubbed his thumb over the cool sterling bracelet around her delicate wrist. "And the bracelet?"

She smiled. "My foster mother gave this to me on

my fourteenth birthday—three months after I ran away from the community. She said she'd never met such a fearless girl before, and that she knew there were great things in store for my life."

She touched the bracelet and their fingers met on the now warmed metal.

"I never take it off. It's a reminder that instead of being sold out by the parents who gave birth to me, I ignored the fear in my heart and was rewarded with a new family and a new life."

Thinking of the scared, brave little girl she must have been, his heart clenched. "You're amazing."

"Not really. Just stubborn."

"No." Gently he cupped the side of her face in his hand. Stroked his thumb down her smooth cheek. "You're more than that. You're absolutely beautiful. Inside and out. I've never met anyone like you before. I'm honored to know you, Brooke Hastings," he said, meaning it from the bottom of his heart.

And then he kissed her.

Chapter 10

Brooke could barely breathe with Dec's mouth on hers, even though the kiss was soft and sweet and . . . reverent.

He'd said they could forget the boss/employee thing for the night, but he'd also said he could never picture her as a friend.

So that left them . . . where?

She took pleasure in his freshly showered scent, his delicious taste, his firm yet gentle touch, and the sense of security he offered without saying a word. When he ended the kiss she felt rattled, needy, and a little more than speechless.

Searching for something relevant, she said, "Thank you for understanding and not judging."

"No one has the right to judge another's life. When I say I admire you, Brooke, I mean it." His thumb slowly stroked across her cheek. "In fact . . ."

Her heart picked up speed as he glanced at the door then brought his gaze back to her.

"Wait right here."

When he went inside the cabin, she did her best to calm her racing heart. For four years she'd wondered what it would be like to kiss him. Now she knew. And now she knew she would never be satisfied with just three kisses. But with the way he'd gotten up and walked away, it seemed he had other ideas.

When he returned and sat down in the chair with his dark brows pulled together, she knew what he was about to tell her couldn't be good.

Exasperated, she couldn't escape fast enough. "I'll go get the dessert."

"Wait." When he reached out and caught her hand, her heart got tangled up in a wicked web of hope. "When we were at that little shop on the pier in Santa Barbara? You know, the one with all the sparkles and frills?"

She nodded.

"I saw something that made me think of you and I knew I had to buy it."

Handing her the small white paper bag, he sat back in the chair and waited for her to look inside.

"You . . . bought me a gift?"

"It's . . ."

Please don't say it's no big deal.

"When I looked across that store and you were trying on fairy crowns, you made me smile." Uncertainty pulled at the corners of his masculine lips. "I realized you do that a lot. And when I saw *that* in the display case it made me smile too because it connected with you. And . . ." He lifted his hands and dropped them down on his thighs. "That's a whole lot of sappy shit right there, but it's the truth."

"I don't know what to say." But she did know that what he'd said touched her down to the very depths of her heart.

"You haven't even seen what it is yet."

"Dec. If there was an empty peanut shell in here I'd love it, because you thought of me and . . . those words you just said weren't sappy at all. They were wonderful." She kissed his cheek. "Thank you."

She unfolded the bag and the tissue inside. The silver chain bracelet with three charms inside made the butterflies in her stomach get up and dance. She lifted it from the box and the firelight caused it to sparkle. She stopped the charms from swinging so she could see what they were. One was a diamond-encrusted heart. Another was of a mischievous-looking Tinkerbell. The third charm made her laugh out loud.

"A bucket?"

"In case you come up with any more items for your list," he said.

"And Tinkerbell?"

"You were wearing a fairy crown in the store at the time." He touched the little charm and sent it swaying. "I know you always wear your *Fearless* bracelet and I didn't buy this to replace it. Fearless says a lot about you. But the heart on this one says a lot about you too. And I've never met anyone before who has such a feisty determination to turn something wrong into something right. In my eyes, you're very much like that little fairy who flies around sprinkling pixie dust on everything to make it better."

Warmth surrounded her heart and gave it a gentle

squeeze. "You'd better be careful saying things like that or I just might fall in love with you."

As if she hadn't already.

"That would be a very bad idea."

"And that just goes to prove that we have two very different opinions." She kissed his cheek again because grabbing him and throwing him down on the table so she could have her way with him probably *was* a very bad idea. "Thank you so much for this. I love it. Will you help me put it on?"

"Of course."

She handed him the bracelet and held out the arm with her *Fearless* bracelet. "I want to wear them together."

He opened the clasp and hooked it onto her wrist.

"They look perfect together," she said, moving her arm so the diamonds flashed in the firelight.

Perfect together.

The same way she saw the two of them.

"But they'll never be as beautiful as you."

Heart as light as air, she chuckled. "Declan Kincade, are you hitting on me?"

"That would be another very bad idea."

But he didn't say *no.*

"How about I go get that dessert?" she asked, knowing that he might be feeling a bit moody right now with all the revelations they'd both just spilled out on the table. She also knew giving him that moment might steal away any of the progress they might have made. And while she might want to give him a push, she'd never take advantage in a moment where he might be emotionally . . . vulnerable. If he gave in, she wanted it to be real.

In the kitchen she grabbed hold of the counter and tried to catch her breath. Her heart had the whole Tarzan chest-pounding thing going on and her knees were wobbly as noodles. When she heard the back door open she snapped upright so fast her neck cracked.

"What's for dessert?" His deep voice rippled through her heart and down to her girl parts like warm, sweet honey.

"Caramel mousse with toasted shredded coconut." She opened the refrigerator and took out the glass dessert bowls. "I was just about to add the coconut. I wanted to wait till just before I served it because I didn't want it to get soggy."

"How about you hold off on that." He came up behind her, close enough to feel the heat emanating from his big, tall, strong body.

Caged between him and the counter, she glanced over her shoulder. "You don't like coconut?"

"There's just something really . . . sexy about a silky mousse." He reached around her, stuck his fingertip in the chilled glass, and licked it off.

Whoa.

If she thought her heart had been pounding before, it just set a new world speed record. Every rapid beat sent a pulse between her thighs and set her desire on high.

"Mmmm." The sound rumbled from his chest and into her back.

"Good?" She tried to sound nonchalant.

"Delicious." He leaned in more. "Have you tried it yet?"

"No."

"No?" He dipped his finger in the mousse again and turned her to face him. "Have a taste."

"You want me to . . . lick it off your finger?"

He gave her a slow nod.

Brooke didn't know what game they were playing and she certainly didn't know the rules. But she wanted this man. And even if she only had him long enough to taste the damn mousse, she was game.

She came fully into his arms and held his hand steady. Instead of licking the mousse off, she looked up at him, closed her mouth over the tip of his finger, and sucked it off.

He closed his eyes and a low growl rumbled in his chest.

"Good?" he asked.

She nodded. "What are we doing, Dec?"

"Sampling dessert."

"Is that all?"

He shook his head slowly. "I've tried to respect that you are the best damn assistant I'll ever find. And I know that if I cross that line I stand a great chance of losing you. I swear to God I've tried not to dream or fantasize about you. But ever since that kiss in the ocean, ever since you woke up wrapped around my body, I haven't been able to think of anything else."

To know he'd been thinking of her like *that* filled her with total and complete exhilaration.

"What if I promise you won't lose me?" she asked.

"I'd still hesitate. But then I'd seriously think about putting a huge dent in the no fraternizing policy."

"Then I promise you won't lose me." She trailed her fingers up the front of his rock solid chest and felt his heart pound against her palm. "So what's your excuse now?"

"No excuse."

"Then exactly what is it you want to do? Right now . . ." She let her fingers play over his abs. "While my body is pressed against yours and every sexual fantasy imaginable is playing in my head?"

"Brooke."

"Dec." She leaned in and felt the hardness of his desire press against her from behind his zipper. Then she pressed her lips against the rapid pulse in his throat. "What do you want to do? Right . . . now?"

Yes, she was walking over hot coals.

Yes, she was daring the devil to come out and play.

And yes, she'd never wanted anything more than she wanted him.

"Right now . . ." His eyes darkened with hunger as they searched her face. "I want to forget I'm your boss. And I want to lick my dessert off every soft, silky, sexy curve on your body."

A strong intake of air lifted his broad chest as he settled his hands on her hips and brought her up hard against him.

She went up in flames.

"But if you tell me I'm overstepping my bounds," he added with a frown tugging his dark brows close, "tell me to go to hell, or tell me no, I'll back off. Right now. Even though it might kill me. And it probably will."

"I'd never tell you no." She looked him straight in the eye. "Don't you know that by now?"

"I promise I'll go slow."

"Dec." She grabbed the front of his shirt with both hands. "I've been waiting for this for four years. Don't disappoint me now by going slow. Give me everything you've got. Fast and hard."

"Fuck. Yes."

All thought flew from her head as he closed his mouth over hers and fed her a long, hungry, pantie-wetting kiss. Her body hummed with need as his hands traveled down her back and gripped her rear end. Without breaking the kiss and with amazing ease, he lifted her up onto the counter.

Now they were eye to eye. Even though he'd stepped between her thighs, the lower parts of their bodies were no longer touching. And Brooke really, really wanted them touching.

His firm, demanding mouth trailed down the side of her neck while his hands roamed her back, sides, and breasts. Her head dropped back to give him better access.

Yes.

She wanted him to devour her.

Completely.

Because when it came her turn, she planned to savor every second, every muscle, every interesting body part he possessed and then some.

Twice.

"You make me so crazy," he murmured against her throat. "I want to take my time with you, but my body is aching for more. It's aching for deep, fast, and hard."

"Oh God." She pulled his shirt up and over his head. When it landed somewhere on the floor she leaned in and pressed her mouth to his chest. She licked his pebbled nipple then sucked it into her mouth. He had a gorgeous physique. Tall. Lean. Firm. Not too overdone. Just right. "Didn't I mention that fast and hard sounded really good right now?"

"You did." He trailed a slow lick with the tip of his tongue up the side of her throat. "But I've been waiting to touch you for so long, I am *not* going to hurry."

When his hand gently cupped her breast and he rolled her nipple between his thumb and finger, a *need it, want it, gotta have it* message shot between her legs.

"Are you sure?" she moaned when he playfully nipped at her throat, an action that sent a direct, razor sharp response to her nipples. "We could always do it again."

"Oh. We will." He lifted his head, looked into her eyes and cupped her face in his hands. "But you don't want to be disappointed and I certainly don't want to disappoint."

"I was joking earlier." Her breath caught in her throat when he slid his hands beneath the straps of her dress and touched her bare skin. "There's no way you could disappoint me."

"I'm not going to take that chance." He grinned like the devil and drew her dress down, exposing her bare breasts to the cool air and his hot eyes.

"You are even more beautiful than I ever imagined," he murmured. "And I am even more turned on that you aren't wearing a bra under this dress." He glanced down. "Panties?"

She slipped her hand down to the zipper of his jeans, pressed her palm against his massive erection, and squeezed. "Would it make you harder if I said no panties?"

"I'm not sure harder is even possible."

"Let's give it go." She squeezed him again. "No. Panties."

He growled. "God, I love the way you think."

"Your body likes the way I think too."

He chuckled deep and sexy. "My body *loves* the way you think."

Not that she'd planned for tonight to go where it seemed to be headed. It wasn't why she had no underwear on beneath her dress. But at this moment her fondness for freedom whenever possible beneath her clothes was working for her. Brooke figured she should probably feel shy about sitting there half naked. She didn't have the most perfect body, but the way Dec looked at her made her feel perfect. And that was really all that mattered.

Now if she could only get him to hurry up and start taking off the rest of his clothes she'd be much happier.

Instead, he again dipped his finger into the caramel mousse. Slowly he drew a circle around her nipple. When the cold of the creamy mix touched her skin, she drew in a breath and let go of a moan. Then he dipped again and did the same for the other side. The heat of his mouth took away the chill as he circled her erect nipple with his hot, moist tongue. She squirmed and nearly slid off the counter. He caught her in time, then he pinned her wrists behind her body, which arched her back and thrust her breasts higher.

"Mmm. Perfect." His warm breath whispered across her skin, fanned the fire, and singed her patience.

Each tug and pull of his mouth caused a response lower in her body. Her thighs squeezed his hips.

"Do I get equal time?" she asked. Her fingers tingled to touch him. She was tired of imagining what his skin would taste like on her tongue. She wanted the real thing.

"You'll get your turn." His fingers curled into the fabric of her dress and he pulled it off over her head in one smooth motion.

Before she could blink, she was buck-naked on his grandfather's kitchen counter while he stood between her thighs still partially dressed.

"*After* I've had my fill," he said then went back to swirling her nipple with his slick, hot tongue.

"But . . ." *Oh damn that felt good.* "I want my hands on you."

"And I want my tongue on you. Everywhere. But especially between your gorgeous legs." His hot, moist mouth moved down her body, teasing and torturing, until he ended up on his knees. His big hands slid over her thighs and then under them as he brought her to his mouth.

He kissed each inner thigh, and then he moved that magical mouth right where she wanted him. Heat exploded through her entire body and she had no option but to drag her fingers through his hair and hang on for dear life.

Briefly he lifted his head and looked up at her. "You're beautiful, Brooke. Everywhere. So soft. So sweet. So tasty." And then he went right back to business, delivering on his promise that he would not disappoint.

The fastest, hardest, most mind-blowing orgasm hit her at mach speed in a wave of silken heat and bubbly tingles. When she completely melted and bonked the back of her head on the cupboard, he kissed his way up her thigh, alternating between light feathery kisses and gently sucking her most sensitive spots. He continued the pleasure up her stomach to her breasts then ended up at her neck again.

"Dec?" she said when she was able to form words.

"Hmmm?" His fingers continued to explore her body, letting her know he was nowhere near done yet.

"Get those damn pants off right now."

A low chuckle of pleasure rumbled in Dec's chest because he'd just satisfied this woman for the first time of the night. "Maybe you'd like to give me a little help?"

"I thought you'd never ask." Brooke slid off the counter and danced her fingers down his chest on their way to his zipper. Before she pulled the tab down she caressed his erection through the denim of his 501s.

"Fuuuuck." His heartbeat kicked up into the red zone as he dropped his forehead to hers. "That feels so damn good. I can't wait to have your hands on me."

Having her beneath his hands, against his tongue, was like some kind of magic he'd never known. Not that he'd ever been a selfish lover, but with Brooke he couldn't seem to get enough. He wanted it all. Right now. He wanted to soak her up in his skin so he'd never have to be without her.

"I don't just want my hands on you," she said. "I want my mouth and my body on you too." She took him by the hand and pulled him into the bedroom.

He'd never been much of a follower, but the hell if he wouldn't follow her anywhere she wanted to go. Especially if it led him to more of whatever this was happening between them.

Because whatever it was, it was fucking amazing.

When they reached her room, she propelled him against the bed until the backs of his knees hit the mattress.

Moochie, who'd been sleeping on the comforter, didn't care for the rambunctious company. She gave them a dismissive sneeze then leaped from the bed and trotted off into the living room.

"I always knew you were great at taking control." He leaned in and playfully nipped at her bare shoulder.

"If you think I'm good in the office, I guarantee this will be better." She slid the zipper tab down then pushed the jeans and his boxer briefs down his thighs.

There was no hiding the effect she had on him now.

She had a body of curves most women would diet away. He was glad she didn't try to cover herself up. She was a real woman and he wanted to look at her just like this, all night long.

Soft, sexy, seductive, and naked.

He reached up and undid the clip holding her long curly hair. When it fell about her shoulders in a golden cloud, she looked like a voluptuous, nude, fairy princess. Like something that should be painted on canvas and preserved as a fine art piece.

Intelligent thought flew from his head when she wrapped her hand around his hard shaft and gave him a firm squeeze. A sumptuous shudder rippled down his back as she moved her palm down his hot skin to the plump head then back up. He pressed deeper into her hand and groaned at the unbelievable sensation that spiraled through his entire body.

When she pushed him back onto the bed and crawled over him like a sleek lioness, he knew what she had in mind. He knew having her lips wrapped around him would be a hot paradise, but all he could think about, all he wanted, was to be buried deep inside her.

Undeterred, he flipped her over on her back and she laughed.

"I thought I was going to be in control."

"Next time." He kissed her sassy mouth. Reached for his wallet on the nightstand and pulled out a condom. "Right now I need to be inside you."

She raised her head and licked the side of his neck. A delicious shiver slid down his back and sent an urgent message to his cock.

"Then at least let me do the honors." She took the packet and tore it open.

Having Brooke roll a condom on his cock in such a sexy, provocative way might go down as one of his most favorite things ever. In fact, the only thing that could top it would be making love to her without a condom.

But he was already taking enough risks.

He was hard and ready to go, but he wanted things to

last as long as possible. And he wanted to taste, touch, and feel her luscious body again. Settled between her legs, he kissed her pretty mouth, her lovely neck, and he suckled each of her gorgeous breasts until she moved beneath him and began to beg as he rocked his cock against her slick, hot opening.

His will broke on her third *"Please, Dec, now,"* and he slid deeply, possessively inside her wetness. Her muscles gripped him and she let go of a long, lusty moan that rolled over him like a heat wave.

He stilled until he could regain control.

Everything in his body said to drive hard and fast, to find release, but that wasn't how he wanted this to go. He pushed deeper into her core, retreated, and rotated slowly as the sensation and steady buildup crept like molten lava through his veins. Brooke wrapped her legs around him and lifted her hips to meet his thrusts in a rhythm that removed all sensation except where their bodies were joined.

A litany of *"Oh God. Oh God. Oh God."* spilled from her lips with each thrust and Dec knew she was close to coming again. In tune with her cries, his hips pumped faster and he reached between them and rubbed her sensitive spot. One last cry of pleasure escaped from her lips as her muscles contracted around him and pulled him in deeper. Each thrust was like a perfectly synced electric explosion of nerves until a storm of heat and sensation swept through his body and he erupted in a long, hot, breath-stealing orgasm.

When his heartbeat decelerated enough for him to be able to regain his senses and move, he drew Brooke into his arms and pulled the comforter over the two of them.

For the first time in his life, he was cuddling a woman after sex instead of putting on his pants and checking out.

That was the exact moment he knew that, more than being just an incredible assistant who kept him going day after day, Brooke meant something really special to him.

He just didn't know how he was going to deal with it come morning.

Chapter 11

*B*rooke woke to a cold and empty bed.

Just as she'd predicted.

Yes, Dec had made love to her several delicious times last night and he'd slept with her snuggled in his arms. But she knew at some point he'd run. The guarded employer in him would make sure of that, even if he'd wanted to roll over the top of her come morning light and repeat everything they'd done last night.

She didn't expect he'd easily throw down his belief that mixing business with pleasure was a bad thing. Nope, he would definitely take some more convincing, teasing, and torturing.

Until he saw things her way.

She got up, put on her fuzzy yellow robe, and then followed the heavenly aroma that drifted from the kitchen.

Except for Moochie, who was curled up in a corner of the leather sofa and snoring, the house was empty and silent. A note on the counter in front of the coffee-maker drew her attention.

> *Coffee is made. Breakfast is in the oven. Moochie has already been fed and walked. Headed to the vineyard office. Please call the marketing contact and see if he has the data pulled together yet.*
>
> *BTW, dessert last night was delicious.*
>
> *D*

She smiled. At least he'd acknowledged that there *was* a last night. Still, it would have been nice if he'd waited around until she woke up.

She didn't know whether she wanted to kiss him for the coffee, breakfast, and taking care of her dog before he'd left, or if she wanted to growl. Because even though he'd acknowledged that they'd *deliciously* stepped over the employer/employee line, she knew exactly why he'd left early.

One step forward, two steps back?

Hopefully not.

Dec was a man who took what he wanted, worked hard for what he needed, and put everything important on a personal level on the back burner. Brooke was a woman who put everything on a personal level at the top of her list and let the chips fall where they may with the rest. Well, she worked hard too, but that wasn't the heart of her life.

Talk about opposites attract.

As she opened the oven door and pulled out a warm

plate piled high with fluffy pancakes, she chuckled. The box of instant pancake batter still sat on the counter next to a bottle of syrup, which explained his sudden cooking abilities. After she poured a cup of coffee, snagged a few pancakes off the plate, and loaded them up with margarine and syrup, she sat down at the kitchen table to make her plans for the day. A long hot shower started the list. Finding a way to get Dec in bed again was next.

Devious?

Maybe.

But her body still tingled from his touch and she wanted more.

Brooke had no doubt he was used to being the aggressor, just as she knew his head would overrule his heart and all his other body parts.

At the office she frequently had to convince him that some things were worth the risk. Apparently old habits didn't change due to location. Sometimes, gorgeous men with big hearts and stubborn heads just needed an extra little nudge toward something they didn't even know they wanted. It was like passing by a candy store and seeing the sweetest lollipop on earth.

Who could resist?

As she headed to the shower, she snatched up her cotton candy scented body wash. If she planned to help Dec break all his bad working habits, she needed all the help she could get.

*J*he office coffeemaker gurgled with a fresh pot as Dec sat across the desk from Ryan, watching his brother sign a check to pay some utility bills for the vineyard.

Jordan wouldn't make an appearance until his ladylove left for work. Ethan had holed up somewhere in the main house doing God knew what. And Parker had a full day of work in his Portland food truck. So currently it was just Dec and his oldest brother, both of whom Dec considered to be the most level-headed of the male siblings.

Well, he'd been level-headed until last night when he'd completely lost his mind and ended up having the single most fulfilling personal and sexual experience of his life.

He'd always been an up early, get to business kind of guy. This particular morning had been completely different. He'd had to drag himself away from Brooke's warm luscious body. For at least an hour he'd lain there watching her sleep.

He'd never done that with a woman.

She was so beautiful, and in slumber she seemed so at peace. With her hand tucked beneath her cheek and the whisper of a smile on her lips, she'd unknowingly presented an offer to him. He could have this. All he had to do was reach out and take it. A woman like Brooke didn't come around every day. He wasn't used to taking things for himself just because he wanted them. Not that Brooke was a *thing*, but he definitely wanted her. When sunshine began to fill the room he knew he had to deal with his newfound feelings.

An apology for last night seemed ridiculous. Yes, he knew that what he'd allowed to happen had been wrong, but it had been so amazing that, deep down, he wasn't sorry at all.

"Stop smiling."

Dec brought his head up and he realized he'd been daydreaming. "What?"

"You're smiling like the cat that licked the cream," Ryan said.

Not quite what had happened, but licking had been involved.

Ryan's eyes narrowed. "So what's up?"

"I wasn't smiling."

"Hell. You were practically drooling." Ryan shoved away the checkbook. "Maybe I don't want to know. I'd probably be jealous."

"We should probably stick to business."

"Now I'm definitely curious." Ryan leaned back in his chair and clasped his hands behind his head. "Brooke?"

"How'd you know?"

His brother chuckled. "Because when she walked in here yesterday your eyes almost came out of their sockets. I've got to admit she's a damned attractive woman."

"She's more than that."

"Details?" Ryan asked full of big-brotherly hope.

"Fuck you. You know I wouldn't tell you that."

Ryan laughed. "I wouldn't expect you to. But you can't blame a celibate guy for trying."

"Well, don't try living vicariously through me."

"So what, you let go and had a little fun and now you don't know what to do?"

"I'll figure it out."

"How about you just keep on living so you can keep on smiling?"

"You know things are never that easy."

"Shit." Ryan leaned back in the chair. "You ran like a little girl, didn't you."

"No."

"Yes, you did. Otherwise you'd still be wrapped up in those sheets with her. I know I would be."

Would it give away his true feelings if he punched his brother in his smartass face?

"Well, you're never going to get that chance. So don't get any ideas."

"Little brother?" The aged chair beneath Ryan creaked as he leaned forward, planted his forearms arms on the desk, and looked Dec straight in the eye. "I know you probably don't want advice from a guy whose wife left him to star in a commercial with toilet paper, but I've got news for you. If you don't make good on those feelings for her you've been wearing on your not-so-secret sleeve, someone else will take your place. It's only your luck that she's crazy about you."

"How the hell do you know that?" And he wasn't even going to think about someone else holding her or making love to her. That image just plain pissed him off.

"Because she wears her feelings on her not-so-secret sleeve too."

He did not want to be having this conversation. What he wanted was to march his ass right back to that cabin and crawl back into bed with Brooke. Hopefully she'd still be warm and asleep, and he could wake her up slowly, using everything he'd learned last night that made her moan and smile.

"You don't think so?" Ryan continued spewing his

unasked for and definitely unwanted advice. "Then sit back and do nothing. But when some other guy—maybe even one of your own brothers—steals her away, don't come crying to me. Or Parker. Or Ethan. We might be very busy."

"Fuck you, Ryan."

"Fuck *you*, Dec." Ryan kicked the trash can under the desk. "I know you're smart as hell. You're my brother and I love you. I care about you. I want to see you happy as a kid with a brand-new red balloon. And honestly I'm envious as hell. But if you don't do something about your feelings for Brooke, she might get frustrated and move on. Did you ever think about that?"

He had.

And he didn't like that idea one little bit.

It had taken a hot shower and three cups of coffee for Brooke to leave her fantasies from the previous night behind and get herself into work mode. She'd made the call to their marketing contact and he'd emailed over the statistics. After she'd printed them out, she dropped them in a manila envelope, petted Moochie on the head, then headed out for a walk up to the vineyard office to deliver the info.

Along the way she couldn't help taking a good look at the gorgeous property. There were acres and acres of green meadows where a few deer were now having a mid-morning snack. And there were just as many acres of forested area where a red-tailed hawk soared high above the treetops. The rolling hills with rugged mountain peaks as a backdrop were enchanting, and Brooke suddenly felt as though she'd been transported to somewhere across the Atlantic.

In her hand she held the data on the marketing statistics. And with that knowledge, she knew exactly what she'd do with the vineyard if it belonged to her.

Halfway up the long curved road, Nicole, Dec's teenage sister, came running down with her dark brown hair flying and her pink Western boots clomping against the gravel.

"Hey there."

Nicole came to a bouncing stop wearing a huge grin. "Are you coming up for coffee?"

"Actually I was taking these papers to the office."

"What are they?"

"The demographics data."

"Oh. Important?"

"I believe so."

Nicole sighed then grinned again. "Too bad. They'll have to wait." She grabbed Brooke's hand. "Come on."

"Where are we going?"

"I want to play you my new song."

Brooke glanced toward the building that contained the vineyard office. She knew she should go directly there, but how could she pass up the chance to hear Dec's sister sing? "I'd love that."

"Oh good. I wrote it for Jordy and Lucy's wedding. I wanted to see what you thought before I played it for them."

"Why me? We barely know each other."

"Yeah, but that will change now that you and Dec are together."

"Whoa." Brooke stopped. "Who told you that? We're not together."

Nicole shrugged then planted her hands on the hips of her flowery dress and laughed. "Are you sure?"

"Yes. I'm . . . Why are you asking? And why would you assume?"

"Because I know my brother." Nicole tucked her arm through Brooke's and got her moving again. "He's never brought a woman home for anything. He's never trailed off to La-La Land in the middle of a conversation. And he arranged for the both of you to stay in our grandfather's cabin."

"Nicole—"

"Nicki."

"Nicki, I don't want you to get the wrong idea. Your brother only brought me here so we could continue to work."

"Weren't you able to manage from the office before when he was here after our parents died?"

"Yes, but—"

"And didn't he drive you up the *romantic* coastline instead of hopping on a plane and renting a car like he usually does?"

"Yes, but—"

"And at the risk of embarrassing himself, didn't he get up to sing karaoke because you wanted him to?"

"Yes, but—"

Nicki's ethereal blue eyes sparkled. "And aren't you crazy in love with him?"

"Yes, but . . . Hey, you tricked me."

"Yes, and it worked." Nicki laughed again. "Now that Lucy is joining the family, I'm finding that I really love having big sisters. Brothers can be so . . ."

"Aggressive?"

"Poopy. They want to tell me what I should do with every aspect of my life. And no boy has ever been brave enough to date me more than once because my brothers scare the life out of anyone who tries."

"That's because they love you."

"Well, sometimes I wish they didn't love me quite so much." Nicki opened the front door to the huge main house, a home designed to look like an old-world castle. "I have a lot of life to live. You can't be a songwriter if you haven't lived life. You need the inspiration. Right?"

"Right." As Brooke stepped inside the front hall of the main house for the very first time, she noticed that everything seemed to be in disarray.

"Excuse the mess," Nicki said. "I'm redecorating."

It struck Brooke as a bit odd that anyone would want to change the home of their parents so soon after they'd died. Then again, she didn't know the relationship and she really had no right to an opinion. Especially since she'd left her parents far behind on that blistering summer night so many years ago.

"This is a beautiful house."

"It really is." Nicki propped her hands on her hips and evaluated the room. "Too bad it was never decorated right. I don't mean to diss my mother, because she tried. But there was no happiness when you came into the rooms. Now that Jordy and Lucy are getting married—here at the vineyard by the way—I've convinced them to move into the house. We made a deal and I'll then be moving into Lucy's little cottage. They need more room. I need more privacy. So Lucy and I have been going over decorating styles and I'm trying to surprise her by painting a few rooms before they move in."

"What a lovely idea. I'm sure she'll appreciate that."

"Lucy's awesome. I can't wait for you to meet her."

"I'm looking forward to it."

"She wants to meet you too." Nicki laughed again. "She knows better than anyone how hard it is to bring down a Kincade brother."

"Sounds ominous."

"Honestly? I have never seen Jordy happier. He gave up being an NHL star to be with her. Not that she asked him to. She'd never do anything like that. She's just Lucy. Kind of understated and totally wonderful. She was my creative writing teacher. If it hadn't been for her and Jordy, I'd never have had the courage to break out of my shell and write music."

"I'm really happy for you."

"I'm really happy for *us*." Nicki excitedly grabbed her arm. "Go Team Brooke!"

"Go *what*?"

"You know, like in the Twilight stories. Everyone was either Team Edward or Team Jacob. Aunt Pippy and I are Team Brooke. No one has signed up for Team Dec yet."

"You're pitting us against each other?"

"Not at all. We're trying to bring you together. We're just betting on who can hold out the longest."

Brooke knew she'd already fallen hard for the middle Kincade brother, but she didn't want to spoil the teenager's enthusiasm.

"You have an unfair advantage," Brooke said. "I've already spilled the beans on how I feel about him."

"Right. But my brothers never do anything the easy way. He's going to be on a roller coaster and do some stupid things. But before his train pulls into the station, he's going to crumble at your feet like a man completely and hopelessly in love."

"Who says I won't crumble before him?"

"You won't." Nicki grabbed Brooke in a hug. "Because you've already had his number for four years. A little while longer isn't going to matter to a smart woman who knows what she wants."

"How did *you* get to be so smart?"

"Believe me, if you'd seen me just a few months ago I was a mess. I didn't talk to anyone. I hated everyone. And things were going downhill on a roller skate. Not that I'm any kind of angel now. But Jordy was persistent and I've learned that I have people around me who truly love me. And I truly love them back. Which is why I want to see Dec happily in love. With *you*."

"That's really sweet, Nicki."

"I know." A big cheesy grin filled the teen's beautiful face. "And as an added benefit I'll have more inspiration for my love songs."

"Well, I am a big country music fan so never let it be said that I wasn't willing to do my part."

As Nicki picked up her guitar, Brooke looked around the living room at the family photos. There were group photos of their parents, the brothers and sister at picnics among the grapevines or at other outdoor events. There were candid shots of the brothers grinning with their arms slung over each other's shoulders. There were photos of Ryan with his daughter, Riley, and obviously a new one of Jordan and his fiancée, Lucy.

A pang hit Brooke in the gut.

She'd always wanted a family like the Kincades. She'd been lucky to find the Hastingses and they'd been wonderful at making her feel like one of them. But the bottom line was she'd been born to another family. And hard as she tried, she couldn't help wishing that they'd seen the error of their ways and done what they could to be good parents and role models. Maybe if they had her sister would still be alive.

Dreaming of a family of her own had been a constant in Brooke's life. She wanted that ideal image of a husband and wife with children they adored. She wanted the whole *Leave It to Beaver* thing. And then she'd gone and fallen in love with a man who had nothing but business on his mind.

Nicki strummed the first chord and Brooke hoped that the young girl didn't get her hopes for Team Brooke up too high. Team Dec was a strong-willed man whose ability to play the game of negotiations had made him a multimillionaire.

Chapter 12

By the time Brooke strolled into the vineyard office, most of the brothers were present. Yet regardless of how much he wanted to keep what had happened between them last night private, Dec couldn't take his eyes off her. Not that she had on anything outrageous; she simply wore a pair of tight jeans and a snug T-shirt that fit like a second skin. But after discovering and appreciating every delicious curve she possessed, all he could do was imagine peeling them off.

"Sorry to interrupt." Her voice was a bit breathy, probably from walking uphill to the winery office. But to Dec's ears, it sounded as sexy as it had last night when she'd begged him for more.

Her sandals slapped rhythmically against the floor as she came into the room and Dec immediately looked down to the blue polish on her toenails. Last night he'd also discovered that her feet were ticklish, as well as several other places on her voluptuous body.

Discovering those areas had been more fun than he'd ever imagined. He'd never known sex could be so playful. And now that he knew, he realized he could come up with all kinds of ideas.

"I received the info you were waiting for." She handed him a large envelope with a polite smile. "I thought you might want it as soon as possible."

"Thank you." He took the envelope, touching her fingers on purpose to see if her smile would shift from all business to the playful Brooke he'd gotten to know so well last night. "Did you get the note I left?"

"I did." The corners of her mouth curled into that smile he wanted to see. He'd never wanted to kiss her more than at that very moment. "And thank you for the pancakes and coffee."

"You're welcome."

When he glanced up his brothers were all staring at him.

"What?"

"Nothing." Ryan grinned. "Not a damn thing."

While Brooke maintained a calm and businesslike presence, Dec felt like he was coming apart at the seams. He couldn't reveal what he felt on the inside or his brothers would dog pile on him like a bunch of adolescents prime for a good old-fashioned razzing. He needed some time to figure things out first. So for the moment, while he might want to wrap Brooke up in his arms and cart her back to bed, he had to get back to business as usual. They had the mystery of Lili MacKay to deal with as well as the flagging state of the vineyard.

Apparently Brooke realized that too.

"I really didn't mean to interrupt," she said to his brothers. "But it was nice seeing everyone again."

As she headed toward the door, Dec felt torn. If she stayed he knew he'd have a hard time focusing on the details of the information they needed to discuss instead of on how pretty she looked with her hair freshly washed and left curly. Or how the neckline of her snug T-shirt dipped close to her cleavage. Or how much attention he'd paid to those perfect breasts just a few hours ago. And if she left, he'd basically be thinking about all the same things.

Damn. He'd never been so happily distracted in his whole life.

"No need to run off, Brooke." Ryan slyly gave Dec a wink. "Have a seat."

Before Dec could offer her his chair, Ethan jumped up and offered his. Dec threw him a back-the-fuck-off glare.

"I really don't want to intrude," Brooke said before she sat down. "I know you have a lot to discuss."

"Nonsense." Dec indicated the now empty chair next to him. "Have a seat and join us. The other day you had some excellent observations about the vineyard. I'd like to hear your thoughts now that we've received the demographics report."

"That's very sweet of you." Her smile was like a ray of sunshine as she sat down. "But I'm no expert."

"Your marketing degree gives you more of an advantage than the rest of us," Dec said to her, trying to keep things in control. "As Ryan said, we'd appreciate your assessments."

He hoped to hell he was sounding like his typical business-minded self. But he doubted it with his heart thundering because she smelled as sweet as cotton candy, and all he wanted to do was take a bite.

"I appreciate that." Her slow blink hinted that maybe he wasn't the only one having a hard time focusing. "I did look over the report, and on the walk over here some ideas did come to mind."

"Then please . . ." Ryan smiled. "Let us know what you think."

"Well, if you insist." Brooke's face lit up with an irresistible smile that made Dec ridiculously proud of her ability to jump into the sandbox with his brothers. "Your primary market falls into three categories. The first are DINKs."

"DINKs?" Ethan laughed. "That doesn't sound too promising."

"Double income no kids," Brooke clarified. "The second category is empty nesters. And on the smaller end of the scale is what they call the cougar/silver fox quotient."

"I know what a cougar is," Ethan said. "Had one hitting on me in Florida last year when I was working the Everglades fire. I'm guessing a silver fox is the man's version?"

Brooke nodded. "Forty- to sixty-year-old wealthy, single, career driven men and women seeking a younger man or woman. So basically what you have are groups of people looking for the dream getaway or romantic rendezvous. You're only minutes from Portland and only a couple of hours from Seattle. Both have a wealth of adults in your target market."

"So basically, we're not looking at twentysomething singles or young families," Ryan confirmed.

"Exactly. Those in your age groups and financial demographics are above middle income. They're looking for somewhere to unwind, enjoy some light activities like golf or hiking, and some pampering with good food and good wines."

"Too bad Jordan isn't here," Dec said. "He suggested a golf course."

"Probably a challenging nine-hole would be sufficient. Or maybe a driving range," Brooke said. "You'll just need to give them something to do afterward—a spa, restaurant, somewhere to sit outside and enjoy the surroundings, maybe listen to some light music. However, even though your audience speaks to a specific range, you could also increase business by making this more of an event venue instead of just hosting the occasional wedding. Bringing in local entertainment would be beneficial too."

"So what kind of theme would be all-encompassing to this demographic?" Ethan asked. "Modern? Country?"

"Actually . . ." Brooke locked her fingers together and cupped them over a knee. "Your main house already has a hint of what I think would work well. It almost looks like an Italian villa. Go for a European flair. Build a few more cottages for your B and B with some old-world charm like those in Ireland, France, or even the Netherlands. Give them a cobblestone path, lots of fragrant flowers, a fountain. Mix in the candlelight and moonlight with good food and your delicious wine and I think you'll transform the place into something magnificent and memorable. If you add in an entertainment area, golfing, and a friendly tasting room you'll be all set. Of course, you'll still need to come up with a marketing and advertising plan. For that I'd recommend visuals, not audio. If you don't already have a website, you'll need one. If you do have a website you'll want to revamp it to reflect the changes you've made. Provide your clientele with a destination. *Show* them what a picturesque place Sunshine Creek is and why they would want to spend their time here."

"Those are great ideas," Ryan said. "And actually we'd already discussed adding an entertainment area and wine club."

"On the upside," Brooke added, "it would give you an opportunity to employ more local people. Economically that's good for everyone."

Dec already knew Brooke was smart, and at the moment he couldn't be more proud. He was impressed that she'd figured it all out while they'd been struggling to find their footing. Much the way she'd figured out that it was time for him to break old habits and learn to add a little more fun into his life.

Last night she'd done a breathless, pleasurable, mind-bending job of making her point.

"I graduated college with an amazing architect who specializes in old-world, Craftsman-style structures," she said. "I'd be happy to give you his number."

"Sounds great." Ryan looked pointedly at Dec. "I hope you realize what a gem you have in her. You'd better not be stupid enough to ever let her get away."

Dec knew Brooke was brilliant and she didn't need anyone else to be a success. And even though he really needed *her*, he realized she didn't really need *him*. But he didn't think that was the context his savvy brother had in mind.

"I'd be completely lost without her," he admitted, even as a twinge of regret for stepping over the line last night slammed down like a fist.

*B*rooke excused herself from the vineyard office with the explanation that she had a ton of work to do when all she really needed was a moment to breathe. In just a few short hours her emotions had hit all the summits and dives of a roller coaster.

At first, she'd been upset that Dec had left this morning without saying a word. His disappearance had skirted the borders of making her feel cheap and used. She figured the breakfast and the note had been his way of smoothing over his disappearing act, and that helped. Then seeing him smile at her in the office had made her feel all warm and fuzzy. But when he'd said he'd be lost without her, the words seemed empty, and they didn't come with a smile.

Was she expecting too much?

Probably.

Was she rational right now?

Probably not.

At this moment, Dec knew her better than almost anyone. He knew what her life had been like. He knew she killed karaoke. He knew every sensitive spot on her body that made her hum with pleasure. That she liked to be kissed on her neck behind her ear. That during lovemaking she loved to be on top. But he didn't know how deeply she felt about him. And that look he'd given her just before she'd walked out of the office had been rife with caution and regret.

Sure, she knew he wouldn't fall easily. She knew he'd drag his feet and that his mind would get tangled up with the arguments of right and wrong.

Why couldn't things just be simpler?

Angrily she kicked a pebble on her way back to the creek-side cabin and ended up stubbing her toe.

"Dammit." She stopped to check out the damage. She'd lost a chunk of her blue toenail polish but otherwise was really no worse for the wear.

"Are you okay?"

She clenched her teeth as Dec strolled closer with his hands in the pockets of his jeans, looking quite casual and unconcerned with a black T-shirt hugging all those finely sculpted muscles she'd had her mouth all over last night.

"I'm fine."

"You don't sound fine." He stopped in front of her, making her back up a step. "In fact, you sound pissed. What's up?"

"Nothing." The man was a genius with numbers. So how could he be so dense with the human aspect? Giving him no enlightenment because, yes, she could be as stubborn as a rusted screw, she turned and trudged back down the road toward the cabin.

He followed. "We probably need to talk."

"Not a good idea right now." Talking would most likely lead to tears—hers—and she didn't want to show any weakness. She wasn't sorry for coming on to him back at the beach and kissing him. She wasn't sorry they'd made love last night. She was only sorry that apparently he appeared to be sorry. "I have work to do."

His heavy footsteps continued to fall on the gravel behind her. Not a surprise. Dec hadn't become successful because he gave up easily. If a client situation challenged him, he saw it through to the end no matter how frustrating or troublesome it became. She imagined that's how he saw her now.

Frustrating and troublesome.

Well, too bad for him.

When she reached the cabin, she opened the door and closed it behind her. A moment later it opened again and he stepped inside.

"Trying to shut me out?"

"As if I could." She went directly into her makeshift office. And, of course, he followed.

"Brooke." She flinched at the strain in his voice. "Seriously. What's wrong? Is it about last night?"

She spun toward him. "If you say last night was a mistake I swear I'll kick you where it hurts."

"Last night was . . . amazing. But—"

"No buts, Dec. It happened and I had a great time."

He jammed his hands in his pockets. "Obviously so did I."

"It's not as obvious as you think when you look like you're about ready to run for the hills."

"I'm not running. But in all honesty, it shouldn't have happened," he said. "You're my—"

"Oh dear God. Give that whole boss/employee thing a rest, will you? Last night we were anything but. Last night we had our tongues in each other's mouths, our hands all over each other, and our body parts were up close and personal. We're both adults. You don't think we can behave as such?"

"I can't look at you the same way as before." He shook his head. "You're a total distraction to me."

"I'll take that as a compliment." She tossed a folder on top of several others on the desk.

"I'm not kidding, Brooke. How do you expect me to get anything done if all I can imagine is stripping off your clothes and bending you over that desk?"

Eye rolls were stupid and immature. She did one anyway.

"So you think if you act like it didn't happen and you don't make the mistake of sleeping with me again, it will change anything?" she asked.

He had the nerve to shrug.

"Huh." She folded her arms.

"What does *huh* mean?"

"If that's how you want to play, so be it."

"It would help if you didn't walk around here in tight pants and skimpy little tops."

"And now you want to dictate what I wear?"

"No. I just—"

"Good." She came around the desk, curled her fingers in his shirt, and forced him to look her in the eye. "Then let's get one thing straight, shall we? I am *not* going to change a thing about myself to accommodate *you*. I am *not* going to stop wanting *you*. And I sure as hell am *not* going to stop trying to make you want me too. Got that, *boss*?"

"You don't play fair."

"Nobody ever said life was fair." She uncurled her fingers and stepped back, giving him a frustrated push. "Especially in love and war. Haven't you ever heard that before?"

For a moment he stood there looking gorgeous and confused.

For a moment she felt bad.

Disbelief curved his lips downward. "Are . . . are you saying you *love* me?"

"Are you saying you don't think you're loveable?"

"No." He shook his head. "I mean yes. I don't think I am."

That crushed her. "Why?"

"I think I fit more into the tyrant category. And who could ever love a tyrant?"

"You're not a tyrant." Anger fled and compassion stepped up. "How do you even come to that conclusion?"

"Don't make a big deal out of it, Brooke. I know who I am."

"Apparently you don't."

"Yes. I do. I'm a workaholic who makes no time for anything outside of work. Everything I do is solitary because I don't make time to make a lot of friends. And I don't make a lot of friends because I don't have time for them. I don't make time for relationships of any kind. Do you understand what I'm saying?"

Each word jabbed her in the heart. She didn't see him like that at all. If she did she'd never have fallen so hard for him. But why would he shut himself off from everyone? What was the actual deep down reason that made him do such a thing?

She didn't understand at all why he held himself back from enjoying life. Or enjoying her. But those were things to be discovered another day when emotions weren't high and the chances of saying something both of them would regret were countless.

"Loud and clear."

"Good." He inhaled a breath that tightened the cotton shirt across his chest. "Then you understand why what happened last night . . . shouldn't ever happen again?"

Dear God. If he could only *feel* the way he was looking at her right now, like he wanted to wrap her in his arms and hold on tight. And, hopeful romantic that she was, she noted that he'd said *shouldn't* not *couldn't*. Two totally different things.

"Loud and clear, *boss*."

"So we're just going to go back to the way things were twenty-four hours ago?"

"You know I'm good at following orders," she said. "But that request is completely delusional."

"And why is that?"

Men. She withheld an eye roll.

"Because within the last twenty-four hours you wanted me. And you gave me this beautiful bracelet as a thoughtful gift. And we had amazing sex. *Four times.* But don't worry, boss man. Like always, I've got everything under control."

"And what exactly does *everything* encompass?"

A crazy sense of relief flowed through her when he didn't deny wanting her.

"It means that in the future I'll plan my work and work my plan." And her plan was to continue to make him see that life didn't revolve around a messy desk–unless that happened to be the place you were having wild monkey sex.

*F*rustration rolled off him like heat waves in the Sahara. Dec left his grandfather's cabin *and Brooke* to get some fresh air. And a drink. He definitely needed a drink and it wasn't even noon. So he settled for a strong cup of coffee and a slice of lemon meringue pie at the Muddy Cup Café in beautiful downtown Sunshine.

Sometimes a guy just needed to clear his head. To figure things out. Because right now he was more confused than when he'd woken up this morning. Why not do it with caffeine and sugar? A sound idea except the coffee made him think of the fresh pot he'd made that morning for Brooke but hadn't stuck around to share, and the sugar made him think of the sweet caramel mousse he'd licked off her delicious body last night.

Now he was on his second cup and trying not to think. At all. Not helping was reading the local trash paper *Talk of the Town*. The front-page headline made his eyes cross.

GUNS OF STEEL:
HOTTEST BICEPS IN HOLLYWOOD

And this had exactly what to do with living in Sunshine Valley?

His family had some previous issues with *Talk of the Town* when the editor, who dreamed of a job working for the *Weekly World News* or the *National Enquirer*, had run an unfavorable story on Jordan and Lucy that nearly destroyed their fragile relationship. Both his brother and future sister-in-law had told off the bitter woman who ran the place, but nothing had changed. The news coming out of the modest building on Main Street was still a pile of garbage and lies and would have been put to better use in a construction site outhouse.

"Can I interest you in another piece?"

Declan looked up to find the middle-aged server with fiery red hair leaning one hip against his table in an obvious attempt to flirt. He wasn't sure whether she was offering another piece of pie or something more personal.

"Thanks. I'm good."

"I'll bet you are." She winked. Then after refilling his coffee cup she said, "If you change your mind, just give me a nod." Luckily she didn't hang around and wait for him to change his mind. Instead she carried the steaming carafe to the next booth and used her same flirting techniques on the two elderly gentlemen enjoying a late breakfast.

Dec folded the so-called newspaper and pushed it across the table. There was only so much nonsense one could take in a day.

He was pretty sure the paper had gone to the extremes of exaggeration when it printed a story about Bill and Hillary Clinton adopting an alien baby. The trouble was, not even these outrageous stories could take his mind off Brooke. Before he left the cabin she'd shut herself inside the office and immersed herself in work. It was exactly what he deserved. He should have let her know how much the night before meant to him. Instead, he'd fallen back on his old ways and told her it couldn't happen again in the future.

The conversation had been another stabbing reminder why he stayed away from personal relationships. He just wasn't any good at them. Even the relationship with his twin brother had deteriorated over the years.

Yes, since the death of their parents and since Jordy had come home, it had gotten better. But there was a time when—without going into the whole twinsie communication thing—they were as close as two brothers could be. But something had happened to Dec when his twin took off for greener pastures and neglected everything in Sunshine. Including his own family.

Though he wanted his brother to be successful, Dec had taken offense. Jordan had always been the more outgoing, the more physical one. While Dec hadn't let any grass grow beneath his feet where the girls were concerned, and without allowing himself to fall into the geek category, he'd studied his ass off. He'd had to. School hadn't come easily for him because of his dyslexia—a secret his parents had taken with them to the grave.

Back in the day, had his brothers known, they would have teased him mercilessly. Not that they didn't love him, but they were rough-and-tumble boys who beat the shit out of each other for fun.

His teachers had misdiagnosed him with ADHD

because he'd been clever enough to figure out how to distract from a situation when he didn't understand something. When he was correctly diagnosed with dyslexia, everything changed. He figured out how to deal with the problem and how to overcome it as much as possible. But while doing so, he'd been reserved and missed out on a lot of social skills—something that continued to this day. As long as he stuck to the one thing he knew— business—he figured he'd always be all right.

He'd never expected an amazing woman would step into his carefully planned world and mix it up so he felt like he had to learn all over again.

When the bell above the café door jingled he looked up. In walked Lili MacKay in a dark pair of sunglasses, black pants, and a black shirt, as though she was trying to be inconspicuous.

The fiery-haired waitress grabbed a menu and escorted the blonde to a booth in the opposite direction. Though she hadn't noticed him, she sat facing him, which gave him ample opportunity to observe her.

She ordered tea, not coffee. Sourdough toast, no butter, no jam. And she didn't remove the dark sunglasses.

Dec's curiosity soared.

Who the hell was this woman?

He watched as she pulled her cell phone out of a black purse, typed something in, and then smiled. Who was she texting? And what would bring such a reticent smile to her face? Why not a full smile?

And why was he so obsessed?

Yes, she was an attractive woman, but that's definitely not what stirred up his attention. At the moment he couldn't think of anyone but Brooke in that sense. But the mystery the woman had brought with her when she'd shown up at the vineyard couldn't be ignored.

He picked up his coffee cup and made his way to her table. "Mind if I join you?"

Startled, she looked up from behind those sunglasses and frowned. "I'd prefer to have my breakfast alone, if you don't mind."

"I do mind." He sat down opposite her and set his cup on the table. "Because I'm curious."

"About?"

As if she didn't know.

"About why you showed up at our family vineyard. About why you seemed surprised when you were told that our father—and mother—were dead. About why you abruptly left without enlightening my brothers and me as to why you were there to see our father." He sipped his coffee. "Among other things."

"And I believe I told you it was personal."

"Actually, you said it was business. So now I'm even more curious."

Lili MacKay's lips flattened into a thin line.

"So which is it, Ms. MacKay? Business? Or personal?"

From behind the dark lenses her eyes darted left and right as though looking for an escape. Too bad he was between her and the door, and she wasn't going anywhere until she told him the truth.

"Why do you care?"

"Because you came to our family vineyard, looking for my father. Isn't that enough?"

"Look, Mr. . . . Kincade. My business isn't with you. And if you don't mind, I'm really not in the mood to share my deepest darkest secrets with a complete stranger."

Dec sat back, the vinyl booth cool against his spine.

"And now you're talking about secrets. So tell me why I shouldn't be curious as hell about you."

"I'm really not all that exciting."

"My father—if he were alive—might disagree. Yes?"

The harsh intake of air she pulled into her lungs said he'd nailed it.

"I think it would be a good idea if you came back to the office with me."

Her head tilted. "Why?"

"How many ways do you want me to say it, Ms. MacKay? You either want something or you have some vital information. I think it's important that my brothers and I know which it is. We've already been dealing with enough after our parents' deaths. I certainly don't see you keeping your *deepest darkest secret* constructive."

She finally removed the sunglasses. "Others might disagree."

Holy shit.

Dec had a feeling he now knew why Lili MacKay had suddenly appeared in their lives. If he was right, it would crush every single thing any of them had ever believed.

Chapter 13

$\mathcal{M}$uch as it happened in a complicated business deal, a change of tactics and demeanor became necessary for Dec to get Lili into his car so he could drive her to where his brothers would meet them at the vineyard office. Not that Dec didn't trust her to drive her own car, but . . . he didn't trust her. She had a scared rabbit look all over her, including the trembling of her hands as she fidgeted with things in her purse.

"No need to be nervous," he said, glancing over at her and for some reason feeling sorry for whatever situation she might be in. He didn't know how forthcoming she might be. He only hoped she'd tell the truth and kill the terrible suspicion rising inside him.

"That's easy for you to say." She brushed her hair back over her shoulder. "You have the upper hand."

"How's that?"

"You aren't walking into the lion's den." Her glare burned him, even from behind her sunglasses. "You *are* the lion's den."

Contrary to his feelings, he chuckled. "You remind me of my sister."

Her eyes popped wide. "You have a sister too? And two brothers?"

"Four brothers. Two weren't there when you came in. But they'll be there now." He could guarantee it.

"Great." She sighed and looked out the window.

The rest of the drive was silent. When they reached the vineyard parking lot, she hesitated before she got out of the car. Dec felt a need to calm her fears but really couldn't figure out why he'd feel protective of her at all. Basically he was only there as a guard to make sure she didn't escape before she clued them all in on her mission.

Once she was outside in the fresh air she seemed to pull herself together. She held her head high, straightened her shoulders, and with her sunglasses firmly in place, walked toward the office with determination.

Inside the office the brothers were waiting. Well, actually they were arguing about whom they thought would win the World Series that year, but that was nothing new. Quarreling seemed to be a daily occurrence. Just one of the many things that made being a sibling fun.

When he and Lili came into the room the conversation stopped and even he felt the force of their displeasure.

"Ms. MacKay." Ryan waved his hand at the empty chair opposite his desk. "Have a seat." The brothers were in various positions around the room, either leaning against a wall, the desk, or sitting with their arms folded. Regardless of their physical positions, they were a united force. If he'd been anyone other than one of them, he might be intimidated as hell.

"I prefer to stand, thank you," Lili said.

"For a quick escape?" Jordan asked. When her head snapped around to glare at him, he said, "Have a seat, Ms. MacKay. And that is *not* a request."

Pressing her lips into a thin line that proclaimed her annoyance, she plopped down in the chair.

Ryan leaned back and steepled his fingers together. "Declan says you've decided to enlighten us about the reason you came to see our father."

"More like I was persuaded to enlighten you."

"Dec is a businessman who *persuades* people to trust him with their money," Ryan said. "And he's very good at it."

"Apparently." She folded her arms and crossed her legs.

Her body language was closed off and Dec hoped they could make some kind of progress before everyone had a meltdown.

"Would you care for some coffee? Tea? A stiff drink?" Ryan tried to use humor to ease the woman's obvious tension.

"What I'd like . . ." She glanced at the faces surrounding her. "Is an introduction to each of you. I always like to know the enemy by name if possible."

"We're not your enemy, Ms. MacKay." Jordan gave her a tight smile he'd probably used on the ice against his opponents. "Yet."

"Who are *you*? Mr. Intimidation? And what is it you do besides give out veiled threats?"

"I like your spunk, kid. Jordan Kincade." He offered his hand, which she timidly shook. "Second in line brother. Fraternal twin to Declan, whom you've already met. Former NHL player for the Carolina Vipers. Currently a pain in the ass to my siblings while I figure out what to do with my life besides marry the woman of my dreams in a few months."

His light banter made her smile as she pointed to the man behind the desk. "And you?"

"Ryan Kincade." He also offered his hand. "Firstborn. Divorced. Father to nine-year-old Riley. General manager for the vineyard."

Next she looked to Parker who, while no question the easiest-going brother, currently wore a scowl. Still, he managed to offer his hand. "Parker Kincade. Fourth in line. Single. Chef and owner of a Portland food truck."

She glanced up to Ethan, who sat perched with one hip on the desk. "And you?"

"Ethan. Baby brother. Single. Firefighter." He grinned. "Nicest of the bunch."

"I call BS on that." Jordan punched his arm.

"Our sister Nicole is missing because we weren't sure what you had to say," Ryan said. "She just turned eighteen and is still quite emotional after the loss of our parents."

"My condolences." Lili swallowed. "There sure are a lot of you."

"True," Ryan admitted. "And when locked together in a room for too long we get a little tense. So maybe you can relieve our curiosity by telling us what business you had with our father."

Ryan might be the quietest brother, but he could also be intimidating as hell. A trait he learned being the oldest, and therefore the one assigned to keep the rest of their sorry asses in line.

Lili took a deep breath, reached in her purse, and pulled out an envelope that she handed to Ryan.

After a brief hesitation, Ryan unfolded the paper inside. In 0.3 seconds his eyebrows jacked up his forehead and Dec's stomach twisted.

Eyes piercing, Ryan glared at Lili. "Is this some kind of joke?"

Lili flinched. "I assure you it's not."

"What the hell is it?" Declan stepped forward and snatched the paper from Ryan's hand. He read the words. Twice. Then he cut a glare across the desk at the blonde who seemed to be shrinking in her chair.

Verification of his suspicion.

Fuck.

"Take off your sunglasses," Dec demanded.

"I'm not sure why that matters."

"Please do it anyway."

Slowly she lifted a hand and removed the sunglasses.

A united gasp and one "holy shit" pervaded the room.

Mystery solved.

Responding to a client email regarding the sad situation of the stock market's effects on retirement funds, Brooke typed in the usual reply.

The stock market is a pendulum. It will swing back the other way. It always does. Don't panic. If you would like me to set up a teleconference with Mr. Kincade, I'd be happy to do so.

She wanted to add *Don't worry, be happy*, but snark with a client was always a bad idea. Everyone had a right to worry about their financial stability. Still, her mind couldn't be less on work. Someone else claimed first place in that category. Thankfully he had placed himself somewhere else for the day. Because frankly, if she were around him the temptation to strangle his big strong neck might be too hard to resist.

Oh sure, she'd known falling for her boss was the absolute worst idea she'd ever followed through with.

No.

The absolute worst idea she'd ever followed through with had been taking off her clothes and hopping into bed with him.

Yes.

That was the worst.

On second thought, believing their relationship could shift from business to pleasure without him freaking out about it? *That* was the worst.

She dropped her head to the desk and thunked it several times against the wood veneer. "Stupid. Stupid. Stupid."

Moochie looked up with a tilt of her head that confirmed Brooke had officially lost her mind.

"I know. I know." She reached down and stroked her hand across her little dog's silky fur. "Your mommy's a complete idiot."

*B*y late afternoon Brooke was eyeballs deep in researching the numbers on an investment deal for a small private company looking to expand their business. She considered getting up and making a fresh pot of coffee even though she'd really like to go out for a run. She needed to get some oxygen to her brain before it dozed off and she had fantasy dreams about her impossibly sexy, frustrating, and delusional boss.

She stood and stretched, but that wasn't going to help. Maybe she should go for that run after all. She didn't figure Dec would be back anytime soon. Even if he did come back, what could there possibly be for them to talk about? He'd made his point.

Then again, they didn't always agree. Points could be argued.

"Right, Moochie my poochy?"

Man's—and girl's—best friend wagged her stub of a tail.

The front door slammed so hard it threatened to rattle the old vineyard family photo off the wall. Moochie took off to hide. Brooke looked toward the door and within seconds Dec appeared.

A frown pulled his dark brows together and crinkled the corners of his eyes.

Good God, what had she done wrong now?

He stood in the doorway, broad chest rising and falling on breaths that looked like he'd run a mile. Or ten. But deep in those blue eyes was a well of distress. In a blink, she knew whatever was troubling him hadn't been caused by anything she'd done.

"Brooke?"

"Yes?"

He came around the desk, pulled her up into his arms, and kissed her like he needed her for air. His embrace was constricting as he hugged her, as if he was afraid she would disappear like smoke.

Her heartbeat thundered in her ears as his kiss moved across her cheek while he held her face between his hands. When his warm lips slid down her neck she couldn't help dropping her head back to give him better access. When that sensuous male mouth came back up to her lips and his thumbs stroked her cheeks she flung herself into the sensation.

He looked deep into her eyes. "Please don't say no."

How could she possibly refuse?

"I won't."

Without another word, he picked her up and carried her into his room. They made it no farther than the door he closed and backed her up against.

Leaning in he pressed his thick erection against the crux of her thighs and rubbed, making her just this side of crazy with need. He fed her wet, hot kisses with tongue tangling passion. His hand traveled down her neck, over her breast, and to her leg, where he hooked his fingers underneath and lifted her thigh up over his hip. He pressed into her and from behind the fabric of his jeans she could feel the hard pulse and heat of his rigid staff.

The T-shirt dress she'd changed into earlier gave him easy access. His hand shot beneath the fabric to cup her sex and massage her with insistent, talented fingers. She grew damp and needy, and she realized that even if she could have *this* every day, she'd never get enough of him.

"I love that you get so wet for me," he murmured against her ear. "So hot. So fucking sexy."

Anticipation tingled down her spine and a whimper

of need crept from her lips as she reached for him, palming his erection then giving it a squeeze that had him dropping his forehead against the door.

"I need you, Brooke," he groaned. "I need you so fucking bad right now."

"Then take me."

His greedy fingers tore the pair of lemon yellow panties from her body and flung them over his shoulder. While his fingers once more slipped between her legs, she unzipped his pants and, along with his boxer briefs, pushed them down his narrow hips. Using the door as leverage, he cupped her bottom with both hands and lifted her until her legs circled his hips and locked in place.

He plunged deep.

A gasp burst from her throat as a guttural groan of intense pleasure pushed from his chest. He leaned into her, panting as if he was holding on for dear life. Or as if he'd finally touched the place he wanted to be.

Brooke clung to his broad shoulders, meeting his thrusts, inhaling his masculine scent, and trying to keep her wits about her when every place on her body he touched turned to fire. Unlike the night before it didn't last long. There was too much urgency. Too much friction. Too much . . . everything.

There was only one thing missing.

A condom.

With a last powerful thrust and groan, Dec dropped his face into the curve of her neck. Against her breasts his heart beat like a wild captured animal. A few heavy breaths later he pulled out and set her feet back on the ground. Then he gathered her up in his arms and just held on.

Brooke held him, stroked his strong, muscular back and the soft silkiness of his hair. And because she knew he would, she waited for him to let her go. Eventually he did, even if he seemed reluctant.

He kicked his pants the rest of the way off, yanked off his shirt, and stood before her completely nude and glorious. Then he slipped her dress over her head until she was naked too.

He held out his hand. "Come lie down with me."

She nodded as he pulled down the bedding and they slipped between the covers. He pulled her close, wrapped his arms around her and tucked her head beneath his chin. For what seemed like forever they lay there without speaking, wrapped in each other's arms.

A million things went through Brooke's mind.

A million questions.

A million worries.

"I'm sorry," he finally said. "I lost control. I didn't use a condom. And I have *never* done that before."

"I'm on birth control. And I haven't been with anyone for . . . well, a really long time."

"Doesn't excuse it." Softly he played with a curled tendril of her hair. Then he drew her closer and hooked a leg over hers.

"You surprised me," she said, stroking the firm definition of his biceps. "After this morning, I—"

"I've never needed anyone like that before. Like this. And I'm not just talking about the sex. I just . . . needed to be close to you."

"What happened?" she asked, because she knew something definitely had. Normally he seemed like he didn't need anyone. He always played it calm and cool, until last night when he'd given in and they'd made love. And even though her body still tingled from having him inside her, she knew right now she needed to be a *friend* he could talk to.

"The woman I told you about that showed up at the office looking for our father?"

"Yes."

"Apparently there's a very good chance she's our sister."

"What?" Surprised, Brooke turned her head and caught him with his eyes closed tight as if he could squeeze away the revelation. "How is that possible?"

"She said that her mother died a month ago after a long battle with ovarian cancer. Her mother made a deathbed confession about the father Lili never knew. *Our* father. She explained that her mother and our father had an affair after meeting at a work function. Her mother knew my dad was married but said there was something too strong between them to ignore. They were together for over a year when she became pregnant."

"While he was married to your mother?"

He rolled to his back, propped an arm behind his head, and nodded. "Which completely blows the belief that our parents had the perfect marriage right out of the universe."

"Does she have proof?"

"A written confession signed by her mother."

"Not a birth certificate?"

"Nope."

"She could be lying."

"We all thought about that. But there's one kicker in the story that raises a whole lot of questions. Like the rest of us, she has our father's blue eyes."

"I'll admit the color of your eyes is unusual. Beautiful. But still, that's not enough to take her at her word, or to believe a letter that could have been written by her. Right?"

"Right. We're hiring an investigator to check out her story. Plus she's agreed to give her DNA to be tested."

"What if she leaves? Did you get her contact info?"

"Ryan did. It's a good guess that if we can eventually follow the paper trail of the stolen money, it will lead to child support payments for Lili."

"You really think so?"

"It all kind of makes sense," he said. "After having five boys, Mom all of a sudden got antsy to get pregnant again. And then Nicki came along. Thirteen years after Ethan was born."

"Maybe your mother found out about the affair and the baby," Brooke said. "Maybe she thought having another child would save their marriage. That's not uncommon."

"Maybe. But if it's true, the bottom line is our father had an affair."

She laid her hand over his heart. "I'm so sorry."

"The thing I'm most worried about is what this will do to Nicki. She knew there was a reason Dad didn't treat her as he should. Maybe it had been because of the guilt he felt for the affair and for not being a father to Lili. Nicki went through a really dark period not long ago. She's just started to come out of it and act like a happy teenager again."

"Does she know about Lili?"

"No. We purposely kept her away because we had no idea what Lili's business was or intentions were. Now that Nicki's eighteen she's a voting member of the board. But in our eyes she's still just a kid whose heart should be protected."

"You're all good big brothers."

"Not really. We've all missed the mark at one time or another. But when one of us screws up, there are four more to take his place."

"I'm sure in Nicki's mind you're all superstars."

He gently squeezed her fingers that lay across his chest. "I appreciate the vote of confidence."

Though there was much to be said, including Declan's insistence that they needed to maintain the fragile, professional only relationship, he rolled to his side, pulled her in close, and fed her a succession of lust awakening kisses.

His touch was gentle. His words were hot and dirty. And he made love to her like she was the most precious thing in his world. He made love to her as if he had all day.

But when she woke up a few hours later, he was gone.

Chapter 14

Declan pulled the sweatshirt hoodie up over his head and scrunched his shoulders against the chilly breeze blowing in off the river a short distance away. As he walked along the path that followed the creek through the vineyard, the clouds moved in and obscured the moonlight.

Good thing he knew this path by heart.

About a quarter mile from the cabin there was a small waterfall. Dec had always enjoyed the sound of the water rushing over the rocks and sand. He found it relaxing. Which was exactly what he needed right now. To grab some quiet time to think things through before he screwed up any further.

When he and his brothers had been younger they'd conned their grandfather into helping them arrange some large boulders at the creek so they had somewhere to sit and drop a pole in to catch fish in the shallow pool. The fish they'd caught had been small and they'd always released them back into the creek. But the thrill of the catch never got old.

He circled around the "No Fishun" sign they'd put up what seemed like a hundred years ago and found his favorite boulder to sit on. The water and night were too cold to dangle his bare feet in, so he settled for leaning back and watching the scattered moonlight dance behind the shifting leaves of the black locust and Norway maples.

He should have brought a bottle of wine with him. But drinking alone had never appealed to him. He should have stayed in bed next to Brooke's soft, warm body. But he had too much on his mind. She'd been sleeping so peacefully and he'd been too restless to do the same.

Brooke deserved so much better than he was able to give.

He should never have walked into the cabin earlier with her there. Before this trip he'd never had weak moments. He'd always been in control. For the sake of his career he'd had to be in control. But when he'd walked through the front door, torn up by the revelation that his father had cheated on his mother and produced a half-sister none of them had been aware of for the past twenty something years, he'd needed a distraction. When he'd added the worry of how Nicki would handle the discovery of why their father had treated her differently, he'd needed . . . Brooke.

All his adult years he'd trained himself to handle things just fine on his own, including the fact that letters didn't always look like letters and numbers didn't always look like numbers. He'd been just fucking fine.

Or so he'd thought.

Now he didn't know what the hell was going on. It seemed as though every day some kind of problem popped up that required him to step out of his neatly arranged life. The drama had quickly become like someone's warped idea of a soap opera and unwittingly, Brooke had become his lighthouse in the storm.

"Looks like we had the same idea."

Dec looked up as Ethan approached and sat down on his own favorite boulder. "You couldn't sleep?"

"Hell no." He lifted a bottle of Foggy Noggin Scotch Ale then pulled another one from the pocket of his hoodie and tossed it to Dec. "Figured a walk and a microbrew would do the trick. Turns out I was wrong."

Dec popped the cap to the bottle and took a long refreshing drink.

"What are you doing all alone?" Ethan asked. "It's kinda romantic out here."

"Yeah, well, don't think about kissing me anytime soon. Unless you want a black eye."

Ethan chuckled. "No worries. You're not my type."

"You've got a type?" Dec teased.

"Thought I did." Ethan slugged down a drink then dangled the bottle between his knees. "Turns out I was wrong about that too."

"What gives?"

His brother shrugged his broad shoulders. "I've been rethinking this whole life thing and how it sure hasn't added up to what I expected."

"How so?" Dec figured he knew where his brother was headed, but he also figured maybe the guy just needed someone to talk to. Since Dec wasn't around all the time and Ethan wasn't one to pick up a phone except to order takeout, maybe it was time for a little one-on-one bro chat.

God knew he could use one.

"By the time I was sixteen I thought I had everything figured out." Ethan took another drink and shook his head. "I thought I'd get engaged to Emily, go to college, get married, build a house, and have some kids. I thought I'd be a Vancouver firefighter. I thought by the time I reached thirty years old I'd be happy as hell and living the good life. Now I'm trying to figure out why I'm fighting fires in the freaking Everglades, dodging alligators and commitment, dealing with the loss of our parents, babysitting a temperamental teenage sister, and discovering that our father cheated on our mom and we possibly have a full-grown sister nobody knew a damn thing about."

Declan let go a heavy sigh. "I hear that."

"What about you?"

"Me?"

"No. The asshole standing behind you. Yes *you*."

"Guess I'm kind of in the same place you are. I thought being a successful businessman and a millionaire by the time I was thirty was going to be enough. Now I'm not so sure. Now I'm trying to figure out why I've always dodged commitment. Why when I go home at night I feel like pulling my hair out. And where the hell I went wrong."

"Does Brooke fit into that scenario somewhere?"

"Brooke fits into that scenario everywhere. But she didn't until Jordy opened his big fat mouth and made me take another look at her."

"Hell, bro, you ought to take several looks at her. She's hot as hell."

"God. Don't you start too."

"Just sayin'."

"Yeah, well don't."

"Uh-oh. How'd you screw up?"

Declan gave him a look.

Ethan cringed. "You didn't."

"Oh. I did," he admitted, waiting for the regret to sink in. But all he felt was need. "Several times."

"I won't ask if it was any good because the look on your face says you'd go back for more if she'd let you."

"That's the problem. She'd let me. I'm the one who keeps trying to put her at arm's length."

"I don't mean to seem dense but . . . why?"

"I've got a million excuses why, but the truth is I don't know." Dec took a drink of ale and shook his head. Something both he and his brother seemed to be doing a lot. "She's perfect. In every way. I've tried to stick to the mind-set of not mixing business with pleasure. I know that doing so has a great propensity to become a major disaster."

"So what's your biggest fear?"

"That I'll lose her."

"You're afraid she'd quit being your assistant?"

"Sure, that. But I'm more afraid that she'll walk out of my life for good."

"And yet here you sit on a stupid rock feeling sorry for yourself." Ethan grinned to take the sting off the truth.

"What about you? When was the last time you talked to Emily?"

"The day she told me she wouldn't marry me because I wanted to be a firefighter."

"That was a long fucking time ago. And maybe you should have thought of a different occupation since her firefighter dad was killed in a fire."

"How long have you known me?"

"Since Mom and Dad brought you home after you were born and stuck your squalling ass in my room."

"Have you ever known me to want to be anything other than a firefighter?"

"Discounting the time you wanted to be a Ninja Turtle, I guess not."

"Well, there you go." Ethan stuck the empty bottle of ale in his hoodie pocket. "I just figured Emily loved me and everything would work out okay."

"I'm sorry it didn't."

"Yeah. Me too."

"So what would you change if you could go back to that time?"

"Honestly?" Ethan tossed a pebble in the creek. "I'd change everything. I wouldn't just accept *no* and walk away. I'd figure it out and make it happen. I've been with a lot of women since then, but the only woman I still dream of is her." He tossed another pebble. "What about you? If you could go back to whenever you first kissed Brooke, would you still kiss her?"

Declan shook his head even though his heart felt something very different.

*B*rooke had taken a cold shower and washed her hair, hoping to take the steam out of her temper. The fact that she was sitting at her computer—fuming—at close to midnight validated that the shower hadn't worked. Neither had the two glasses of wine she'd drunk, nor the cup of chocolate chip ice cream she'd devoured. At the moment she was riding high on aggravation, alcohol, and sugar.

Bad combination.

She'd packed her clothes and gathered Moochie's belongings while she debated finding a nearby motel or catching the next flight back to Southern California. But she didn't have a ride to either a motel or the airport, and it was too late at night to ask anyone in the Kincade household. That's when she got the idea to call a taxi, only to discover that Sunshine didn't have a taxi company. They didn't have Uber either. Which left her stuck unless she wanted to steal Dec's car, which was parked outside. But he had the keys and she'd never learned to hotwire a car. And the airport was probably closed by now anyway.

Frustration crawled up the back of her neck as she navigated through the airlines' websites to find the next flight out of Portland. Trying to focus on business was impossible when all she really wanted to do was cry.

She'd thought she could change him. Or at least change the way he saw things between them. But he'd made it clear that all the thinking she'd done along those lines had been her own twisted version of what could happen. She'd thought she could handle his business side as well as his romantic side. Unfortunately she hadn't taken into consideration his aloof side. The one that kept making her feel like she needed to be the one doing all the work to bring them together. He either wanted it or he didn't.

She saw that now.

She knew he was confused about the events that had sprung up with Lili MacKay, and what hurt the most was that he'd confided in her yet he didn't trust her enough to stick around so she could actually be there for him. A woman in love could forgive many things. But the one thing she could never forgive was being made to feel insignificant.

An hour later when the front door finally opened, she took a deep breath for courage and met him in the living room. Arms folded she prepared for battle. She hated the fact that he looked so miserable. Judging by the tension around his eyes, he was tortured by what had transpired this afternoon with Lili MacKay.

But that wasn't her problem.

Not because she didn't care. Not because she wouldn't help. Simply because he'd never ask her. He'd always made it clear that he could handle anything. Alone. She had to believe that he would. Even though it broke her heart.

She needed more from a man she loved. She needed him to trust her. She needed him to need her for more than the temporary solace he found in her body. She needed the care and respect to be mutual. She needed him to love her back as much as she loved him. Once the good feelings backed off, she had to admit that no matter what rosy picture she painted around him, she doubted Dec could ever let go enough to reciprocate those feelings.

He looked up as she came into the room. "Hey."

"Hey?" She clenched her jaw. "That's it?"

"I should apologize." He stuck his hands in the pocket of his hoodie.

"Ya think?"

"I'm sorry," he said without looking at her.

"And I'm sorry that I can't accept your I'm sorry."

"What?" He looked at her then, frown lines deepening in his forehead and creases breaking out from the outer corners of his eyes. "Why not?"

"Because I don't even know what you're apologizing for and neither do you. You're only saying it because you think you should and you think I think you should."

"I'm confused."

"Well, that makes both of us." She tightened her folded arms.

For an uncomfortably silent moment they stood there staring at each other.

She waited for him to say something, to explain why he kept making love to her then running like a fire-breathing dragon was after him. She'd never asked him for a commitment, never asked him for anything. But he stood there, saying nothing, and her heart shattered.

"I need a ride to the airport," she said curtly.

"The airport? Why?"

"Because I'm leaving. And you'd better not ask me why or I'll be tempted to come over there and punch you."

"I don't need to ask why. I know you're mad."

"Mad?" Affront barked from her throat. "I'm not *mad*. I just don't like being used. And the fact that I let it happen twice says more about me than it does you."

"And what is that?" Hope sparked from his eyes, which she quickly extinguished.

"It means that . . . I can't work for you anymore."

"What?" He flashed the panicked look she'd expected.

"Look, Dec, it's not news that I care for you. That you mean something to me. It's just as obvious that you don't return those feelings. You made it perfectly clear that you didn't want to mix business with pleasure and I didn't listen. But then you kept blurring the lines and I got confused."

He started to speak and she held up her hand.

"Let me finish. It's not that I've been with a lot of men, but I've never had such an amazing time making love with someone only to have them run out on me, not once, but twice. I'm convenient for you, and that's not okay with me. I need to be more." She turned to get her belongings.

"I care about you, Brooke." He'd taken several steps toward her. "I don't want you to quit. I need you. You're a huge part of what makes my business a success."

"You don't need *me*. Anyone with half a brain and decent organizational skills can do my job." Brooke imagined pulling the dagger from her heart and dropping it to the floor dripping with blood. Because all she wanted to hear him say was that he truly needed *her*, not her stupid executive skills.

"I'm sorry about all the troubles you're going through with your family. I really am. And I'd have loved to help you through the situation. But I don't want to just be a part of making your business a success."

"What do you want then, Brooke? Because right now, I'm so fucked up in the head and heart I have no clue."

"I want you to quit hiding behind the whole boss/employee thing because that's just an excuse. The truth is you won't let me in. I *need* you to let me in, Dec."

Her admission led only to his silence, so she gave it one last try.

"I want to be a part of your life that makes you happy to come home. I want to be there to help you through troubled times. I want to make you smile. I want to love you. I *do* love you. But that's my problem, not yours. I'm perfect for you, but you'll never see that. And so . . . I have to go."

Because she couldn't stand to look at him anymore without breaking down in tears, she went into the bedroom, grabbed her things, and hooked Moochie's leash onto her collar. When she returned to the living room, Dec stood there with his hand clasped to the back of his neck, looking at the floor as if it held some kind of miraculous answer.

His head came up with a frown. "You really are leaving?"

"Have you ever known me to lie?"

"No."

"Then why would I start now?" She resettled Moochie's leash in her hand. "If you don't want to take me to the airport, I can drive myself. I'll leave your car in the parking lot, and drop off the key with security."

"Brooke . . ." He pulled the keys out of his pocket and held out his hand. "Fuck. Just take the damn car."

"I'll have my office cleared out before you get back." She grabbed the keys from his hand and strode toward the door. Her little dog trotted by her side with a sad puppy face.

"Brooke?"

Her heart gave a hard, painful thump as she stopped but didn't turn.

"I really am sorry," he said.

"You should be."

She closed the door behind her and kept her head held high until she put all the bags and her little wide-eyed dog into the car. She slid into the driver's seat and fastened the seat belt as if it was any other day. She made it all the way to the driveway of the main house before she hit the brakes and let the tears fall.

A tap-tap-tap on the driver's side window forced Brooke to look up from crying into Moochie's fur. But it wasn't Dec who stood there. She wiped her fingers beneath her eyes and rolled down the window. "Hi, Ethan."

"I was looking for a lady in distress." He gave her a smile. "Have you happened to see one around here?"

She gave a sad chuckle. "Look no further."

"Mind if I get in?" He rubbed his arms up and down the sleeves of his hoodie. "It keeps getting colder out here."

"Actually I was . . . heading to the airport."

"At this time of night? I don't even think it's open."

"I don't know."

"Come on. I promise I won't kidnap you or anything. And I haven't renewed my serial killer license so I think you're safe."

"It's not that."

He went around to the passenger side and climbed in anyway. Moochie excitedly leaped to the newcomer's lap.

"My brother's an asshole," he said without hesitation. "Believe me, no one knows that better than me. So how about you drive us up to the house and we have a talk?"

"It's late and I—"

"Tell me about it. So let's not waste any more time, okay?"

"I really don't think your brother's an asshole."

"Well, then you have to at least give me the chance to prove to you that he is."

With nearly black hair and bright blue eyes, Ethan was as gorgeous as the rest of the Kincades. She knew that no matter what he said, he loved his family tremendously. And if a wave of exhaustion hadn't poured over her head she would have tried harder to convince him to get out of the car and let her escape.

"I'll go to the main house with you," she said. "But only if you promise to make some coffee. Or at least hot tea."

"Deal."

She put the car in DRIVE and headed toward the big house. Within a minute after Moochie did her business on the lawn, they were walking into the dark, silent house. As good as his word, Ethan filled the coffee carafe with water and poured fresh grounds into the filter. While they waited for it to brew, she sat down at the long family size kitchen table.

It was nearly one o'clock in the morning and Ethan looked tired, which only made Brooke feel even guiltier.

"You look like you could use some sleep," she said.

"I'll admit it's been a long, weird day." He stood at the counter by the coffeemaker with two mugs in front of him. "But that doesn't explain my brother's problem."

"I'm not sure we should be talking about him."

"Are you kidding? We all talk about each other and give each other crap. That's what families do."

She wouldn't know. All she'd ever received from her birth family were orders. There had never been laughter in the home except between her and her siblings. Come to think of it, even a smile on her mother's face had been rare. She'd learned about familial love from the Hastingses, but they didn't have a loud and boisterous house either.

"I saw Dec down at the creek earlier," Ethan said. "We had a talk. I'm guessing when he went back to Grandpa's cabin it didn't go well between the two of you."

"I quit my job."

"Seriously?"

She nodded and accepted the steaming cup of joe he'd just poured.

"What did he say to make you quit?" He brought his own cup to the table and sat down next to her.

"It wasn't what he said. More like it was what he didn't say."

"Dec can be a man of few words, that's for sure.

He's a lot like Ryan in that sense. Jordy, Parker, and I are more alike."

"The rowdy and flirty type?"

"Rowdy for sure." A smile appeared from within a five o'clock shadow that dusted the lower half of his face. "I'll let you be the judge of the flirty part."

"What's going on?" Nicole scuffed into the kitchen wearing cat print pajamas, a frog print robe, and duck slippers.

"I'm so sorry." Looking at the teen's bleary eyes, Brooke felt horrible. "Did we wake you?"

"No. Fezzik decided my nose was his new favorite plaything and woke me up. Then I heard some murmuring down here and thought I'd check it out."

"What if it had been a burglar?" Ethan wanted to know.

"Then I'd either use all those self-defense moves you guys have always taught me, or I'd grab a knife, or I'd run like a cheetah."

Ethan shook his head. "I need to leave you with a babysitter when I go out."

Nicole speared her brother with a glare that informed him of the ridiculousness of his idea.

"Or I can always ask Aunt Pippy to come back and live in the house." He grinned like he knew the comment would push her buttons.

"Please don't. All she wants to do is watch reruns of *Magnum, P.I.* and drool over Tom Selleck."

"It could be worse. She could have you dancing go-go moves to the Beach Boys."

"I like the Beach Boys."

"See? It will work perfectly if she's here." Before Nicole could argue Ethan asked her, "Coffee?"

Nicole gave Brooke a look of concern that made her want to cry all over again.

"Somehow I think a drink might be more appropriate right now," Nicole said.

"Yeah, well, you're not legal yet." Ethan ruffled her messy hair. "So it'll have to be coffee or milk."

"You're not the boss of me, Ethan Kincade." She gave Brooke another sympathetic look. "Mind if I join you?"

"Please do." Brooke pulled out the chair on her other side. "I'm actually just having a cup of coffee and then I'm off to the airport."

"Oh God." Nicole put her head in her hands. "What did Dec do now?"

"Brooke quit her job," Ethan said much more casually than Brooke felt.

"Seriously?" Nicole high-fived Ethan. "That'll teach him a lesson. But you shouldn't go back to Cali," she said to Brooke. "You need to stick around so he knows what he's missing."

"Why would I stay?" There was only one reason she'd want to stay, but that six-foot-three, tall, dark, and handsome reason didn't want her around. At least not for anything more than as someone to keep his work organized and be conveniently available for a quickie when he felt the need. Disgust for putting herself in this position dug at Brooke like dragon claws. She reached down and lifted Moochie onto her lap for comfort.

"*Why* would you stay?" Nicole tilted her head at Brooke like a puzzled kitten. "Where do I start?"

"At the beginning's always a good place," Ethan said. "Unless you'd rather commence slicing and dicing our dear brother first."

"You know what she should totally do?" Nicole asked Ethan, then answered her own question without hesitation. "She should stay here in the house with you and me. And then to make Dec jealous maybe Parker can ask her out and—"

"Why can't *I* ask her out?" Ethan wanted to know.

Brooke didn't find it entertaining that they were talking about her like she wasn't there. "You guys, I'm not—"

"You can take her out too." Nicole's eyes widened at her brother and a smile burst onto her face. "In fact, you both should. Oh my God. You could like totally fight over her and—"

"Whoa. Whoa. Whoa." Brooke raised her hands. "I don't approve of lies and deception. Especially when it would be forcing someone to take me out just to make someone else jealous. And making your brother jealous is impossible because he doesn't care."

"Who said I'd be forced into taking you out? And just for reference, *this* is my flirty side." Ethan winked. "You're gorgeous, sweet, and fun. Sounds like a perfect date to me. And if you think Dec doesn't care, let us prove to you that he does."

"That's really not necessary."

"Yes it is. And I am totally writing a song about this." Nicole raised her hand and high-fived Ethan again. "Go Team Brooke."

"No. No Team Brooke." Brooke doused the growing

energy on the brother and sister celebration party. "The last thing I want is to be a wedge between you and him."

"It's not a problem, believe me," Nicole said.

"But I—"

"You did hear me say he and I talked, right?" Ethan asked Brooke.

"I don't think—"

"I know he cares about you," Ethan said.

"He just doesn't know it," Nicole added. "Or at least he won't acknowledge it yet."

"But he won't—"

"Sometimes people just need a little push in the right direction." Ethan grinned and sat back, folding his arms across his wide chest.

"Or a good, hearty shove," Nicole added.

"Look." Brooke pulled in a deep breath. This family had way too much going on to be concerned with her love life. Or lack thereof. It was obvious Nicole hadn't been told yet about the possibility of their father's affair and subsequent other daughter. Brooke wasn't about to add more fuel to their bonfire by whining about the man she loved not loving her back. "It's not that he doesn't care. I know he cares. The problem is he won't let me in. So while I appreciate all your concern and your creative thinking, I really just need to get home."

"But you're in love with Dec, right?" Nicole wanted to know.

"Yes, but—"

"Then you're already home, silly." Nicole covered Brooke's hand with her own. "You're a stand and fight kind of girl. Not a run and hide kind, right?"

Brooke looked down at the sparkling bracelet Dec had given her and the one she'd worn ever since she'd taken control of her own destiny.

Fearless

She thought of her sister, who'd never had the chance to find love. Her sister, who'd been repeatedly raped by the man she'd been forced to marry. Her sister, who'd succumbed to her own misery before she'd even reached the age of twenty, leaving the children she did love behind for another poor victim to raise.

Years ago Brooke had found the courage to seek a better life. She'd be doing a disservice to herself—and her sister—if she didn't continue to fight for what she wanted. She'd make a mockery of herself and her past. And then she thought about the number one item on her bucket list.

Marry the love of my life.

How could that ever happen if she tucked tail and ran? If she didn't give him a real chance to let her in? Not that she was some lunatic who'd continue to pursue a man who didn't want her, but Dec showed interest. When he made love to her and let himself go, she knew they were absolutely right for each other. So how could she be happy for the rest of her life if she didn't at least give them a chance?

Maybe it would work.

Maybe not.

She'd never know unless she gave it her best shot.

Chapter 15

Declan didn't need an alarm clock or the crow of a rooster to wake him because he hadn't been asleep. By the time the sun peeked through the window of his grandfather's cabin, he had already consumed an entire pot of coffee. His hands had progressed into the jittery stage as he unfolded the newest edition of *Talk of the Town* and shook his head at the ridiculous headline.

HOLLYWOOD PSYCHIC ARRESTED.
CLAIMS SHE DIDN'T SEE IT COMING.

He flipped through the rest of the paper looking for something of value but wasn't surprised when he found nothing more than a five-dollar-off coupon for pizza. Tossing the rag paper across the table, he lifted the nearly empty cup of coffee to take a sip. Realizing it was cold he set it back down.

He didn't need more caffeine. He didn't need stupid trash paper headlines. He needed to know where the hell Brooke was and if she was safe. He should never have let her go. He needed to know she didn't hate him. He needed to prove to her that he could let her in, even if he wasn't a hundred percent sure he could. But most of all he just needed her there so he could touch her, hold her, kiss her, and soak in all the goodness that made her so special.

It hadn't taken him long to realize that she was right. He'd been hiding behind the whole don't-mix-business-with-pleasure rule. Needing her had *nothing* to do with her executive skills.

All the mornings he'd walked into his office to see her smiling face, he knew his relief hadn't come from knowing she'd put together his workday with masterful dedication. He knew the extra beat in his heart hadn't been because he wouldn't have to worry about anything because Brooke would have it all figured out.

All the joy that encompassed his days revolved around *her.*

In reality he could find another suitable assistant. Maybe they wouldn't be as on the ball as Brooke or have her personality or energy. But he'd be fine. There was only one Brooke, and he didn't want her to just be in his office every day. He wanted her in his life. All the ping-ponging he'd done about mixing business with pleasure had brought him the one thing he feared most.

Losing her.

He grabbed his cell phone and tapped her name in

his contact list. When she didn't answer he figured she was still angry. He couldn't blame her. Only a coward backed away from what he really wanted. If he were honest, he'd admit he'd had deep feelings for her long before Jordan had put the thought in his head.

A shot of panic hit his spine.

What if she wasn't answering her phone because something had happened to her? What if she was in danger?

Dammit.

He should never have let her leave in the middle of the night.

Hell, he should never have let her leave at all. He should have wrapped his arms around her and just told her how she made him feel.

He should have let her in.

When he called the office next and was told Brooke hadn't checked in yet, panic set in. They didn't know she'd quit. But at least he knew now she was still MIA.

He jumped up from the table and dashed out the door to find someone to drive him to the airport to see if his car was parked in the lot as Brooke had informed him it would be. If it was, he'd call every airline that flew out of Portland until he found her. He'd call her roommate to check but he didn't even know the guy's last name, let alone his number.

On a normal day the path up to the main house was a brief walk. Today it seemed like miles. When he got close he was staggered to see his car parked in the driveway. Relief washed over him. Hopefully she'd changed her mind and stayed there for the night just to clear her head. Hopefully she was safe and snug in one of the spare bedrooms and had forgiven him for being such a dunce.

When he heard footsteps in the distance, he turned around.

On the path that wound between the grapevines, he saw Brooke's blond ponytail swinging behind her back as she jogged beside Ethan. The two were carrying on a playful conversation. Ethan teasingly bumped her shoulder then took off running backward while she tried to catch up. When she did, Ethan tweaked her ponytail and she laughed.

What. The. Hell?

They didn't see him as Dec planted his hands on his hips to observe his baby brother's obvious flirtation. Not usually an issue when it was with any other woman. Problem? Judging by the smile on her face, Brooke was flirting back. While Dec was relieved she was safe, he was also annoyed as hell that while he'd been worrying, she'd been goofing off with his brother.

The two kept a steady pace as they jogged off and disappeared into the rows of grapevines. Dec tamped down his emotions and continued on to the house to wait for them to return. He and Brooke needed to have a talk about what had occurred last night. Then he needed to have a little chat with his brother.

When he opened the door and went into the kitchen to wait, he found Nicole at the table eating a bowl of Froot Loops while scanning through Facebook on her tablet. She looked up as he entered the room.

"You look like hell." She grinned. "Trouble sleeping?"

"Did Brooke stay here last night?"

"Maybe." Nicki dug her spoon into the cereal, took a bite, and spoke through a full mouth. "What's it to you if she did?"

"Not that it's any of your business, but I've been worried about her."

"You wouldn't have had to worry if you hadn't acted like such an ass."

"Hey. Watch your mouth."

"I can watch my mouth, but apparently you can't stop being an ass. So who's worse?"

"Good God. You're not going back to bitchy Nicki, are you? I thought we left her behind."

"*We* didn't do anything. *I* did it all with Jordy's help. And no, I'm not going back to being pissed off at the world. I'm just pissed off at *you*. I like Brooke. And I hated seeing her upset last night."

"How did you get her to stay?"

"I didn't. You can thank Ethan for that." She shoveled another spoonful of cereal into her mouth. "He found her upset, crying, and trying to leave. He convinced her to come inside. They got to talking and, well, let's just say those two really hit it off."

Brooke had been crying.

Fuck.

His sister was right. He was an ass.

"What do you mean by they *really hit it off*?"

One dark eyebrow lifted quizzically. "Do you really want me to give you the details?"

"Yes." No matter how ugly they may be. He needed to know.

Nicki stood and picked up her bowl. "Maybe I'll finish breakfast in my room."

"Not so fast." He snagged her by the neck of her frog robe. "Define 'hit it off.'"

"Not my story to tell." She unwound her robe from his grip. "You should talk to Ethan. Or Brooke. Or maybe it would just be easier to talk to both of them at the same time. Because since last night they've been together every single minute."

𝐸than Kincade not only happened to be very good-looking, he was very good company. After the scene with Dec last night Brooke didn't think she'd be laughing so much, so fast. But Ethan had an easy way about him that opened a door to friendly conversation and plenty of jokes at his brother's expense.

However when Ethan told her about Emily—the one who got away—her heart broke. He didn't have to say anything to make it clear he was still in love with his ex. When he mentioned her name his blue eyes lit up even as regret shadowed his handsome face.

"Not saying I haven't moved on, but . . ."

"It's hard to forget a love like that," Brooke said.

"Yeah." Ethan slowed his stride as they jogged along the greenbelt beside the river, close to beautiful downtown Sunshine. The path was lined with gigantic shade trees. Mounds of cheerful flowers bordered the grass.

"It's hard to erase all those crazy plans you made up in your head for the two of you when you know no one else will ever come close," he said. "Which is why I want to help you with Dec. Or at least I want to help my stubborn ass brother realize what he might miss if he doesn't use the brain God gave him."

"Thank you. But using his brain is the problem," Brooke said as they rounded a curve. "He needs to learn how to use and trust his heart."

"Agreed. He's never had a serious relationship that lasted more than a few months at the most. It's like he's afraid to—"

"Ethan!" Brooke hated to interrupt the intriguing conversation but something caught her eye and her imagination flew into overdrive. She pointed to a large commercial building with a large fenced area. A "For Sale" sign was posted on both the building and chain link fence. "What is that?"

"It used to be some kind of distribution center. Place has been empty for a couple of years."

"Do you know how much they're asking for it?"

"Why?" Ethan chuckled. "Looking for a place to bury Dec's body if he doesn't wise up?"

"No." She jogged over to the building, stood on her toes, and looked inside a window. "It's perfect."

"For what?"

She turned to him and couldn't contain her smile. "The dream I've had for more than half my life."

*O*utside on the patio Dec flipped through a house and garden magazine without actually seeing anything printed on the pages. Sunshine bounced off the glass as he glanced down at his watch. Again. Agitated he looked up at the surrounding vineyards where several workers inspected the vines.

Where the hell were they?

He snapped the magazine closed, folded his arms, and leaned his head back to let the sun beat down on his face. A second later his phone chimed and he answered it without looking at the caller's name.

"I just wanted you to know I changed my plans. I'm taking the next flight back to the East Coast."

With his mind solely focused on Brooke he pulled the phone away from his ear and looked at the caller name.

Lili MacKay.

Fuck. Like he needed one more complication today?

"What changed your mind?" he asked bitterly. "Afraid the truth won't be in your favor?"

By her hesitation he knew he'd pissed her off. Not his intention. At least not until they got the facts straight.

"I'm afraid you and your brothers won't be able to handle the truth. My mother was a wonderful person. She wasn't a liar and I'm not either. I'm also not overly fond of being a dart board for your sarcastic remarks or spiteful behavior."

"I'm sorry. I didn't mean to snap at you. There's a lot going on here and—"

"Not my problem." An audible sigh whispered through the phone. "Look, you have my number. I'm not asking anything from any of you. I just wanted to meet the father I never knew. Since that's no longer an option, there's really no need to stay. I have absolutely no hope that any of you would ever accept me, and I'm not so sure I care anyway."

The call disconnected.

"Fuck!" Dec threw his phone down on the table and jammed his fingers into his hair. "Can I get a fucking break?" He looked out over the vineyard again and finally spotted Brooke and Ethan jogging his way. Something dark stuck its nails in the back of his neck.

Or maybe it was something green.

Face flushed from exertion, Brooke's little gray tank top clung to her like a second skin as she ran up the steps to the patio. When he stood to tell her he wanted to talk, she jogged right past him and went into the house.

Ethan stopped, which was great because Dec planned to wring his neck.

"S'up, big bro?" Ethan grinned as he dropped into a patio chair.

"What the hell are you doing?"

"Trying to catch my breath. Long run. I was done a couple miles back but Brooke . . ." He grinned as his thought trailed off. "Brooke is just full of energy and wanted to keep going."

"I don't care if you ran to Timbuktu. I want to know what the hell you're doing with her."

"Brother? I just told you. We were running." Ethan leaned back in the chair and lifted his face to the sun. "Don't get your panties in a wad with me over your own stupidity. And don't get pissed off if others see the opportunity you tossed aside."

"What the hell does *that* mean?"

"It means you fucked up and I'm taking Brooke out to dinner tonight."

"The hell you are." Jealousy curled into a fist and delivered a vicious punch to Dec's heart.

"Yep. We're driving into Portland . . ." Ethan continued like Dec wasn't glaring at him and contemplating murder. "Made reservations at the City Grill. Great food, great views, romantic atmosphere, and they serve our wine. What could be better for getting to know someone?"

"You're not taking Brooke anywhere." Dec knew the thirtieth floor restaurant well. It overlooked the city, the Cascade Mountains, and was known to be one of the most romantic spots in the area. No way in hell would he let his little brother take Brooke there or anywhere else.

"Sure I am."

"No, you're not." He tossed his cell phone to Ethan. "You're calling Lili MacKay and talking her out of skipping town."

"Skipping town? Why's she doing that?"

"Because we treated her like shit yesterday when she hadn't even asked us for anything."

"Looks like there's a lot of that going around." Ethan glared at Dec then picked up the phone. "What do I say to her?"

"I'm sure you'll figure something out." Dec turned to go into the house.

"And where are *you* going?" Ethan asked.

Dec did not miss the mischievous grin planted on his brother's puss.

"To make sure Brooke *never* goes anywhere with *you*."

* * *

Dec walked through the living room, den, and kitchen but Brooke was nowhere to be seen. He climbed the stairs then went room-to-room pressing his ear to each door to find her. He struck pay dirt when he reached the bedroom he'd once shared with Jordan. Through the door he could hear her talking to someone on the phone. Eavesdropping had never been his thing, so when he tapped on the door and she didn't respond, he simply let himself in.

At the small desk, she sat with the phone tucked between her ear and the sweet slope of her bare shoulder, writing down information on a piece of paper. He waited until she finished her call.

"When would I be able to look at it?" she asked the person on the other end of the line. A silent moment passed before she said, "That sounds perfect. I'll see you then."

When she disconnected she looked up with a frown.

"I don't remember asking you to come in."

Her tennis shoes were tinged with dust and her forehead was still moist from the run. And Dec thought she looked beautiful.

"Who were you talking to?"

She huffed out a laugh. "None of your business."

"Brooke, I—"

"Save it." She went to the door, opened it and stood there as if waiting for him to leave. "I think you said enough last night."

"I didn't say nearly enough." He shut the door and leaned a hand on it so she couldn't escape. The action brought them face-to-face. She didn't back down, and that was just one of the things he admired about her. "I especially didn't say I'm sorry."

"You did. In a half-assed kind of way. Exactly what are you sorry about?" Her chin came up in that stubborn way that made him want to grab her and kiss the fury right out of her. "That we had sex—again—and you bailed on me—again—like I was some kind of . . . hooker? An unpaid one to boot."

She took a step closer and jammed her hands down on her hips. Challenge darkened her eyes and furrowed her brow. "Or are you just sorry that I quit?"

Dec's heart gave a hard thump. He needed to be honest—with her and himself. "Both."

"Fine. Then say what you need to say and then please leave. I have an appointment and I don't want to be late."

He kept his hand firmly planted on the door when he really wanted to wrap it around her waist and pull her against him. "Dammit, Brooke. I don't know how to do this."

"*This?* What *this*?" Her hands flew upward. "Apologize?"

"Yes." He jammed his hand through his hair. This was turning out all wrong. "No."

"Well, which is it?"

"You confuse the hell out of me," he growled. "And I can't figure things out. I feel like everything is spinning out of control and I can't get a handle on it."

She folded her arms and shifted her weight to one luscious hip. "Sounds like a personal problem."

"Exactly!"

"Well, now you're confusing *me*. So maybe we should just leave things unsaid and move on." Her chest rose on a full intake of air, then she walked into the adjoining bathroom and closed the door.

He waited, thinking she'd come back out. He waited, thinking by the time she did he'd know exactly what to say so he wouldn't sound like such a stupid ass. But when the shower turned on he knew he'd be waiting awhile.

Fine by him.

He planted himself on the bed, leaned against the headboard, crossed his feet at the ankles, and propped his hands behind his head. When the image of Brooke naked, covered with sweet smelling soap and droplets of warm water flooded his imagination he locked his fingers together so he wouldn't be tempted to open that door and show her exactly how he felt.

Without one damn word.

Chapter 16

The water in the shower could never be cold enough to cool down the temptation to run back out there, grab Dec, and show him how she felt. But this time the man would have to figure things out on his own. She'd already shown him. She'd already told him. She'd already laid her heart at his feet. And she'd be angry as hell if he didn't seem truly mystified about what was going on in his head and heart.

For the first time since she'd known him, Declan Kincade appeared to be completely bewildered.

In his normal day-to-day life he was solid. Thanks to her professional skills he knew exactly what to expect out of his day. He knew how it would begin and how it would end. She'd thrown a glitch into the works, and now for the first time he had to change things up. He had to take himself off autopilot and figure out where to go from here.

Yes, this could all backfire on her. But if he didn't

give their situation considerable thought, it wouldn't matter. She might be ready to find love and live happily ever after, but maybe love had never been on his agenda. Maybe happily ever after for him truly only meant a successful business. He might be her dream man, but maybe his dream woman was someone completely . . . not her.

With more on her mind now than when she'd first gotten in the shower, she rinsed the conditioner from her hair, shut off the water, and toweled off. Refocusing as she stepped out onto the plush bathroom mat, she formulated a plan in her mind regarding the property she was about to see.

Right now, although her heart might not agree, there were more important things in this world than Declan Kincade.

Toweling the moisture from her hair she opened the door to the bedroom. The first thing she saw was a gigantic pair of feet propped casually on the bed. Her eyes shot to the man stretched out as if he owned the place with her traitorous dog stretched across his lap. His blue eyes shot to the embarrassing detail that she was completely naked.

"Oh my God." She rushed back into the bathroom. "Dec! What are you still doing here?"

She flinched at his low chuckle.

"Waiting for you."

"I kicked you out." She came back into the bedroom wrapped in a towel. "You aren't supposed to be here."

"But look what I'd have missed had I left."

"Exactly." She exhaled. "Could you go now? Please?"

"I have nowhere to go. My assistant bailed on me and I have no idea what's on my agenda."

"I'll tell you what's on your freaking agenda." She swung her arm and pointed to the door. "Get the hell out!"

A slow smile tilted the corners of his lusciously masculine lips. "You can't kick me out of my own room."

"Your what?"

"This is *my* room. *My* bed. You can't kick me out."

"Are you always this obstinate?"

"You should know." His heated gaze dipped to where she had the towel tucked between her breasts. "We've worked side by side for four years."

"Right. I guess you just hid the major part of your jerkiness from me all this time."

He unfolded his hands from behind his head, swung his legs off the bed, and sat up. Brooke took a step back because she now realized that the closer he got the more her IQ sank to a disastrous *need him, must have him now* level.

He captured her by her elbows and pulled her in. The delicious scents of his warm body and sandalwood aftershave mixed together with her citrus shampoo and honey body soap and made her light-headed.

"Avoidance is never a good response, Brooke. And neither is running away. I've recently become painfully aware of that." His grip was firm but his fingers were tender on her skin. "We need to talk."

"No can do." She lifted her chin and looked into his devastatingly blue eyes surrounded by thick dark lashes. "I have an appointment. And I'm not coming back to work for you. So there's really nothing to talk about."

"You're wrong." His fingers gently caressed the side of her face, tucked her hair behind her ear. "There's plenty to say. Starting with the fact that I plan to win you back."

"Did you not just hear me?" She backed away from his touch. She couldn't take it without the fear of crumpling like a wad of paper. "I'm not coming back to work for you. Ever."

"And I wasn't talking about work," he said as a parting shot before he walked out the door.

*B*rooke putt-putted up to the commercial building in Aunt Pippy's VW. She was grateful Dec's aunt had been generous enough to let her borrow it again. All it had taken was a quick explanation of her intentions with this viewing and Aunt Pippy was strongly on board Team Brooke.

After Dec's declaration that he planned to win her back, she wondered exactly what he intended. She didn't mind admitting that his insistence was quite a turn-on. Still, she had to make plans for her life.

With or without him.

She might want Dec in her life, but she didn't believe in putting life on hold until someone else made up their mind whether they wanted to be a part of it or not.

As she parked the VW in the lot, an elderly woman in a red blazer and dark blue pants got out of the Lexus in the next space.

"Mrs. Carr?" Brooke extended her hand. "It's nice to meet you."

"The pleasure is all mine."

The woman's bluish-gray bubble hairdo was sprayed stiff and her perfume was overly strong, but she seemed nice enough. All that really mattered was that the interior of the building would fit what Brooke had in mind and the price was right.

"Let's take a look inside, shall we?" Mrs. Carr held out her hand for Brooke to lead the way. When they reached the door, she unlocked it, reached inside, and flipped some switches that shed overhead light on the interior. "The building has a total of twelve thousand square feet with twenty-four parking spaces out front."

On the wall near the door a series of offices had been constructed, which gave Brooke a head start on what she would need later. The rest of the interior was completely open space. On two sides a series of garage door type windows would let the light in once the vertical blinds were removed. And the optimum height ceiling would allow for taller and bulkier structures without overwhelming the space.

Exhilaration springboarded through Brooke's blood. "It's perfect."

"I'm so glad." By the size of the agent's smile, Brooke figured she smelled a sale. "Let's take a look at the outdoor space. The bare land equals a little over an acre."

Mrs. Carr stood near the building while Brooke walked around the property. A parking lot was already paved. There was no concrete to tear up. It was all fresh ground and ready to go for what she had in mind. Not for the first time did she appreciate all the financial advice Dec had given her. She appreciated even more that she had been smart enough to listen. Because right now she had a nice sum sitting in the bank waiting for such an opportunity.

Fingers crossed, she returned to the real estate agent. "Let's talk price and negotiation."

A little while later Brooke headed back to Sunshine Creek in Aunt Pippy's VW, barely able to contain her excitement. A million ideas swirled through her head and she made mental notes for everything she needed to do in the coming days.

But before all that, she had a date.

People could say what they wanted, but when Dec made up his mind, he steered straight in that direction. Wondering what Brooke's appointment and phone call had been all about he'd waited in the house until she'd driven away in his aunt's car. Curiosity made him consider following her, but that just seemed too stalkerish. Hopefully his brother would enlighten him on what had Brooke in such a hurry.

Outside on the patio, he found Ethan at a table with a cell phone still pressed to his ear, his face turned toward the sun, his feet kicked up on the chair next to him, and a glass of wine on the table. His brother currently looked the epitome of relaxed.

Dec was about to change all that right now.

He stood behind Ethan, towering over him, waiting for the phone call to end. Had it not been an important one, Dec would have interrupted. But with a very edgy Lili MacKay on the other end of the line, Ethan's charm was crucial.

"You could continue to stay at the Salty Seagull," Ethan was saying, "but you might consider moving over here to the B and B."

Pause.

"No. I'm not kidding. While we wait on the reports, you might as well get to know all of us. After all, if we are family, you'll have to decide whether you want to be an active member or run like hell." Ethan brushed a honeybee from the sleeve of his T-shirt. "As an added bonus, if you're nearby I can pre-warn you about which brothers are the scariest."

Ethan chuckled.

"All right then. I'll check back with you tomorrow. For dinner give Mr. Pickle Buns a chance. And make sure you order the cheese stuffed Doritos. I promise you won't be sorry."

"You invited her to stay *here*?" Dec asked when Ethan ended the call.

"Best way to keep an eye on her, right? Besides, if she actually agrees to it, that might be a sign that she's really interested in getting to know the family. Someone who was scamming wouldn't necessarily do that."

"You're a genius." Dec sat down, literally stunned that Ethan had come up with that solution. Not that his brother was dense by any means, just that his mind didn't usually travel to resolutions other than ones that involved firefighting. "Why didn't I think of that?"

"Because your head is too far up your ass about Brooke to think straight. No worries, big bro. I got this."

Dec wanted to wipe the smirk off Ethan's face. "Speaking of Brooke. FYI, you're *not* taking her out tonight."

"Yeah. I am."

"Not if you want to be able to walk tomorrow."

Ethan grinned. "Are you threatening me?"

"Yes."

"Because you just want to pull a power play? Or because you really care about Brooke?"

"Because I really care about Brooke."

"Not because she's a challenge or something you feel the need to control?"

"She *is* a challenge, and that's one of the things I love about her. Shit, the woman had me up on a stage singing karaoke in front of a bar full of drunks. Who else could get me to do that?"

As his brother shrugged, Dec realized the words he'd said. The truth hit him like a bulldozer.

He loved her.

He was *in* love with her.

Damn.

"Why would I feel the need to control her when she's perfect the way she is?" Dec asked. "I've been blind and stupid for too long. It's time to grow up and work hard for the one thing—the one person—I can't live without."

"About damn time." Ethan folded his arms and leaned back in his chair. "So what's your plan?"

*B*rooke felt decidedly overdressed as she got ready to meet up with Ethan downstairs at the main house. Nicki had taken on a little sister role and insisted on helping with her makeup and hair. Then she insisted Brooke wear the little black dress she'd bought to go with her new pair of Ariat cowboy boots. Though they wore the same size clothes, Nicki's feet were smaller and Brooke opted to wear the one and only pair of high heels she'd brought on the trip. By the time Nicki was done, Brooke looked in the mirror, pleased to see the woman looking back.

Her hair had been styled in loose shiny curls and her makeup had been accented with the smoky eye look. A sheer red gloss coated her lips, silver hoops sparkled from her ears, and not an ounce of the panic she felt showed on her face.

"He's not going to know what hit him," Nicole said, giving Brooke a nod of approval.

"*He* meaning . . ."

"Dec. Of course."

"But Dec won't be there."

Nicole shrugged. "We'll see."

Brooke had never been agreeable to deception of any kind, but Ethan insisted his brother needed an extra little push to get him to open his eyes. Brooke thought if Dec didn't open his eyes on his own what was the point? Still, she'd been unable to talk Ethan out of the date. He'd suggested that either way, they both needed to eat dinner so why not have an enjoyable experience at a top-rate restaurant. With her stomach empty and rumbling she was now glad she'd finally agreed.

Ethan waited at the foot of the stairs in a light blue button-down shirt and gray slacks. His hair had been casually styled. And if she had been any other woman he would have stolen her breath.

Ethan grinned. "Absolutely gorgeous."

"Are you sure about this?" she asked him as he offered her his arm and escorted her to his SUV.

"Never been more sure in my life. And believe me . . ." He opened the passenger door and waited for her to slide in. "That's saying something."

Half an hour later they were in the elevator making their way to the thirtieth floor restaurant. When they arrived, Ethan approached the hostess and gave her his name. As they were about to be seated, Ethan's phone chirped. He pulled it from his pocket, glanced down, and apologized for having to take the call. He asked the hostess to go ahead and seat Brooke and said he'd be right back.

Brooke knew there was a lot going on in the Kincade family with the business and the sudden appearance of a possible secret sibling. Not to mention the possibility of a connection between the missing money and the secret sibling.

With a hospitable smile the hostess led Brooke to a private table by the window. The City Grill was classically decorated with natural elements. A slate wall with a trickling waterfall divided their seating from the next table and a portion of the restaurant. While the hostess set the menus down, a server delivered two glasses of ice water. Brooke looked out over the city view where the lights sparkled in the clear night and reflected off the waters of the Columbia River. The scenery was incredible, but it didn't stop her conscience from drilling at her that she should not be there.

Nervous, she nudged the napkin wrapped silverware on the linen tablecloth and took a breath. The best thing to do to get through the night was to try to actually enjoy it.

"The view may be stunning, but *you* take my breath away."

Brooke's heart took a stuttered step. She looked up. The man smiling down at her before he took the seat across the table from her was not her date.

"What are you doing here?"

Declan's dark eyes glittered as a server delivered a bottle of Sunshine Creek Vineyard Titania Private Reserve Cabernet with two glasses to their table. There was only silence from the man across the table as the server poured a small amount and allowed Dec to sample it before he poured full glasses. When the server left, Dec raised his glass and prompted her to do the same.

He tapped his glass to hers. "You didn't really think I'd let my little brother take you out for a romantic dinner, did you?"

"Why would you care who I go out with?" She sipped the wine that hinted of black cherry, vanilla, and mocha. "Or is it merely a case of sibling rivalry?"

"It has nothing to do with that." He sipped his wine

then looked at her over the rim of the glass. "And everything to do . . . with you."

For the life of her she tried not to let that matter. "Why the change of heart?"

"Not a change of heart at all," he said. "Let's call it an awakening."

Brooke refused to get her hopes up. She'd put herself out there only to get knocked down. He'd said he planned to win her over. While she had a great imagination, she had no idea what that meant. Still, she loved him, and she knew she'd give him more chances than he probably deserved.

"I'm not going to make this easy on you." She leaned in and put on her best flirt. "In fact, I'm going to run you through every test I can think of to see if you're really sincere or full of BS."

"Test me. Challenge me." He leaned in and the corners of his sexy mouth lifted. "Just give me a chance. I'm letting you in, Brooke, and I'm up for anything you send my way."

The declaration and the dare sizzled through her as powerfully as if his hot tongue was licking her core.

"Anything?"

Before he could respond, the server showed up to take their dinner requests. Dec sat back in his chair and ordered for the two of them. No seared ahi this time. Of course he knew what she liked. They'd shared meals over many business meetings. But that he took charge and proceeded to order several delicious entrées to make sure she'd have anything she desired turned her on in an unreasonable way.

He wasn't just ordering to impress her. He was letting her know that he knew her, that he was thinking of her and not just absently rattling anything off the list. Each entrée ordered sounded full of flavor but light, instead of something heavy that might make her drowsy.

What did he have in mind for after dinner?

"Anything," he said, returning to their conversation when the server left. "Although, if you *give it to me* while leaning in a little more, that would make it even better."

She glanced down and realized that her position gave him quite an eyeful of cleavage. Instead of straightening and tugging the neckline up, she leaned in more. "Like this?"

A low, sexy chuckle rumbled from his chest. "Exactly like that."

He reached across the table and took her hand. He traced featherlight caresses across her fingers with his thumb. "It looks as if you already have a challenge in mind."

"Maybe I do." Letting the anticipation build, she slid her hand away, lifted her wineglass, and sipped her wine. "Maybe I'll find out how sincere you really are right now."

"You won't scare me away."

"We'll see about that." She took another drink and set her glass down on the white tablecloth. "Ready?"

"For you?" He smiled. "Always."

Oh, he really was very good at flirting when he set his mind to it.

"All right then. I should probably remind you right

now that no matter how much you wine and dine me, and no matter how lovely the compliments, I am not now nor am I ever going to come back to work for you."

"I believe you made that clear."

"And you took me seriously?"

His dark hair gleamed beneath the overhead light as he slightly tilted his head in acknowledgment. "I always do."

"I'm looking for a partner," she said.

"What kind of partner?"

"Does that scare you?"

"Not even a little."

"Looks like I'll have to try harder."

"Harder sounds good."

She chuckled, then hit him with exactly what she had in mind. "I'm looking for a lifetime partner. Someone who will be there during the good times and the bad. Someone who will love me and be the love of my life. Someone who will build a life with me and raise a family. Someone who will take care of me when I need them. Someone who won't waste my time with games and promises they never intend to keep. Someone who will let me into their soul as much as I'll let them into mine."

"That's a long list."

"I'm very good at making lists."

"I know you are."

"So let me ask you, Dec . . ." There was only one way to approach this and find out exactly where he stood. "Could the someone I'm looking for be you?"

She took another small sip of wine and held his

gaze, waiting for him to either back down or get up and run.

Disappointed when he said nothing, she shook her head. "I didn't think so."

She downed the rest of the wine in her glass then reached for the bottle.

"Hold on. Don't discount me so fast." He reached out and took the bottle from her hand. "I'm all in."

"All in?" She snorted with disbelief. "Then why the hesitation? And why do you look like a ghost just chased you from a haunted house?"

"Truth?" The broad shoulders beneath his gray coat shrugged. "Because I've never thought of any of that before. I've never dated a woman for more than a couple of months. I've never thought about marriage, or having babies, or growing old with someone. It's a new concept for me."

"Then why are you here?"

"Because now that I've thought about those things, I want them to be with you. And only you."

Once upon a time she'd thought hearing him say those words was all she'd ever want. But he'd mentioned nothing about love. Brooke knew you couldn't force someone to love you. They either did or they didn't. And while she did believe Dec truly did care for her, she didn't believe he was in I-want-to-spend-the-rest-of-my-life-with-you love with her.

Before she broke down and cried, she decided to steer the conversation in a different direction.

"That's nice of you to say that."

His eyes narrowed. *"Nice?"*

She nodded.

"I didn't say that to sound *nice*. I said it because I mean it."

"Well, now I have another challenge for you. I'm also looking for a business partner. They can be active or silent; it's entirely up to them. I'd like to give you the first crack at the opportunity."

"Changing the subject isn't going to make me forget." His jaw clenched. "I'm not done with the first part of this conversation."

"Call it a small detour."

"What kind of business are you considering?" he asked.

"Are you interested?" she pushed, again noting his slight hesitation. She knew she was completely taking him out of his comfort zone. He was a numbers guy through and through. He'd never agree to anything until he could perform a full evaluation. She also expected him to tell her she was crazy because she didn't know the first thing about running a business. But she did. She'd done her homework. And what she didn't know, she'd learn.

"Brooke? Right now I'm very interested." His eyes locked onto hers. He leaned in slightly and kept his voice low. "I'm interested in slipping that little black dress over your head to see what you have on underneath. I'm interested in sliding my tongue down the side of your neck until I reach those tempting breasts you keep taunting me with. And I'm interested in letting my hands and my mouth worship your body. I know where all your hot spots are, and I'm interested in setting fire to each and every one of them. And afterward, I'm interested in holding you close and never letting you go."

The need to fan herself with the cloth napkin became as crucial as taking her next breath. But that would show weakness, and then he'd pounce.

He'd say no to her proposal. And then she'd know that his sincerity only ran skin-deep. She didn't actually need a business partner, but she needed to know exactly where he stood.

"Are you trying to distract me?" she asked. Because it was almost working.

"Absolutely not." He reached for her hand again. "I'm just letting you know I'm interested . . . in *anything* you have to offer. I just want you to know something about me first. Something only my parents knew and took to the grave with them."

He sounded so serious and looked so guarded her nerves kicked in like a rocket.

"It took me a while to figure things out," he said. "To understand why I've been so . . . solitary. Why I've been so focused on only one thing."

"What is it?"

"When I was a kid, I had problems with school. My grades were always low and I got into a lot of fights with kids who made fun of me. I had zero confidence. And I figured someday I'd let my anger and frustration get the best of me and end up in jail. After years of being told I had ADHD and that someone should just give me a pill to calm me the hell down, finally a teacher made a suggestion to my parents to have me tested. Turns out I'm dyslexic."

"That must have been very hard for you."

"To find out I had a learning disorder?" He shook his head. "It was the best news I'd had in a long time. At least it answered the question of why I couldn't see letters and numbers correctly. Still, I was embarrassed that I wasn't like my brothers. I wanted to be like them. I wanted to finish my homework fast so I could run outside and play just like they did. But it took me a lot longer to do anything, and eventually I just kind of retreated into my own environment."

"You were protecting yourself."

"I guess you could call it that. I made a promise to myself that I wouldn't let it drag me down. I promised that I'd figure it out and I'd become successful, the best at whatever I did, even when all I really wanted was to be more easygoing like my brothers."

"Oh Dec." The pressure in her chest intensified and squeezed her heart.

"Somehow I got lost in that single-minded focus. I forgot to look around and see what else was out there. I still struggle, especially when I'm tired. But my eyes are open now, Brooke. And all I see is you."

It wasn't a declaration of love. It was better. Because it was as deeply honest as she'd ever seen him. And she knew that what he'd said had come from his heart.

"I'm never going to be perfect," he said. "I'm always going to have challenges when I have too many things on my plate. But if you want a partner? I'm your man."

That was the moment Brooke melted into a complete pile of starry-eyed goo.

* * *

They tabled the discussion when the server brought their entrées. Throughout the dinner and then the butterscotch cheesecake and vanilla bean crème brûlée desserts, Brooke questioned him about his past. He was more open and honest with her than he'd ever been with anyone in his life.

But she hadn't reopened the door to the discussion they'd had previous to him telling her about his dyslexia.

He didn't feel like she was judging him, but her silence definitely made him question the sanity of revealing his Achilles' heel.

As they headed back to Sunshine over the N. Steel Bridge, Dec asked her, "Where would you like to go now?" The bridge lights flashed inside the darkened car while the deck made thu-thump sounds beneath the wheels. "We don't have to go back home if there's something you'd like to do."

Her smooth, sleek eyebrows lifted. "How good are you at following directions? And no, that's not a slight about the dyslexia."

"You should know how I am following directions. You give me orders every day."

"Not anymore."

The reminder that she would no longer be his right arm sank like a stone in the pit of his stomach. "True. So what do you have in mind? A walk in the park? A boat ride?"

"Let's stick to business for now."

While she gave him directions to somewhere in Sunshine, he couldn't help being disappointed by her response. Maybe that's what she'd had to deal with from him all along. All business. No play.

Brooke wasn't an all business kind of woman. She was free-spirited and fun. She was the type to come up with bucket list items that anyone else might consider ridiculous for a woman not yet thirty years old to do. But he understood why. He also understood that he'd been the one to take her spark away.

Now he had to give it back.

No matter what or how long it took.

And he had to convince her that his feelings for her were true.

No matter what or how long it took.

For the rest of the drive, she kept her gaze out the window. But as soon as they drove into Sunshine, her foot started tapping nervously. Two blocks off Main Street, she told him to pull the car over to the curb. As soon as he parked she got out and stood on the sidewalk looking at a dark, empty building behind a chain link fence.

When he joined her, he dropped his coat over her bare shoulders to guard her against the chill. "What do you see when you look at this building?"

"My future." She walked up to the chain link fence and curled her fingers around the wires. "I see a place where families can go together to have fun. A place where teens can go so they don't get in trouble because they're bored. I see a place I can be proud of and a chance for me to be a member of a community. I see a place where I can . . . belong."

"You see all that in a concrete building and a patch of dirt?"

She nodded. "Confession time for me now."

She turned toward him and what he saw in her eyes was something he'd never seen in her before.

Shame.

This night was turning out completely different than he'd imagined.

"Growing up in the community I wasn't allowed to read anything except the Bible. I never saw television or movies. I was never allowed to run outside and play or use my imagination like a normal child. I was forced to study and to serve. And that was it."

She took a breath.

"When I escaped I had to learn to have fun. I had no idea what it was like to play make-believe or sit down at a table and play a board game. I had no clue what it felt like to swing up into the sky or climb a tree and pretend to be a monkey. That's why I keep pushing you to make that bucket list. That's why I keep trying to push you out of your comfort zone. Because I want you to see and feel all the things you've sheltered yourself from. I had all those fun things locked away from me, but you've done that to yourself. I want you to have the best life possible." She touched the sleeve of his jacket. "With or without me."

Love, pure and simple, radiated from her dark eyes and beautiful smile.

Dec had never met a more unselfish person in his life. She loved him. And if he let her go, he'd never have the pleasure of sharing in all those wild and crazy things she wanted to do from that bucket list.

She turned her attention back toward the concrete

building. "I see brightly colored neon lights. I hear the sounds of splashing water, music, and laughter. I smell popcorn and pizza."

"All that from a concrete building?"

"It's more than a concrete building to me. I want to build a family fun zone with bowling, miniature golf, arcade games, and a snack bar with everything from corn dogs to onion rings. I want others to have the fun with their loved ones that I never had."

Silence passed between them as he looked at the structure.

"Can you see it, Dec?" Joy flitted in her eyes. "Can you see my dream?"

"Of course I can." He caught her smiling face between his hands and pressed his lips to hers. "And if anyone can make their dream a reality, it's you."

Chapter 17

A light rain began to fall when Dec dropped Brooke off at the front door of the main house. Their relationship had taken a wonderfully dramatic turn, but Brooke wasn't ready to jump back into old habits. Both of them could use a little more thinking time before they moved forward, which was why she'd decided to remain at the main house instead of going with him back to his grandfather's cabin.

A little starry-eyed when she walked into the house, she almost jumped out of her skin when she found a painting party going on in the living room. Aunt Pippy had beige paint in her fireball hair and there were khaki colored paw prints all over the plastic drop cloth. Several teenage girls wore splotches on their T-shirts and even more had paint on their faces.

"Hi!" Nicki came down a ladder to give Brooke a hug. "This is Brooke," she said to the others in the room gathered around a game of Twister. "She's the one my brother Dec is hot for."

Oh my God.

"I'm not sure I—"

"Brooke! I've been dying to meet you." An attractive woman with a ponytail and dark-framed glasses came to shake her hand. "I'm Lucy."

"I'm a hugger," Brooke said and Lucy complied with a chuckle. "It's so good to meet the beauty who tamed the beast."

"Thank you." Lucy positively beamed. "It wasn't an easy task, but worth it. Nicki says you're rowing the same boat."

"Trying to."

Lucy sympathetically patted her shoulder. "The Kincade men do have a way of keeping us guessing, don't they."

"Agreed."

"Just don't give up." Lucy bent down and dipped her paintbrush in the paint tray. "That's the main thing. I promise it will be worth the trouble he puts you through."

"Thanks." Brooke grinned at the woman with whom she could see becoming fast friends. "I'll keep that in mind when my brain and heart feel like scrambled eggs."

"We're having a painting party," Nicole explained, then proceeded to introduce Brooke to her girlfriends. In the middle of all the chaos was Moochie, slurping the chin of a dark-haired girl wearing a paint splattered WSU sweatshirt.

"When we get done painting we're going to have a slumber party and an all-night chick flick festival," Nicki announced. "Want to join us?"

How could she possibly say no? Besides, going

upstairs to crawl into bed alone with nothing to think about but Dec didn't sound like much fun.

"I'd love to. Let me go upstairs and change."

"How'd *the date* go?" Nicole whispered.

"I was tricked. Dec showed up. Did you know about that?"

"Moi?"

"The hand on your chest and the fluttering eyelashes do not make you look less guilty."

"Hey. Told you. I'm Team Brooke. But I'm a little Team Dec too." Nicole gave her a squeezy hug. "Go get changed and promise you'll come back down."

"I'll do my best." She tweaked Nicole's nose. "You little sneak." It was hard to be mad at the girl when the evening had turned out so wonderful.

As soon as she closed the bedroom door and kicked off her shoes, her cell phone rang.

Dec's number popped up on the screen before she answered. "Miss me already?"

"Yes." His deep, sexy voice sent a tingle straight into her panties. "What are you wearing?"

She chuckled. "The same thing I had on when you dropped me off at the house minus the shoes."

"That's not what you're supposed to say."

"Oh?" She loved the playfulness in his tone. "Pray tell, what am I supposed to say?"

"That you're wearing nothing but a pair of lace panties and high heels, and that you were thinking about me and just about to get down to business."

Laughter bubbled up from her throat. "Is that right? And what, may I ask, are you wearing?"

He paused and her curiosity spiked.

"Socks."

"Just socks?"

"Nope. Now I'm wearing nothing."

"Seriously?" She'd seen him naked and it was a glorious sight. That tall, lean body, and all those tightly rippled muscles. Mmmm.

"Want to come check?" he asked.

"What if I said yes?"

"I'd tell you to hurry the hell up."

She liked this playful banter and she hated for it to end.

"I'm supposed to put on my pajamas and go downstairs for a slumber party with Nicole and her friends to watch chick flicks."

"Sweetheart, if you're looking for romance, I can do better than watching a movie."

"Is that right?"

"Mmm-hmm. But for now, I just wanted to say that I'm behind you and your dream one hundred percent. You inspire me. And I admire you for the courage it took to kick a boring job aside and go for it."

"I never really found my job with you boring. In fact, you taught me how to stay on my toes."

"All the better for you to kiss me."

"Now how am I supposed to go downstairs and watch chick flicks with *that* on my mind?"

"You'll think of something." He sighed. "And now I'm going to go to bed, think of you, and . . ."

"And?" Why did all kinds of dirty thoughts race through her head?

"And figure out exactly where I can fit into that amazing dream of yours."

*W*ay before morning came, Dec gave up trying to sleep. All night he'd been haunted with a list of things out of his control and a list of things he'd screwed up. Both had grown quite extensive, which verified that it was definitely time for a change.

He kicked back the covers and strode to the window in his favorite gray sweatpants—the only article of clothing he owned that showed any real sign of wear and tear. Everything else in his closet had been pressed and starched to within an inch of its life. Everything in his dresser drawers had been folded neatly and color-coded. True, not by him, but that didn't make him any less pathetically organized to the point of dreary.

Through the window he noticed dawn had not yet peeked above the mountains and a light drizzle soaked the ground. He went out into the kitchen and began to make a pot of coffee before he realized he was already fully awake. Right now caffeine wasn't what he needed.

He needed Brooke.

Last night had been too quiet without her and Moochie in the house. His bed had been cold. His arms and his heart had been empty. He'd told her he needed to figure out where he could fit into her future and he'd meant it. While the clock ticked toward morning, he'd taken a careful overview of his life.

His days were a staid routine, altered only by how

many times Brooke came into his office and flashed her dimples. His nights had been a string of lifeless conversations with women he appreciated but didn't really care about.

He wanted to care about someone.

He wanted to need someone. He didn't want his gravestone to just say *He made a lot of money for people.* Brooke breathed life into everything she did. Somehow she'd taken herself out of the hell she'd been living in and found a way to be free in heart and soul. Without her, everything seemed meaningless.

Instead of consuming caffeine for an adrenaline rush, he decided to go for a run. Exercise always made him feel better. And if he couldn't feel good by making love to Brooke right now, at least a run would clear his head and give him a little more clarity about his future.

As soon as he stepped out onto the path through the grapevines, his shoes squished in the mud. Running might not be such a good idea in these conditions. The drizzle had become heavier and the last thing he needed to do was break a leg. But a walk would do.

Realizing it wouldn't really do much to keep him dry, he pulled the hoodie up over his head anyway. Dawn had barely begun to touch the sky with shades of pink and gold, but around him he could see the grapevines coming into full bloom. The air smelled sweet and earthy. And as he turned at the corner of the pinot gris, he saw Brooke in the distance.

Wearing the floral dress she'd been wearing the night they'd first made love, she danced in the rain beside her little dog. The fabric clung to her wet body like a second skin. When she lifted her face to the sky, held out her arms, and twirled in a circle, Moochie danced at her feet and barked.

The sound of Brooke's laughter tickled the center of his chest and made him smile. An overwhelming need to hold her quickly moved his feet in her direction.

He snuck up from behind and pulled her into his arms. She squeaked with surprise before realizing it was him. Then her surprise turned to laughter.

"What are you doing out here?"

He captured her face in his hands. "Watching the most beautiful creature on earth dance like a fairy princess among the magical vines." He lowered his head and pressed his lips to hers. As the rain fell around them she curled her arms around his neck, lifted to the toes of her red rain boots, and leaned into his body.

The air was cool, but he shivered for an entirely different reason when she opened up to him and answered his kiss with the sweet slide of her tongue and a sigh.

God, he could kiss this woman all day.

All night.

He tipped his head back, stroked her cheekbones with his thumbs, and looked deep into her eyes. "Teach me," he said, his voice rough from the spiraling passion.

Confusion moved across her face. "Teach you what?"

"How to dance in the rain. How to separate life from work. How to be the man you want and need me to be."

"Oh Dec."

"Before you walked out the door the other night, you said you were perfect for me. You were right." He pressed his mouth to her cool, damp forehead. "Please teach me how to be perfect for you."

Tears blurred the beautiful chocolate of her eyes.

"You don't have to change for me."

"I know." Gently he kissed the rain from her lips. "I want to change. For *us*."

Chapter 18

A majority of women longed to hear three little words from the person they loved. Brooke's heart soared with the sound of one.

Us.

"You know what's on my bucket list?" Rain dripped from his hair as he touched his forehead to hers.

"Mud wrestling?"

He laughed. "No."

"Then what?"

"This." He scooped her up into his arms and took long strides through the mud. After a rain-spraying body shake, Moochie trotted behind them.

"Exactly what is *this*?" Brooke laughed at the sound of his shoes squishing with each step.

"Carrying you off to make love to you all day with the rain beating down on the roof."

"All day?" Oh how she liked the sound of that.

He kissed her lips. "And then some."

"What about food?" she teased. "If we're going to make love all day, we'll need nourishment."

"You can have anything you want as long as you stay naked and in my arms."

"It could get messy," she said, tightening her arms around his neck.

"It *will* get messy."

"Awesome. You're off to a good start, Mr. Kincade."

"I plan to finish well too."

When they reached his grandfather's cabin, he kicked off his muddy shoes, opened the door, and carried her across the threshold.

Once Moochie shook off beneath the awning and the door closed behind them, Dec set Brooke's feet on the ground. Then he backed her up against the door, leaned into her, and kissed the breath from her lungs. Beneath his sweatpants, his erection was thick and hard. His greedy hands and fingers caressed her through the wet fabric of her dress. They touched, teased, caressed. His mouth left her lips and with impatient hunger he kissed his way down her neck.

Smooth and sure, his hands slipped beneath the dress and pulled it over her head. It landed with a soggy plop on the floor. Dec wasted no time in returning his hands to her body. His touch made her hot and the friction warmed her up even more. When his lips covered her nipple and he sucked it inside his mouth where it was warm and wet, the sizzle took a cliff dive right down between her legs.

"All day starts right now." His teeth gently tugged her erect nipple while he pushed his pants off his lean hips. "I need to be inside you."

"Yes." To her own ears her voice sounded strangled. "Take me right here. Right now."

His big hands gripped her bottom and he lifted her. "Wrap your legs around me."

Without hesitation, she locked her legs and the red rain boots around him. He plunged inside her slick heat with such pleasure-minded commitment they both moaned with gratification.

"God." He exhaled and dropped his forehead to hers. "I definitely want this to last all day."

"Me too." The way he moved inside her was as if his body knew exactly where to touch.

"But it's not going to this time." He kissed her. "I just want you too damn bad."

Smooth, steady strokes and passionate kisses set the pace, as if they couldn't get enough of each other. As if the world were about to end and they only had moments to love each other. He whispered naughty things in her ear and she whispered back.

"Wrap your arms around me," he said, his hands clasping her rear end tighter. "I need more." Buried deep inside her, and with her arms and legs securely wrapped around him, he carried her into the bedroom. Creatively he managed to get them horizontal without breaking their bond. After a few slow thrusts, he left her body to slide down and put his mouth between her legs.

The magical things he did with his tongue sent a shock wave through her nerves and the tingles that began at her toes slowly moved upward.

"Dec? Please come back inside me. Now!"

He raised his body over hers, pushed inside, and filled her completely. The tingles spiraled into the hottest, most powerful orgasm of her life. She knew God didn't exactly have anything to do with it, but she couldn't stop praising him over and over and over.

Dec's powerful body stilled and a low, satisfied groan rumbled from deep within his chest. Their hearts pounded together, separated only by flesh and bone. He pushed inside her several more times until his orgasm stopped pulsating.

And then they laughed. Because the power of the release for both of them was like lighting a firework and dancing naked beneath the fiery sparkling shower.

Dec rolled to his back and took her with him. He wrapped his arms around her and held her tight. And all she could think was she'd found the place she wanted to be forever.

*S*ex was supposed to be satisfying. Otherwise you were either doing it wrong or wasting your time. But Dec knew the kind of satisfaction that now curled around his heart wasn't like anything he'd known before. All at once he felt the need to protect, to please, to adore, to hang on to this woman forever and never let her go.

He settled his hand at the back of her head and brought her face down so he could kiss her. "Have I won you over yet?"

"Your body has." She chuckled. "The rest of you I'm not so sure about."

"I guess that means I'm going to have to prove I can cook breakfast."

"Forget breakfast. I guess that means you're going to have to prove you're not wearing running shoes anymore."

"My feet are bare." He wiggled his toes against her leg.

"You know what I mean."

He rolled to his side and tucked her against him before he pulled the comforter over both of them. He wasn't a spooning kind of guy, but with Brooke he was more than willing to become one.

"I'm not going anywhere. I'm staying right here . . ." He dropped a kiss on her bare shoulder. "Snuggled up with you."

She giggled.

"What's so funny?"

"I've never heard you say *snuggle* before."

"I plan to get very good at it." He wrapped his arm around her waist and pulled her closer.

Just as he was about to doze off, she whispered, "Dec?"

"Hmmm?"

"If I wake up and you're not here, I will hunt you down and squash you like a bug."

He kissed her shoulder. "Nowhere to go when the only place I want to be is with you."

The rain cleared by late afternoon and the stillness of the weather brought a certain peacefulness and contentment inside the cabin. Brooke had woken up first and nearly cried with relief when she found herself still wrapped in Dec's arms. For a long time she lay there watching him sleep. His nearly black hair was mussed, his thick dark lashes fanned over his cheeks, his beard scruff was sexy as hell, and a satisfied smile had settled on his lips. He was a gorgeous man. But there was so much more that was special beneath the surface of all that tan, smooth skin.

She'd never imagined he'd had so many troubles growing up. He should be proud of the man he'd become—she knew she was. It was easier, now that he'd explained, to see how the dyslexia had controlled everything he'd done. Or hadn't done, for that matter. Now he wanted to learn to have fun. To be free. To enjoy life.

She was only too happy to help him along that path.

Lifting a lock of her now dry hair, she tickled his nose. In response, he wrapped his long arm around her and rolled her beneath him.

"Were you faking?" she asked.

"Faking isn't worth my time." He bent his head and would have kissed the pants off her if she'd had any on. "From now on, everything you get with me is the real deal."

"I can't wait."

He nudged his erection against her mound and grinned. "Neither can I."

Sometime after dark they finally took a shower and rummaged through the cupboards for something to eat. When they came up empty, Brooke fed and walked

Moochie while Dec got dressed so they could grab some dinner. To her amazement, not a single restaurant in Sunshine delivered. In Brooke's mind that classified the town as quaint. Dec—who lived in the middle of Southern California's to-go paradise—called it inconvenient.

A few minutes later as they walked out to his car, a blond-haired woman went into the cabin next door.

"Shit."

Brooke looked up. "What's wrong?"

"I totally forgot about her."

"Her?"

"Lili MacKay."

"That's your *maybe* sister?"

He nodded. "Ethan invited her to stay here until we find out if she's for real or not."

"She's gorgeous."

"In case you didn't notice, she's also blond and fair skinned. You see anyone else like that in our family?"

"No, but . . ." Okay, the man, and most likely the rest of the Kincades, were clearly in denial. "Genetics don't always follow a pattern. Yes, all of you have very dominant dark hair and blue eyes, but I have married friends who have one daughter that looks exactly like the dad—light curly hair, fair skinned, and green eyes, while the other daughter looks exactly like the mom, who's Hispanic."

With his hand on the car door, he turned to look at her. "Is that true?"

"Yes." She glanced over at the cabin. "Maybe we should invite her to grab something to eat with us."

Uncertainty tightened the muscles in his jaw.

"Come on." She rubbed her hand down his arm. "Now's a great time for starting to let go of the old ways. Have a little fun. Step out onto that ledge and jump."

"You wouldn't mind?"

"Of course not. I've had you to myself all day."

He hooked his arm around her and brought her up against his solid body. "You'll have me all night too."

"I like the sound of that." She gave him a quick kiss. "Go on over there and ask her. All she can do is say no, right?"

*L*ittle Shop of Pizza sat at the end of Main Street near the river, and featured vintage décor in black and white with upside-down galvanized buckets as lightshades. You could choose to sit at the counter on stools or at small wooden tables with bright red chairs. An obligatory drawing on the kitchen door revealed a man-eating plant with the face of a pizza in case anyone didn't get the reference to *The Little Shop of Horrors*. The place was perfect for a casual sit-down meal with someone you weren't quite sure you were related to or not.

"I'm so glad you could join us," Brooke told Dec's *maybe* sister while he pulled out chairs for both of them.

There were no sunglasses now to cover her blue eyes and just looking at her brought a new level of unease to Dec's soul.

He could hardly blame her for who might or might

not have been her parents, but the reality that his father could have cheated on his mother pinched a nerve at the back of his neck and made his head ache. In the past he may not have had marriage on his own mind, but one thing he did believe, and that was that if you chose to say *I do*, you didn't fool around with others.

The possible deceit weighed heavy on his mind. But nothing could be done until they had proof one way or the other.

"Thanks for inviting me." Lili slid into a chair and set her purse down on the floor next to her. "Other than playing the intimidation game the other day at the vineyard office I haven't really had anyone to talk to since I got here."

"Lili's from Philadelphia," Dec said, mentioning one of the few things he knew about her.

"What do you do in Philly?" Brooke asked.

"I started out as a florist. A skill I learned from my mother. She owned her own shop until she got too sick to work. We needed the money for the medical bills so she had to sell it. By then I'd kind of moved on to being an event planner." Lili shrugged. "When you're a florist and make deliveries, you learn where all the main party venues are. You meet the caterers. It just kind of naturally evolved."

Dec knew they were planning to hire a full-time planner for the vineyard, but he wouldn't mention that to Lili until they knew who she really was. No sense trying to make her a part of anything if she was an imposter.

"So do you like it here?" Brooke asked.

"It's very different. A lot more laid-back."

"That's exactly what I enjoy about it most. Dec and I both live in Southern California, although I'm about to make a change and move here."

"She's trying to get away from me." Dec put down the menu. "But it won't work."

"You're really going to leave Southern California?" Lili asked. "I thought everyone was trying to move there. Not away."

"How else am I going to create and run a business here?" Brooke said. "I can hardly do that from hundreds of miles away."

What Dec had said to Brooke just before they'd fallen asleep earlier, after having the best, most soul fulfilling sex of his life, was true. There was nowhere else to go when the only place he wanted to be was with her. If she planned to move to Sunshine, he needed to figure out exactly how to make it all work.

"Know what's on my bucket list?" he asked her.

She shook her head.

He pointed to the menu. "Eating a chili and lime pizza."

"Nice detour."

"You said I needed to learn to have more fun." He leaned in and kissed her cheek. "What says party better than a chili and lime pizza?"

"You could start slow, you know. I'm not sure—"

"I wonder if they serve margaritas here too." He looked around the restaurant then realized they had to go to the counter to order. "Name your poison, ladies."

"Diet Pepsi," Brooke said.

"Same," his *might be* sister said.

"Party poopers." He got up and went to the counter. Ordering wasn't the main thing on his mind. Figuring out what to do about his—scratch that—*their* future topped the list. While he waited for their drinks he tried to put his mind to work. But just like with his dyslexia, everything seemed completely backward.

When he turned away from the counter with their drinks and their pickup number for the pizza, he almost dropped the tray.

Beside the table where his *might be* sister was seated stood Nicole—the sister he and his brothers had kept in the dark.

Chapter 19

"I barely kept Nicole from finding out about Lili," Dec said to his brothers in the vineyard office the following morning. Last night when he and Brooke had dropped Lili off at her cabin, he'd gone inside their own and put out the *code red* call to all of them. "Luckily Nicki's friends were waiting in the car and she was just picking up a to-go order. I did my best to rush her out the door."

"Close call," Ethan said.

"Tell me about it." Dec sat back in the chair, his heart pumping as hard then as it had the night before. He and Brooke had finished off a bottle of wine before he finally felt its effects. Brooke's naked and sensual ministrations had helped too.

Sex.

Best. Medicine. Ever.

"I call bullshit on this hush-hush thing with the baby dragon," Jordan said, using his affectionate nickname for their sister. He leaned forward and settled his elbows on his bent knees. "Nicki's the one who's been dealing with Dad's emotional abandonment all this time. Why are we keeping this a secret from her? She deserves to know."

"And she will as soon as the facts come in," Parker said. "But there's no need to throw her in the spin cycle until necessary."

"Hold up. I think I get what Jordy's saying." Dec looked over at his twin brother. "Nicole already feels like she's been ostracized from this family because of Dad's behavior toward her. So in trying to *protect* her, aren't we doing the same thing?"

"Exactly." Jordan pointed at Dec. "I really don't think she'd want to be kept in the dark. She's a big girl now. She's planning her future. She's smart. Let's give her some credit for that and let's stop treating her like she's a two-year-old. Yes, she can be an emotional time bomb. Believe me, no one knows that better than me. But given the circumstances, she should have the right to explode. When she calms down she'll be more reasonable to deal with."

"I agree," Dec said even as his stomach twisted with agony for all his little sister had to deal with lately: the feelings of abandonment, the loss of her parents, being ping-ponged between brothers for adult supervision, among other typical teenager issues.

"I don't know." Ryan got up from his chair behind the desk, ran a hand through his hair, and paced the floor. Finally he stopped and sat back down. "Who's going to clean up the tidal wave if it all goes south?"

"We all will." Dec knew from the bottom of his heart that no matter what the DNA said about Lili, they all loved Nicole, and they'd be there to help her figure things out. "We can be a hell of a support system if we work together."

In that moment, Dec realized what he really missed about being with his brothers. He missed their stupid arguments, their competitiveness, the way they all talked over one another at the dinner table. He missed the way one of them would clamp a hand over his shoulder when something was troubling him, and then they did what they needed to do to help pull him out of his own messes. He missed how they'd all come together in hard times like they'd done when their parents had been killed. He and Jordan had reconnected after a long absence away from each other, but they hadn't connected nearly enough. Dec needed—wanted—more time.

Family first.

Though a shadow of deception hung over their father's legacy, his motto came back to Dec as strongly as it would have if his father had spoken it from the grave.

"Family first," Dec said, and they all agreed.

"The private lab said they should have the results to us by this afternoon." Ryan twirled a pencil through his fingers. "Guess we need to get together with Nicki and let her know what's going on."

"If you guys don't mind, I'd like to have Brooke here. She and Nicki have gotten fairly close and it might do well for her to have another female close by."

"Is there another reason you want her here?" Ethan asked.

"Might be."

His knowing brother grinned.

"I'll have Lucy come too," Jordan said. "Nicki and Lucy are like peas in a pod. Having both Lucy and Brooke here should give her an added support system."

"Might as well bring Aunt Pippy too then," Parker said. "Since she's the one who's been guarding the family secrets all this time."

"Anyone want a drink first?" Ethan asked.

"Fuck *one*." Dec scoffed. "Bring on a whole damn bottle."

"Are you kidding me?" Nicole jumped up from her seat at the kitchen table. "Our father treated me like crap because he already had another daughter?"

"At the moment, it's only a possibility," Dec explained. "The DNA results will give us the truth."

"The truth?" Nicki snarled. "I'll give you the truth. Our jackass of a father cheated on our mother. He had another child he blew off and completely ignored. Just like me."

"He loved you, Nicki." Ryan tried words to calm her down but they only added more fuel to her fire.

"No. He loved *you*, Ryan. And the rest of you. He tolerated me even though I did nothing to turn him against me except being born."

She crossed her arms over her stomach as if she was in physical pain and a sob burst from her chest. Dec got up and went to her. She might try to push him away, but he wouldn't let that happen. She'd suffered enough, and the need he felt to protect her was a living, breathing thing.

He wrapped his arms around her. Instead of pushing him away, she melted against him. "It's okay, sis," he whispered. He softly stroked her hair, and while he rocked her in his arms, he thought about Brooke. In his sister's heartbreak, he imagined Brooke's as she'd realized what her father intended to do and how she'd been forced to run for her life.

Whoever said women were the weaker sex had never taken a good enough look. They were far braver than any of the males in this room.

Him included.

"It's okay," Dec said to her while his brothers came to her and they all ended up in a huge group hug. "We love you. And we'll figure this out together."

*I*n Brooke's dark past, family meetings never occurred. As a child you were told by your parents and the elders what you were going to do whether you liked it or not. In her mind, the *nots* outweighed the *likes* by many. Not that she was ever asked her opinion. She was told how she would think. How she would behave. And even how she would feel. Brooke had broken every boundary they'd put in her way.

The Hastingses had taught her love, hard work, and to dream big, but they'd never had family meetings either.

The Kincades were a different breed. They argued

as hard as they loved. And heaven help anyone who tried to come between them.

This was the reason Brooke felt so bad for Lili MacKay. As soon as the brothers let Nicole in on the situation, Lili would walk through the door with a target on her heart and soul.

Nothing about the young woman seemed deceptive and Brooke believed Lili was telling the truth. She didn't believe the young woman would be the type to show up and try to con a family like the Kincades. Why put yourself through the heartache? And for what? A few dollars? Lili just didn't seem the type. She had a sweet but feisty personality. She'd made it clear that she was self-sufficient and wasn't after money. She simply had wanted to meet the man her mother finally revealed as the father she'd never known.

Only Lili had arrived too late.

For Nicole, the bomb was about to drop. Brooke liked the teen. She was sweet, funny, and very talented. And she loved her brothers so much she was willing to push them in a direction they may never consider. Life wasn't a fairy tale, but Brooke still wished she had a magic wand she could wave that would take away all the sadness and complications this family had gone through.

Now the brothers, Aunt Pippy, Lucy, and Brooke had all gathered in the freshly painted living room of the main house. Because of the current renovations, items and photos had been boxed up and all that remained were the pieces of leather furniture. The disorder of the room seemed to mirror the chaos in the family's lives and the emptiness brought an emotional chill.

Brooke had tried to convince Dec that she had no business being at such a personal event. But he'd insisted that he needed her there. Now he sat beside her on the sofa, holding her hand, their fingers locked together like a lifeline.

Murmured conversation in the room stopped when Nicole came down the stairs with her little gray kitten, Fezzik, at her feet.

"Well, that's encouraging." Nicole glared. "Were you all talking behind my back?"

"Don't flatter yourself, squirt." Jordan caught her in a headlock then kissed the top of her head. A smile never touched the teen's lips. It was as though she knew the sky was about to fall.

"Nicki, come on in and sit down." Ryan waved a hand toward an empty chair. "We have something to discuss with you."

"There's more?" Dark brows slanted over her blue eyes. "Jesus." She dropped into the chair then patted her legs for Fezzik to jump onto her lap.

As the oldest, and therefore the undeclared leader, Ryan took charge of the discussion. "The DNA results are back. We've contacted Lili and asked her to join us. That way we can find out the truth together."

Nicole's eyes widened as she absently stroked the little cat on her lap.

Beside Brooke, Dec squeezed her hand. She gave his a reassuring squeeze back.

"So . . ." Nicole spoke up through the unsettling quiet. "You're saying that any minute a woman who might or might not be my father's illegitimate daughter is going to walk through that door and you expect me to just sit here?"

"Yes," Ryan said. "It won't take long. While we waited for the results, Ethan convinced her to stay at the cabin next to grandfather's."

Nicole speared a glare in Ethan's direction then dropped a heavy sigh with the drama of an atomic bomb. "And now you're telling me that at any point in time in the last couple of days I could have run into her and—"

"Actually, you did run into her," Dec said. "At the pizza place. She was sitting at our table."

"The *blonde*?" Nicole tossed a look at Brooke. "Sorry. No slight on your hair color."

"Yes," Dec confirmed. "The blonde."

"Then how can it be that you'd believe she's related? Have you seen us?" Nicole swept her hand at all of them. "How could a *blonde* possibly come from our father?"

Brooke bit her lip. Now was not the time to go into a lesson about genetics. But right now, someone needed to hold the poor girl. Whether from anger or fear, she was trembling. Brooke nudged Dec in the side and gave a nod toward his sister. She mouthed, "Hug her."

Without hesitation, he got up and went to Nicki's side. When his sister looked up at him with a desperate look in her eyes, he leaned down and hugged her. Brooke couldn't stop the tears from welling up in her eyes. Especially when Dec kneeled on the floor beside the chair and held Nicki's hand.

"We're about to find out if that's possible," Dec said.

"And no matter what the results are, we're family. We stick together. Every single one of us—Brooke and Lucy included—are here for you."

Nicki looked hard at Dec, then she shared that same scowl with her other brothers. "I love you guys. But if that test comes back positive, I'm not going to be the only one who's going to have to adjust. A positive test means Dad positively cheated on Mom. And that creates a whole new breeding ground for open wounds and mistrust."

She glared at their Aunt Pippy, who'd sat through the entire conversation peeling the orange polish off her fingernails.

"A DNA test might tell us one thing," Nicki said. "But it's not going to tell us the whole story. And, Aunt Pippy, like it or not, you're going to have to open that can of worms and talk."

"I know." Their aunt nodded nervously. "I should have told you sooner. I just didn't want to betray your father."

"Why not?" Nicki asked. "He betrayed the rest of us."

Before Pippy could respond, Ryan's phone rang. As he answered the call he became the focus of the entire room. Feeling the pressure, he got up and walked out of the house.

"Guess he wants to hear the results in private first," Parker said.

"He's going to have to tell us anyway," Ethan added. "Why hide?"

"Because everyone needs to hear it at the same

time." Parker seemed like he was trying to keep the *duh* from his tone. "And there's a person missing from the puzzle."

Nicole sighed and Dec squeezed her hand.

A few minutes later Ryan came back into the room. "That was the lab. Lili's on her way up to the house now."

Brooke's heart stuttered. Whatever the results, everything in this family was about to change. She looked at the man she loved with all her heart and wondered exactly how it all would affect him.

By the time Lili came through the door, Jordan and Lucy had tucked Nicole between them on the sofa. She kept her head down, refusing to look at the young woman who'd entered the room. Dec understood how she felt. Well, he tried to understand. In Nicki's mind she'd been treated unfairly by their father and Lili could be the entire reason for that. However, if that was the truth, Lili had suffered the same mistreatment.

It wasn't fair.

And it didn't make sense that their father could have been capable of something like this. But it was a fact they all might have to deal with.

Lili gave everyone a timid smile, but she stopped in her tracks when she spotted Nicole. Dec shot Lili a warning look but he knew that she was in as tough a place as the rest of them. No one should be silenced here. And the only person who should bear the force of their wrath was the one person who couldn't be here to explain himself.

"I'm so sorry," Lili said to Nicole, who refused to look up. "I really didn't come here to hurt anyone," she said to the rest. "This wasn't something I've known about for years and only now decided to investigate. My mother died just a few weeks ago. So believe it or not, this is as painful for me as it is for you."

"I doubt that." Nicole's head finally came up with a snap. "*If* you're our father's daughter, and what you say is the truth, you haven't lived with his deceitfulness all your life. I've had to live with being ignored by him because of *you* my whole life. Try feeling *my* pain."

"I'm sorry, Nicole." Lili gave her a sympathetic look. "As much as I'm sorry for your pain, you're wrong. I *have* suffered deceitfulness and alienation. Just like you."

Ryan offered Lili a seat but she chose to stand.

Dec liked the young woman, but if she'd come here for any other reason than the truth, he'd make her sorry she'd ever stepped foot in Sunshine. On the other hand, if her truth was validated by the DNA test, Dec had a lot of things to consider.

He glanced at Brooke and was glad he had her by his side. He wanted her by his side always. He wanted to make her happy the way she made him happy. He'd protect her at any cost. He loved her more than he'd ever thought possible.

Now Dec understood why Jordan had given up his multi-million dollar hockey career to be with Lucy. With the situation at hand, Dec couldn't help wondering if their father had ever felt that way about their mother.

If he had, what the hell had gone wrong?

Anticipation intensified as Ryan stood near the fireplace and faced them.

"The lab is mailing each of us a notarized copy of the DNA results in case we have any questions. But the bottom line is . . ." Ryan turned his eyes toward Lili, who stood near the door, nervously wringing her hands. "Based on DNA retrieved from several items belonging to Dad and Lili's sample, the results are 99.99 percent *positive* that Lili is his daughter."

Nicole gasped. Shrieked. And ran from the room.

Lili slid to the floor covering her face.

And Dec didn't know which way to run first.

Chapter 20

"What a clusterfuck." Parker peeled the label from his Rock Bottom Red Ale.

Ryan grabbed the bottle of Jameson and poured several shots into his glass.

"Pour one for me too," Dec told him.

"Me three," Ethan said.

Jordan held up his bottle of Naked Blonde Ale. "You know we're not going to find any solutions by sitting here getting shitfaced."

"I'm not getting shitfaced," Parker insisted. "I have to drive home and then sleep on a houseboat all night. Drunk doesn't go well with a floating house."

"Then move to dry land for God's sake and quit your whining." Ethan punched Parker in the arm.

"I'm not whining."

"Dude, you totally are."

Dec groaned. "You guys are a bunch of idiots. But I love you."

"Don't you start getting all sappy and shit," Jordan said. "That's Parker's job."

They all laughed even though there wasn't a damn thing in the world funny right now. They'd left Brooke and Lucy up at the main house with Nicole to help calm her down because she'd refused to see her brothers right now. The diss hurt because Dec only wanted to help. But Nicole, being Nicole, made it perfectly clear that the male species in her life were not needed or wanted right now. Neither was Aunt Pippy, nor their newfound sister who, as soon as the arguing began, had quietly disappeared out the front door.

Brooke had calmly taken Dec aside and given him her promise that between her and Lucy they'd talk Nicki down off the wall. And then they'd find Lili and help her out too.

His heart squeezed.

God, he loved that woman.

There were so many facets to her personality. She could belt out a karaoke tune so horribly it was unrecognizable. Dance in the rain to the song in her head. And completely melt his heart. She could be mad and spitting fire one minute then love him until his eyes crossed with pleasure the next. She was not the woman he'd once thought she was.

She was more.

She was a woman who'd survived a dreadful life and come out the other side with an enthusiastic outlook on the future. And she inspired him to do the same.

And yet he hadn't told her he loved her.

That needed to happen ASAFP.

"I'm asking Brooke to marry me," he announced to his half-drunk brothers who were crowded together in his grandfather's living room.

"When the fuck did all this happen?" Parker wanted to know. "I was going to ask her out."

"Do and I'll have to break your pasta making fingers," Dec said.

"Proud of you, bro." Jordan clamped his hand over Dec's shoulder. "You finally got it figured out."

"Yeah. With my help." Ethan grinned as he raised his glass. "Here's to smart little brothers pushing stupid big brothers in the right direction."

"I'm not drinking to that." Dec tossed a magazine at him. "You are not smarter than me."

"Says you."

Ryan—Mr. Serious—piped in. "You sure about this, Dec? You've only been together for a short time."

"We've been together for four years. We've only been sleeping together for a short time." Dec drained his glass. "I know her better than anyone I've ever known, excluding present company. And she knows me."

"Yeah." Parker scoffed. "So she'll probably say no."

"Have you even told her you love her yet?" Ryan asked.

"Nope. Just figured it out."

"Thought you were planning to open an office in Chicago," Ryan said.

"Change of plans." Dec held out his glass to Ryan for a refill. "Brooke wants to buy a piece of property over on Parkway just off Main Street to build a family fun center."

"Sounds like a great idea." Ryan nodded. "This area could use something to help the kids burn off energy. And that comes from the dad of a lively nine-year-old."

"So how are you going to manage a long-distance marriage?" Parker asked. "I mean, with you in Southern California and her in Sunshine, she might need a little company now and again, right?"

Dec knew his brother was teasing him, but his threat remained the same. "I guess you really don't need those fingers to use for cooking on that food truck of yours."

"My fingers are staying right where they belong."

"On a hot blonde?" Ethan asked, laughing. "Redhead? Or brunette?"

"All of the above," Parker answered. "And all at the same time if I'm lucky."

"Oh God." Jordan laughed. "The shit is getting deep now."

"I'll be moving here too, jackass," Dec said. "Don't see why I can't open that second office in Portland or Vancouver."

"Damn, bro." Ethan slapped him on the back. "You *are* serious."

"Always." Dec looked at his chirping phone. "Now get the hell out of my house because my woman's coming home. And I'd much rather look at her pretty face than your ugly mugs. We can figure out what to do about our new sister another day."

"*W*here exactly are we going?" A day later, Brooke studied the concentration on Dec's face as he sat behind the wheel of Jordan's borrowed SUV. The road had turned from paved to gravel to dirt as they climbed higher and higher up the mountain.

"It's a surprise."

"What if I said I don't like surprises?"

He chuckled then reached across the armrest and held her hand. "You *love* surprises."

"How do you know that? Maybe I'm like you and appreciate a well-planned-out day."

"I'm turning over a new leaf, remember? I'm the new fun guy."

"Oh. Right."

Moochie crawled up from the backseat and into Brooke's lap.

"I'll bet that's hard to keep in mind with everything that's been going on lately," Brooke said, knowing that with all he'd been through, it must be like trying to keep a canoe from tipping over.

"It's been challenging." He squeezed her fingers. "With Nicki going back into her sullen mood and Lili going back to the East Coast, everything seems to be splitting in different directions."

"How are you holding up?"

"I've got you." He kissed the backs of her fingers. "And you've got me. We're together and that's all that matters right now."

"Awww. I like this new sweet side of you."

"Great. Because we're here."

"And *here* is exactly where?" Brooke looked up just as the sun dropped below the mountain ridge and lit up the blue sky in shades of pink and gold. Tall stands of pine trees stood among aspens, ferns, and wildflowers in every color. "Wherever we are, it's beautiful. I feel like we're on top of the world."

"Almost." He opened the car door. "Come on."

Moochie leaped off Brooke's lap and into the tall grass to sniff around. Brooke stepped out of the SUV and inhaled a breath of crisp, cool air. "Like I said before, exactly where are we? And now I'll add, and what are we doing here?"

He opened the back of the SUV and pulled out several plastic crates filled with camping supplies and food. Then he brought out two sleeping bags and pillows. He placed everything in the center of the clearing then came back to where she stood, still beside the SUV. He took her hands in his and her heart filled with love. The way he looked at her now was completely unguarded. And though he hadn't said the words, the way he looked at her was filled with love.

"On the drive up the coast you told me the top things on your bucket list," he said. "You said you wanted to see the aurora borealis, sleep under the stars on the top of a mountain, kiss the Blarney Stone, and own your own business. I can't provide the aurora borealis right now, but I can provide this amazing sunset. I can't help you kiss the Blarney Stone, but you can kiss me."

"Even better." She wrapped her arms around his neck and showed him how much better.

"And you're on your way to owning your own business," he said with another quick kiss on her lips. "So now, I'm offering you the chance to sleep under the stars on the top of a mountain."

"Oh Dec. I can't believe you remembered all that." She hugged him tight. "That's so thoughtful. I love you for thinking of this."

"Do you love me, Brooke? The mess that I am? The workaholic I can be?"

"Yes. I love you, Dec. The new fun guy who wants to dance with me in the rain, who doesn't laugh at my horrible karaoke, and who loves his family so much that he wants to make everything better for all of them. I love *you*, Dec, whoever you happen to be at any given moment."

He wrapped her in his arms and kissed her so sweetly her heart nearly pounded from her chest. That he did not return the words stung only slightly, because she knew that someday when he was ready to completely let go, he would.

She hoped.

When the kiss ended they stayed in each other's arms, rocking to a song they could only hear in their hearts.

"I realized something," he said.

"What's that?"

"That I've missed my family. And I've realized that more than they need me, I need them. So I'm scrapping the Chicago office idea and I'm planning to build one either in Portland or the Vancouver area."

"Really?" Brooke leaned her head back and looked up at him. "When did you decide this?"

"The moment I realized I couldn't be without you for one minute." He tucked his fingers beneath her chin. "The moment I realized that for four years

I've been crazy in love with you but I've been too afraid to break the bonds between work and home to admit it."

"You . . . love me?" How could her heart keep beating when she felt like time had just stopped?

"I love you, Brooke. I'm *in* love with you. More than I can ever even try to define."

"Oh my God." She reached for him but he held her hands tight.

"Hang on, karaoke queen. I'm not done." He kissed her fingers. "You also said that the number one thing on your bucket list was marrying the love of your life."

"You're right. I did."

"You want to know the number one thing on my bucket list?"

"Absolutely."

"Marrying the love of my life. If she'll have me."

Brooke's heart turned somersaults as he dropped to his knee, reached in the pocket of his hoodie, and pulled out a sparkling diamond ring.

"I love you, Brooke Hastings." He kissed the backs of her fingers. "Build a life with me. Have children with me. Let me be the hand you want to hold in good times and bad and I promise I'll do everything in my power to make sure you smile every day. Please say you'll marry me."

It was hard to speak through all the tears pouring from her eyes, but somehow Brooke managed. "I will, Declan Kincade. And do you know why?"

He nodded. "Because we're perfect for each other."

"Indeed we are." He slipped the ring on her finger

just as the moon rose in the sky above them and the first star twinkled. As he swept her up into his arms, Brooke knew that if perfection was in the eye of the beholder, she was never going to have to wear rose-colored glasses.

Don't miss Jordan's story and the beginning of Candis Terry's Sunshine Creek Vineyard series in

a better man

Meet the Kincade brothers: they'll do what it takes to protect their legacy—but what happens when love gets in the way?

Hockey star Jordan Kincade wasted no time ditching Sunshine Valley and everyone who mattered for a career in the NHL—a truth Jordan confronts when his parents' deaths bring him home. Now he's back to make amends, which begins with keeping his younger sister from flunking out of school. It's just his luck that the one person who can help is the girl whose heart he broke years ago.

Lucy Diamond has racked up a number of monumental mistakes in her life, the first involving a certain blue-eyed charmer. She has no intention of falling for Jordan Kincade again, but when he shows up asking her to help one of her students, Lucy just can't say no. Worse, the longer he's back the more she sees how much he's changed. And so when a blistering kiss turns to more, she can't help wondering if her heart will be crushed again . . . or if she'll discover true love with a better man.

The pungent scent of sweat-soaked bodies and the ice beneath Jordan Kincade's skates filled his nostrils. He devoured the energy, the thrill of the game, and the barely controlled chaos like a perfectly grilled steak. Queen's "We Will Rock You" and anticipation vibrated through the jam-packed arena as he skated to face-off with his opponent on a power play. The Carolina Vipers might be down by a goal, but he knew the high-decibel, foot-stomping boost from the home crowd would pull them through.

It always did.

After an earlier vicious cross-check delivered by Dimitri Pavel, Jordan—much to the crowd's delight—racked up five for fighting. Now it was time to cut the shit and focus. He couldn't allow Pavel's toothless sneer to tempt him into chalking up any more penalty points. There was just too damn much at stake.

"Gonna vipe smile off dat pretty face, kinky man."

Pavel spat when he spoke, a habit that tempted his opponents to dodge the spray and miss the drop. Jordan, who had mercifully retained all his own teeth, imagined it was hard to speak properly when you had the gums of an infant. Still, Pavel could have strings of snot hanging from his nose and Jordan wouldn't care. He didn't dodge anything if it meant he'd lose the face-off.

"Your saggy jock calls bullshit," Jordan shot back. Yeah, okay, the bait had been too strong to resist the smack talk. So sue him.

Like a wolf focused on its prey, Jordan's attention sharpened as the ref lifted his hand and dropped the puck in front of Jordan's skates. Jordan wasted no time in pushing the biscuit across the ice into Tyler Seabrook's stick. The center took control. Dodging sticks, skates, and elbows, he managed to set up a shot in the sweet zone. Jordan snagged the pass and slapped it through the five-hole before the goalie could get his glove on it.

Red lights flashed behind the net and the horn blew, signaling the goal. The crowd leaped to their feet in an ear-splitting roar as the players came together for congratulatory slaps on the back. Nothing felt better than a team celebration after an important goal. The one he'd just scored had been vital and hopefully took the burn off the penalties he'd drawn earlier. With the score now tied, the Vipers would have to quickly score once more or win it in overtime. The chances of either were iffy.

The shift change gave Jordan a chance to catch his breath and rest his legs. During a regular season game he didn't usually tense up. But the closer they got to making the playoffs, the more he tended to tighten every muscle to the extreme. By the time he made it home tonight he'd feel like he'd been hit by a bullet train. Once his team claimed victory and made it into the locker room, he'd need to have his favorite masseuse make a house call. Lucky for him his favorite masseuse came with a pretty smile, long blond hair, a taste for fine whiskey, and preferred to work in the nude.

A smile curled his mouth as he watched Beau Boucher press his opponent into the corner boards with a glass-quaking thud. The hulking defenseman used his weight and muscle to steal the puck and slide it across the ice to power forward Scott O'Reilly. O'Reilly sank it into the net so fast the goalie barely saw it flash by.

With only two seconds remaining on the play clock, the Vipers bench emptied and the entire team roared onto the ice to celebrate the win. Unless a miracle materialized for the other team in the next blink of an eye, the Vipers were one step closer to the Stanley Cup.

Hallefreakinglujah.

REL 0317

At Avon Books, we know your passion for romance—once you finish one of our novels, you find yourself wanting more.

May we tempt you with . . .

- **Excerpts** from our upcoming releases.

- Entertaining **extras**, including authors' personal photo albums and book lists.

- Behind-the-scenes **scoop** on your favorite characters and series.

- **Sweepstakes** for the chance to win free books, romantic getaways, and other fun prizes.

- Writing **tips** from our authors and editors.

- **Blog** with our authors and find out why they love to write romance.

- **Exclusive content** that's not contained within the pages of our novels.

Join us at
www.avonbooks.com

Give in to your Impulses!

**These unforgettable stories only take a second
to buy and give you hours of reading pleasure!**

Go to *www.AvonImpulse.com* and see what we
have to offer.

Available wherever e-books are sold.

AVON**IMPULSE**

IMP 0811